PEACOCK BOOKS

Editor: Kaye Webb

NIGHTFRIGHTS

Is your world nice and safe, and even a bit too ordinary? Are you curious about the unexplained and fascinated by the darkness of the human soul? Then this anthology is just the thing for you.

Peter Haining has gathered together a formidable collection of weird, eerie and downright frightening stories, all good for a giant-sized shudder, and guaranteed to make you look at least twice at your family and friends and the most ordinary things around you, for who knows what is happening beneath their innocent and placid exteriors? If you like to feel your cheeks pale and your blood run cold, then read on.

The star-studded list of authors includes such masters of the horror story as Edgar Allan Poe, Sheridan Le Fanu, M. R. James, Ray Bradbury, Bram Stoker, John Wyndham and Agatha Christie.

Recommended for Peacock readers with nerves of steel and a taste for the macabre.

NIGHTFRIGHTS

An anthology of macabre tales that have terrified
three generations

Edited by Peter Haining
with illustrations by David Smee

PENGUIN BOOKS

Penguin Books Ltd, Harmonsdworth, Middlesex, England
Penguin Books Australia Ltd, Ringwood, Victoria, Australia
Penguin Books Canada Ltd, 41 Steelcase Road West, Ontario, Canada
Penguin Books (N.Z.) Ltd, 182–190 Wairau Road, Auckland 10, New Zealand

—

First published by Victor Gollancz 1972
Published in Peacock Books 1975
Selection and original material
Copyright © Peter Haining, 1972

—

Made and printed in Great Britain
by Hazell Watson & Viney Ltd
Aylesbury, Bucks
Set in Linotype Baskerville

For my sons,

RICHARD and SEAN

because they might enjoy these tales

and

MY PARENTS

because they did

Contents

Acknowledgements

The editor is grateful to the following authors, agents and publishers for permission to include copyright material in this anthology: The Executors of the Estate of H. G. Wells for 'The Valley of the Spiders'; The Executors of the Estate of M. R. James for 'The Haunted Doll's House'; The Public Trustee and A. P. Watt for 'The Transfer' by Algernon Blackwood; The authoress and Hughes Massie Ltd for 'The Lamp' by Agatha Christie; Scott Meredith Literary Agency for 'The Lonesome Place' by August Derleth; Dennis Dobson Ltd for 'Close Behind Him' by John Wyndham; Scott Meredith Literary Agency for 'Enoch' by Robert Bloch; The Executors of the Author's Estate for 'Same Time, Same Place' by Mervyn Peake; A. D. Peters Literary Agency for 'The Small Assassin' by Ray Bradbury; and Joan Aiken for her story 'Furry Night'.

Editor's Foreword

M. R. JAMES, whom many critics regard as the finest of all ghost story writers, not only encouraged the widespread interest in such stories by his own work, but was also a great believer in their power to entertain audiences of all ages – particularly young people. Indeed, he wrote perceptively on one occasion, 'Nothing is more common in old-fashioned books than the description of the winter fireside, where the aged grandam narrates to the circle of children that hang on her lips, story after story of ghosts and horrors and inspires her listeners with a pleasing terror.' This quotation, you may perhaps be surprised to learn, was written something like half a century ago, yet who would deny that in principle it still remains true today? That while there may not be as many grandparents actually reading night by night to their grandsons and granddaughters – distracted as we all invariably are by television – the allure of the ghost story, the story of terror, is still as strong as ever. I am certainly sure that it is – and in a way you've demonstrated the fact by picking up this book.

However, instead of just providing a collection of really fine stories here, I've tried to be a little more adventurous, and indeed original, by bringing together tales that, in a nutshell, have 'terrified three generations'. I have researched back to the turn of the century (and a little beyond) to discover what was giving our grandparents 'the shivers' when they were children, then in turn looked at the literature of our parents during their youth and finally, just to underline what a continuing tradition the 'tale of terror' is, I have provided a group of stories which I believe will give you the same sensations your parents and grandparents enjoyed. Altogether I believe the items show how each passing generation likes much the same kind of thrill and that despite all the progress of knowledge and science, there's at least some degree of 'fear of the dark' in us all. And I think that's not such a bad thing either, for a little relief from the mundane quality of so much of our day-to-day life can only be for the good.

Still, this is all of no real importance: it is the stories themselves which count. I hope you will find both the oldest and the newest equally entertaining and thrilling. I don't expect for a moment that each reader will shudder at the same thing, for such is the nature of mankind that we are all affected by different things in different ways, and nowhere more so than in the ghost or horror story. I hope, too, that the stories will give you at least a glimpse or two of the times in which your predecessors lived and worked.

Let me add, finally, that there are an awful lot more stories that could have been included here and plenty more authors from all three periods of time who, but for the strictures of book-length and availability, might well have appeared. But if you enjoy what you read here, do go and search for more – there is a rich storehouse of 'night frights' ready and waiting on the bookshelves for anyone bold enough to explore.

PETER HAINING
Birch Green, Essex
April 1972

I

Tales That Frightened Your Grandparents

Robert Louis Stevenson (1850—94)

The Body-Snatcher

*No story perhaps created more nightmares among our
grandparents than the now legendary 'Dr Jekyll and Mr
Hyde'. Only overshadowed in horror fiction by the much
earlier 'Frankenstein' of Mary Shelley (which, like it, has
been the subject of innumerable films, television plays and
radio broadcasts), it nonetheless has a more compulsive
style and developing atmosphere that still makes it terrifying reading even today. Robert Louis Stevenson, the
author of this macabre masterpiece, is forever ranked
among the greatest of our writers for his 'Treasure Island'
and a variety of endlessly inventive short stories such as
'Markheim' and 'The Isle of Voices'. There can, then, be
no more suitable author to begin our collection and what
more terrifying subject to write about than of men who
come under the silent cover of darkness to steal the bodies
of the dead?*

EVERY night in the year, four of us sat in the small
parlour of the George at Debenham – the undertaker,
and the landlord, and Fettes, and myself. Sometimes
there would be more; but blow high, blow low, come
rain or snow or frost, we four would be each planted
in his own particular armchair. Fettes was an old
drunken Scotchman, a man of education obviously,
and a man of some property, since he lived in idleness.
He had come to Debenham years ago, while still

young, and by a mere continuance of living had grown to be an adopted townsman. His blue camlet cloak was a local antiquity, like the church spire. His place in the parlour of the George, his absence from church, his old, crapulous, disreputable vices, were all things of course in Debenham. He had some vague Radical opinions and some fleeting infidelities, which he would now and again set forth and emphasize with tottering slaps upon the table. He drank rum — five glasses regularly every evening; and for the greater portion of his nightly visit to the George sat, with his glass in his right hand, in a state of melancholy alcoholic saturation. We called him the doctor, for he was supposed to have some special knowledge of medicine, and had been known, upon a pinch, to set a fracture or reduce a dislocation; but, beyond these slight particulars, we had no knowledge of his character and antecedents.

One dark winter night — it had struck nine some time before the landlord joined us — there was a sick man in the George, a great neighbouring proprietor suddenly struck down with apoplexy on his way to Parliament; and the great man's still greater London doctor had been telegraphed to his bedside. It was the first time that such a thing had happened in Debenham, for the railway was but newly open, and we were all proportionately moved by the occurrence.

'He's come,' said the landlord, after he had filled and lighted his pipe.

'He?' said I. 'Who? — not the doctor?'

'Himself,' replied our host.

'What is his name?'

'Dr Macfarlane,' said the landlord.

Fettes was far through his third tumbler, stupidly fuddled, now nodding over, now staring mazily around him; but at the last word he seemed to awaken, and repeated the name 'Macfarlane' twice, quietly enough the first time, but with sudden emotion at the second.

'Yes,' said the landlord, 'that's his name, Dr Wolfe Macfarlane.'

Fettes became instantly sober; his eyes awoke, his voice became clear, loud, and steady, his language forcible and earnest. We were all startled by the transformation, as if a man had risen from the dead.

'I beg your pardon,' he said; 'I am afraid I have not been paying much attention to your talk. Who is this Wolfe Macfarlane?' And then, when he had heard the landlord out, 'It cannot be, it cannot be,' he added; 'and yet I would like well to see him face to face.'

'Do you know him, doctor?' asked the undertaker, with a gasp.

'God forbid!' was the reply. 'And yet the name is a strange one; it were too much to fancy two. Tell me, landlord, is he old?'

'Well,' said the host, 'he's not a young man, to be sure, and his hair is white; but he looks younger than you.'

'He is older, though; years older. But,' with a slap upon the table, 'it's the rum you see in my face – rum and sin. This man, perhaps, may have an easy conscience and a good digestion. Conscience! Hear me speak. You would think I was some good old, decent Christian, would you not? But no, not I; I never canted. Voltaire might have canted if he'd stood in my shoes; but the brains' – with a rattling fillip on his bald head – 'the brains were clear and active, and I saw and made no deductions.'

'If you know this doctor,' I ventured to remark, after a somewhat awful pause, 'I should gather that you do not share the landlord's good opinion.'

Fettes paid no regard to me.

'Yes,' he said, with sudden decision, 'I must see him face to face.'

There was another pause, and then a door was closed rather sharply on the first floor, and a step was heard upon the stair.

'That's the doctor,' cried the landlord. 'Look sharp and you can catch him.'

It was but two steps from the small parlour to the door of the old George Inn; the wide oak staircase landed almost in the street; there was room for a Turkey rug and nothing more between the threshold and the last round of the descent; but this little space was every evening brilliantly lit up, not only by the light upon the stair and the great signal-lamp below the sign, but by the warm radiance of the bar-room window. The George thus brightly advertised itself to passers-by in the cold street. Fettes walked steadily to the spot, and we, who were hanging behind, beheld the two men meet, as one of them had phrased it, face to face. Dr Macfarlane was alert and vigorous. His white hair set off his pale and placid, although energetic, countenance. He was richly dressed in the finest of broadcloth and the whitest of linen, with a great gold watch-chain and studs and spectacles of the same precious material. He wore a broad-folded tie, white and speckled with lilac, and he carried on his arm a comfortable driving coat of fur. There was no doubt but he became his years, breathing, as he did, of wealth and consideration; and it was a surprising contrast to see our parlour sot – bald, dirty, pimpled, and robed in his old camlet cloak – confront him at the bottom of the stairs.

'Macfarlane!' he said somewhat loudly, more like a herald than a friend.

The great doctor pulled up short on the fourth step, as though the familiarity of the address surprised and somewhat shocked his dignity.

'Toddy Macfarlane!' repeated Fettes.

The London man almost staggered. He stared for the swiftest of seconds at the man before him, glanced behind him with a sort of scare, and then in a startled whisper, 'Fettes!' he said, 'you!'

'Ay,' said the other, 'me! Did you think I was dead, too? We are not so easy shut of our acquaintance.'

'Hush, hush!' exclaimed the doctor. 'Hush, hush! this meeting is so unexpected – I can see you are un-manned. I hardly knew you, I confess, at first; but I am overjoyed – overjoyed to have this opportunity. For the present it must be how-d'ye-do and good-bye in one, for my fly is waiting, and I must not fail the train; but you shall – let me see – yes – you shall give me your address, and you can count on early news of me. We must do something for you, Fettes. I fear you are out at elbiws; but we must see to that for auld lang syne, as once we sang at suppers.'

'Money!' cried Fettes; 'money from you! The money that I had from you is lying where I cast it in the rain.'

Dr Macfarlane had talked himself into some measure of superiority and confidence, but the un-common energy of this refusal cast him back into his first confusion.

A horrible, ugly look came and went across his almost venerable countenance. 'My dear fellow,' he said, 'be it as you please; my last thought is to offend you. I would intrude on none. I will leave you my address, however——'

'I do not wish it – I do not wish to know the roof that shelters you,' interrupted the other. 'I heard your name; I feared it might be you; I wished to know if, after all, there were a God; I know now that there is none. Begone!'

He still stood in the middle of the rug, between the stair and doorway; and the great London physician, in order to escape, would be forced to step to one side. It was plain that he hesitated before the thought of this humiliation. White as he was, there was a dangerous glitter in his spectacles; but, while he still paused uncertain, he became aware that the driver of his fly was peering in from the street at this unusual scene, and caught a glimpse at the same time of our little body from the parlour, huddled by the corner of the bar. The presence of so many witnesses decided him at once to flee. He crouched together, brushing on the wainscot, and made a dart like a serpent, striking for the door. But his tribulation was not yet entirely at end, for even as he was passing Fettes clutched him by the arm and these words came in a whisper, and yet painfully distinct, 'Have you seen it again?'

The great rich London doctor cried out aloud with a sharp, throttling cry; he dashed his questioner across the open space, and, with his hands over his head, fled out of the door like a detected thief. Before it had occurred to one of us to make a movement the fly was already rattling towards the station. The scene was over like a dream, but the dream had left proofs and traces of its passage. Next day the servant found the fine gold spectacles broken on the threshold, and that very night we were all standing breathless by the bar-room window, and Fettes at our side, sober, pale, and resolute in look.

'God protect us, Mr Fettes!' said the landlord, coming first into possession of his customary senses. 'What in the universe is all this? These are strange things you have been saying.'

Fettes turned towards us; he looked at each in succession in the face. 'See if you can hold your tongues,' said he. 'That man Macfarlane is not safe to cross; those that have done so already have repented it too late.'

And then, without so much as finishing his third glass, far less waiting for the other two, he bade us goodbye and went forth, under the lamp of the hotel, into the black night.

We three turned to our places in the parlour, with the big red fire and four clear candles; and, as we recapitulated what had passed, the first chill of our surprise soon changed into a glow of curiosity. We sat late; it was the latest session I have known in the old George. Each man, before we parted, had his theory that he was bound to prove; and none of us had any nearer business in this world than to track out the past of our condemned companion, and surprise the secret that he shared with the great London doctor. It is no great boast, but I believe I was a better hand at worming out a story than either of my fellows at the George; and perhaps there is now no other man alive who could narrate to you the following foul and unnatural events.

In his young days Fettes studied medicine in the

schools of Edinburgh. He had talent of a kind, the talent that picks up swiftly what it hears and readily retails it for its own. He worked little at home; but he was civil, attentive, and intelligent in the presence of his masters. They soon picked him out as a lad who listened closely and remembered well; nay, strange as it seemed to me when I first heard it, he was in those days well favoured, and pleased by his exterior. There was, at that period, a certain extramural teacher of anatomy, whom I shall here designate by the letter K. His name was subsequently too well known. The man who bore it skulked through the streets of Edinburgh in disguise, while the mob that applauded at the execution of Burke called loudly for the blood of his employer. But Mr K— was then at the top of his vogue; he enjoyed a popularity due partly to his own talent and address, partly to the incapacity of his rival, the university professor. The students, at least, swore by his name and Fettes believed himself, and was believed by others to have laid the foundations of success when he had acquired the favour of this meteorically famous man. Mr K— was a *bon vivant* as well as an accomplished teacher; he liked a sly illusion no less than a careful preparation. In both capacities Fettes enjoyed and deserved his notice, and by the second year of his attendance he held the half-regular position of second demonstrator or sub-assistant in his class.

In this capacity the charge of the theatre and lecture-room devolved in particular upon his shoulders. He had to answer for the cleanliness of the premises and the conduct of the other students, and it was part of his duty to supply, receive, and divide the various subjects. It was with a view to this last – at that time very delicate – affair that he was lodged by Mr K— in the same wynd, and at last in the same building, with the dissecting-rooms. Here, after a night of turbulent pleasures, his hand still tottering, his sight still misty and confused, he would be called out of bed in the black hours before the winter dawn by the unclean and desperate interlopers who supplied the table. He would open the door to these men, since infamous throughout the land. He would help them with their tragic burden, pay them their sordid price, and remain alone, when they were gone, with the unfriendly relics of humanity. From such a scene he would return to snatch another hour or two of slumber, to repair the abuses of the night, and refresh himself for the labours of the day.

Few lads could have been more insensible to the impressions of a life thus passed among the ensigns of mortality. His mind was closed against all general considerations. He was incapable of interest in the fate and fortunes of another, the slave of his own desires and low ambitions. Cold, light, and selfish in the last resort, he had that modicum of prudence, miscalled morality, which keeps a man from inconvenient drunkenness or punishable theft. He coveted, besides, a measure of consideration from his masters and his fellow-pupils, and he had no desire to fail conspicuously in the external parts of life. Thus he made it his pleasure to gain some distinction in his studies, and day after day rendered unimpeachable eye-service to his employer, Mr K—. For his day of work he indemnified himself by nights of roaring, blackguardly enjoyment; and when that balance had been struck, the organ that he called his conscience declared itself content.

The supply of subjects was a continual trouble to him as well as to his master. In that large and busy class, the raw material of the anatomists kept perpetually running out; and the business thus rendered necessary was not only unpleasant in itself, but threatened dangerous consequences to all who were concerned. It was the policy of Mr K— to ask no questions in his dealings with the trade. 'They bring the body, and we pay the price,' he used to say, dwelling on the alliteration – '*quid pro quo*.' And, again, and somewhat profanely, 'Ask no questions,' he would tell his assistants, 'for conscience' sake.' There was no understanding that the subjects were provided by the crime of murder. Had that idea been broached to him in words, he would have recoiled in horror; but the lightness of his speech upon so grave a matter was, in itself, an offence against good manners, and a temptation to the men with whom he dealt. Fettes, for instance, had often remarked to himself upon the singular freshness of the bodies. He had been struck again and again by the hang-dog, abominable look of the ruffians who came to him before the dawn; and, putting things together clearly in his private thoughts, he perhaps attributed a meaning too immoral and too categorical to the unguarded counsels of his master. He understood his duty, in short, to have three branches: to take what was brought, to pay the price, and to avert the eye from any evidence of crime.

One November morning this policy of silence was put sharply to the test. He had been awake all night with a racking toothache – pacing his room like a caged beast or throwing himself in fury on his bed – and had fallen at last into that profound, uneasy slumber that so often follows on a night of pain, when he was awakened by the third or fourth angry repetition of the concerted signal. There was a thin, bright moonshine; it was bitter cold, windy, and frosty; the town had not yet awakened, but an indefinable stir already preluded the noise and business of the day. The ghouls had come later than usual, and they seemed more than usually eager to be gone. Fettes, sick with sleep, lighted them upstairs. He heard their grumbling Irish voices through a dream; and as they stripped the sack from their sad merchandise he leaned dozing, with his shoulder propped against the wall; he had to shake himself to find the men their money. As he did so his eyes lighted on the dead face. He started; he took two steps nearer, with the candle raised.

'God Almighty!' he cried. 'That is Jane Galbraith!'

The men answered nothing, but they shuffled nearer the door.

'I know her, I tell you,' he continued. 'She was alive and hearty yesterday. It's impossible she can be dead; it's impossible you should have got this body fairly.'

'Sure, sir, you're mistaken entirely,' said one of the men.

But the others looked Fettes darkly in the eyes, and demanded the money on the spot.

It was impossible to misconceive the threat or to exaggerate the danger. The lad's heart failed him. He stammered some excuses, counted out the sum, and saw his hateful visitors depart. No sooner were they gone than he hastened to confirm his doubts. By a dozen unquestionable marks he identified the girl he had jested with the day before. He saw, with horror, marks upon her body that might well betoken violence. A panic seized him, and he took refuge in his room. There he reflected at length over the discovery that he had made; considered soberly the bearing of Mr K——'s instructions and the danger to himself of interference in so serious a business, and at last, in sore perplexity, determined to wait for the advice of his immediate superior, the class assistant.

This was a young doctor, Wolfe Macfarlane, a high favourite among all the reckless students, clever, dissipated, and unscrupulous to the last degree. He had travelled and studied abroad. His manners were agreeable and a little forward. He was an authority on the stage, skilful on the ice or the links with skate or golf club; he dressed with nice audacity, and, to put the finishing touch upon his glory, he kept a gig and a strong trotting-horse. With Fettes he was on terms of intimacy; indeed, their relative positions called for some community of life; and when subjects were scarce the pair would drive far into the country in Macfarlane's gig, visit and desecrate some lonely graveyard, and return before dawn with their booty to the door of the dissecting-room.

On that particular morning Macfarlane arrived somewhat earlier than his wont. Fettes heard him, and met him on the stairs, told him his story, and showed him the cause of his alarm. Macfarlane examined the marks on her body.

'Yes,' he said with a nod, 'it looks fishy.'

'Well, what should I do?' asked Fettes.

'Do?' repeated the other. 'Do you want to do anything? Least said soonest mended, I should say.'

'Someone else might recognize her,' objected Fettes. 'She was as well known as the Castle Rock.'

'We'll hope not,' said Macfarlane, 'and if anybody does – well, you didn't, don't you see, and there's an end. The fact is, this has been going on too long. Stir up the mud, and you'll get K— into the most unholy trouble; you'll be in a shocking box yourself. So will I, if you come to that. I should like to know how any one of us would look, or what the devil we should have to say for ourselves, in any Christian witness-box. For me, you know, there's one thing certain – that, practically speaking, all our subjects have been murdered.'

'Macfarlane!' cried Fettes.

'Come now!' sneered the other. 'As if you hadn't suspected it yourself!'

"Suspecting is one thing –'

'And proof another. Yes, I know; and I'm as sorry as you are this should have come here,' tapping the body with his cane. 'The next best thing for me is not to recognize it; and,' he added coolly, 'I don't. You may, if you please. I don't dictate, but I think a man of the world would do as I do; and, I may add, I fancy that is what K— would look for at our hands. The question is, Why did he choose us two for his assistants? And I answer, Because he didn't want two old wives.'

This was the tone of all others to affect the mind of a lad like Fettes. He agreed to imitate Macfarlane. The body of the unfortunate girl was duly dissected, and no one remarked or appeared to recognize her.

One afternoon, when his day's work was over, Fettes dropped into a popular tavern and found Macfarlane sitting with a stranger. This was a small man, very pale and dark, with coal-black eyes. The cut on his features gave a promise of intellect and refinement which was but feebly realized in his manners, for he proved, upon a nearer acquaintance, coarse, vulgar, and stupid. He exercised, however, a very remarkable control over Macfarlane; issued orders like the Great Bashaw; became inflamed at the least discussion or delay, and commented rudely on the servility with which he was obeyed. This most offensive person took a fancy to

Fettes on the spot, plied him with drinks, and honoured him with unusual confidences on his past career. If a tenth part of what he confessed were true, he was a very loathsome rogue; and the lad's vanity was tickled by the attention of so experienced a man.

'I'm a pretty bad fellow myself,' the stranger remarked, 'but Macfarlane is the boy – Toddy Macfarlane I call him. Toddy, order your friend another glass.' Or it might be, 'Toddy, you jump up and shut the door.' 'Toddy hates me,' he said again. 'Oh, yes, Toddy, you do!'

'Don't you call me that confounded name,' growled Macfarlane.

'Hear him! Did you ever see the lads play knife? He would like to do that all over my body,' remarked the stranger.

'We medicals have a better way than that,' said Fettes. 'When we dislike a dead friend of ours, we dissect him.'

Macfarlane looked up sharply, as though this jest were scarcely to his mind.

The afternoon passed. Gray, for that was the stranger's name, invited Fettes to join them at dinner, ordered a feast so sumptuous that the tavern was thrown into commotion, and when all was done commanded Macfarlane to settle the bill. It was late before they separated; the man Gray was incapably drunk. Macfarlane, sobered by his fury, chewed the cud of the money he had been forced to squander and the slights he had been obliged to swallow. Fettes, with various liquors singing in his head, returned home with devious footsteps and a mind entirely in abeyance. Next day Macfarlane was absent from the class, and Fettes smiled to himself as he imagined him still squiring the intolerable Gray from tavern to tavern. As soon as the hour of liberty had struck, he posted from place to place in quest of his last night's companions. He could find them, however, nowhere; so returned early to his rooms, went early to bed, and slept the sleep of the just.

At four in the morning he was awakened by the well-known signal. Descending to the door, he was filled with astonishment to find Macfarlane with his gig, and in the gig one of those long and ghastly packages with which he was so well acquainted.

'What?' he cried. 'Have you been out alone? How did you manage?'

But Macfarlane silenced him roughly, bidding him turn to business. When they had got the body upstairs and laid it on the table, Macfarlane made at first as if he were going away. Then he paused and seemed to hesitate; and then, 'You had better look at the face,' said he, in tones of some constraint. 'You had better,' he repeated, as Fettes only stared at him in wonder.

'But where, and how, and when did you come by it?' cried the other.

'Look at the face,' was the only answer.

Fettes was staggered; strange doubts assailed him. He looked from the young doctor to the body, and then back again. At last, with a start, he did as he was bidden. He had almost expected the sight that met his eyes, and yet the shock was cruel. To see, fixed in the rigidity of death and naked on that coarse layer of sackcloth, the man whom he had left well clad and full of meat and sin upon the threshold of a tavern, awoke, even in the thoughtless Fettes, some of the terrors of the conscience. It was a *cras tibi* which re-echoed in his soul, that two whom he had known should have come to lie upon these icy tables. Yet these were only secondary thoughts. His first concern regarded Wolfe. Unprepared for a challenge so momentous, he knew not how to look his comrade in the face. He durst not meet his eye, and he had neither words nor voice at his command.

It was Macfarlane himself who made the first advance. He came up quietly behind and laid his hand gently but firmly on the other's shoulder.

'Richardson,' said he, 'may have the head.'

Now, Richardson was a student who had long been anxious for that portion of the human subject to dissect. There was no answer, and the murderer resumed: 'Talking of business, you must pay me; your accounts, you see, must tally.'

Fettes found a voice, the ghost of his own: 'Pay you!' he cried. 'Pay you for that?'

'Why, yes, of course you must. By all means and on every possible account, you must,' returned the other. 'I dare not give it for nothing, you dare not take it for nothing; it would compromise us both. This is another case like Jane Galbraith's. The more things are wrong, the more we must act as if all were right. Where does old K— keep his money?'

'There,' answered Fettes hoarsely, pointing to a cupboard in the corner.

'Give me the key, then,' said the other calmly, holding out his hand.

There was an instant's hesitation, and the die was cast. Macfarlane could not suppress a nervous twitch, the infinitesimal mark of an immense relief, as he felt the key between his fingers. He opened the cupboard, brought out pen and ink and a paper book that stood in one compartment, and separated from the funds in a drawer a sum suitable to the occasion.

'Now, look here,' he said, 'there is the payment made – first proof of your good faith; first step to your security. You have now to clinch it by a second. Enter the payment in your book, and then you for your part may defy the devil.'

The next few seconds were for Fettes an agony of thought; but in balancing his terrors it was the most immediate that triumphed. Any future difficulty seemed almost welcome if he could avoid a present quarrel with Macfarlane. He set down the candle which he had been carrying all this time and with a steady hand entered the date, the nature, and the amount of the transaction.

'And now,' said Macfarlane, 'it's only fair that you should pocket the lucre. I've had my share already. By the by, when a man of the world falls into a bit of luck, has a few shillings extra in his pocket – I'm ashamed to speak of it, but there's a rule of conduct in the case. No treating, no purchase of expensive class-books, no squaring of old debts; borrow, don't lend.'

'Macfarlane,' began Fettes, still somewhat hoarsely, 'I have put my neck in a halter to oblige you.'

'To oblige me?' cried Wolfe. 'Oh, come! You did, as near as I can see the matter, what you downright had to do in self-defence. Suppose I got into trouble, where would you be? This second little matter flows clearly from the first. Mr Gray is the continuation of Miss Galbraith. You can't begin and then stop. If you begin, you must keep on beginning; that's the truth. No rest for the wicked.'

A horrible sense of blackness and the treachery of fate seized hold upon the soul of the unhappy student.

'My God!' he cried, 'but what have I done? and when did I begin? To be made a class assistant – in the name of reason, where's the harm in that? Service wanted the position; Service might have got it. Would *he* have been where *I* am now?'

'My dear fellow,' said Macfarlane, 'what a boy you are! What harm *has* come to you? What harm *can* come to you if you hold your tongue? Why, man, do you know what this life is? There are two squads of us – the lions and the lambs. If you're a lamb, you'll come to lie upon these tables like Gray or Jane Galbraith; if you're a lion, you'll live and drive a horse like me, like K—, like all the world with any wit or courage. You're staggered at the first. But look at K—! My dear fellow, you're clever, you have pluck. I like you, and K— likes you. You were born to lead the hunt; and I tell you, on my honour and my experience of life, three days from now you'll laugh at all these scarecrows like a High School boy at a farce.'

And with that Macfarlane took his departure and drove off up the wynd in his gig to get under cover before daylight. Fettes was thus left alone with his regrets. He saw the miserable peril in which he stood involved. He saw, with inexpressible dismay, that there was no limit to his weakness, and that, from concession to concession, he had fallen from the arbiter of Macfarlane's destiny to his paid and helpless accomplice. He would have given the world to have been a little braver at the time, but it did not occur to him that he might still be brave. The secret of Jane Galbraith and the cursed entry in the day book closed his mouth.

Hours passed; the class began to arrive; the members of the unhappy Gray were dealt out to one and to another, and received without remark. Richardson was made happy with the head; and, before the hour of freedom rang, Fettes trembled with exultation to perceive how far they had already gone towards safety.

For two days he continued to watch, with an increasing joy, the dreadful process of disguise.

On the third day Macfarlane made his appearance. He had been ill, he said; but he made up for lost time by the energy with which he directed the students. To Richardson in particular he extended the most valuable assistance and advice, and that student, encouraged by the praise of the demonstrator, burned high with ambitious hopes, and saw the medal already in his grasp.

Before the week was out Macfarlane's prophecy had been fulfilled. Fettes had outlived his terrors and had forgotten his baseness. He began to plume himself upon his courage, and had so arranged the story in his mind that he could look back on these events with an unhealthy pride. Of his accomplice he saw but little. They met, of course, in the business of the class; they received their orders together from Mr K——. At times they had a word or two in private, and Macfarlane was from first to last particularly kind and jovial. But it was plain that he avoided any reference to their common secret; and even when Fettes whispered to him that he had cast in his lot with the lions and foresworn the lambs, he only signed to him smilingly to hold his peace.

At length an occasion arose which threw the pair once more into a closer union. Mr K—— was again short of subjects; pupils were eager, and it was a part of this teacher's pretensions to be always well supplied. At the same time there came the news of a burial in a rustic graveyard of Glencorse. Time has little changed the place in question. It stood then, as now, upon a crossroad, out of call of human habitations, and buried fathoms deep in the foliage of six cedar trees. The cries of the sheep upon the neighbouring hills, the stream-lets upon either hand, one loudly singing among pebbles, the other dripping furtively from pond to pond, the stir of the wind in mountainous old flower-ing chestnuts, and once in seven days the voice of the bell and the old tunes of the precentor, were the only sounds that disturbed the silence around the rural church. The Resurrection Man – to use a byname of the period – was not to be deterred by any of the sanc-tities of customary piety. It was part of his trade to despise and desecrate the scrolls and trumpets of old tombs, the paths worn by the feet of worshippers and mourners, and the offerings and the inscriptions of bereaved affection. To rustic neighbourhoods where love is more than commonly tenacious, and where some bonds of blood or fellowship unite the entire society of a parish, the body-snatcher, far from being repelled by natural respect, was attracted by the ease and safety of the task. To bodies that had been laid in earth, in joyful expectation of a far distant awakening, there came that hasty, lamp-lit, terror-haunted resur-rection of the spade and mattock. The coffin was forced, the cerements torn, and the melancholy relics, clad in sack cloth, after being rattled for hours on moonless byways, were at length exposed to uttermost indignities before a class of gaping boys.

Somewhat as two vultures may swoop upon a dying lamb, Fettes and Macfarlane were to be let loose upon a grave in that green and quiet resting-place. The wife of a farmer, a woman who had lived for sixty years, and been known for nothing but good butter and a godly conversation, was to be rooted from her grave at midnight and carried, dead and naked, to that far-away city that she had always honoured with her Sunday best; the place beside her family was to be empty till the crack of doom; her innocent and almost venerable members to be exposed to that last curiosity of the anatomist.

Late one afternoon the pair set forth, well wrapped in cloaks and furnished with a formidable bottle. It rained without remission – a cold, dense, lashing rain. Now and again there blew a puff of wind, but these sheets of falling water kept it down. Bottle and all, it was a sad and silent drive as far as Penicuik, where they were to spend the evening. They stopped once, to hide their implements in a thick bush not far from the churchyard, and once again at the Fisher's Tryst, to have a toast before the kitchen fire and vary their nips of whisky with a glass of ale. When they reached their journey's end the gig was housed, the horse was fed and comforted, and the two young doctors in a private room sat down to the best dinner and the best wine the house afforded. The lights, the fire, the beating rain upon the window, the cold, incongruous work that lay before them, added zest to their enjoyment of the meal. With every glass their cordiality increased. Soon Macfarlane handed a little pile of gold to his companion.

'A compliment,' he said. 'Between friends these little d—d accommodations ought to fly like pipe-lights.'

Fettes pocketed the money, and applauded the sentiment to the echo. 'You are a philosopher,' he cried. 'I was an ass till I knew you. You and K— between you, by the Lord Harry! but you'll make a man of me.'

'Of course we shall,' applauded Macfarlane. 'A man? I tell you, it required a man to back me up the other morning. There are some big, brawling, forty-year-old cowards who would have turned sick at the look of the d—d thing; but not you – you kept your head. I watched you.'

'Well, and why not?' Fettes thus vaunted himself. 'It was no affair of mine. There was nothing to gain on the one side but disturbance, and on the other I could count on your gratitude, don't you see?' And he slapped his pocket till the gold pieces rang.

Macfarlane somehow felt a certain touch of alarm at these unpleasant words. He may have regretted that he had taught his young companion so successfully, but he had no time to interfere, for the other noisily continued in this boastful strain:

'The great thing is not to be afraid. Now, between you and me, I don't want to hang – that's practical; but for all cant, Macfarlane, I was born with a contempt. Hell, God, devil, right, wrong, sin, crime, and all the old gallery of curiosities – they may frighten boys, but men of the world, like you and me, despise them. Here's to the memory of Gray!'

It was by this time growing somewhat late. The gig, according to order, was brought round to the door with both lamps brightly shining, and the young men had to pay their bill and take the road. They announced that they were bound for Peebles, and drove in that direction till they were clear of the last houses of the town; then, extinguishing the lamps, returned upon their course, and followed a by-road towards Glencorse. There was no sound but that of their own passage, and the incessant, strident pouring of the rain. It was pitch dark: here and there a white gate or a white stone in the wall guided them for a short space across the night; but for the most part it was at a foot pace, and almost groping, that they picked their way through that resonant blackness to their solemn and isolated destination. In the sunken woods that traverse the neighbourhood of the burying-ground the last glimmer failed them, and it became necessary to kindle a match and re-illuminate one of the lanterns of the gig. Thus, under the dripping trees, and environed by huge and moving shadows, they reached the scene of their unhallowed labours.

They were both experienced in such affairs, and powerful with the spade; and they had scarce been twenty minutes at their task before they were rewarded by a dull rattle on the coffin-lid. At the same moment, Macfarlane, having hurt his hand upon a stone, flung it carelessly above his head. The grave, in which they now stood almost to the shoulders, was close to the edge of the plateau of the graveyard; and the gig lamp had been propped, the better to illuminate their labours, against a tree, and on the immediate verge of the steep bank descending to the stream. Chance had taken a sure aim with the stone. Then came a clang of broken glass; night fell upon them; sounds alternately dull and ringing announced the bounding of the lantern down the bank, and its occasional collision with the trees. A stone or two, which it had dislodged in its descent, rattled behind it into the profundities of the glen; and then silence, like night, resumed its sway; and they might bend their hearing to its utmost pitch, but naught was to be heard except the rain, now marching to the wind, now steadily falling over miles of open country.

They were so nearly at an end of their abhorred task that they judged it wisest to complete it in the dark. The coffin was exhumed and broken open; the body inserted in the dripping sack and carried between them to the gig; one mounted to keep it in its place, and the other, taking the horse by the mouth, groped along by wall and bush until they reached the wider road by the Fisher's Tryst. Here was a faint, diffused radiancy, which they hailed like daylight; by that they pushed the horse to a good pace and began to rattle along merrily in the direction of the town.

They had both been wetted to the skin during their operations, and now, as the gig jumped among the deep ruts, the thing that stood propped between them fell now upon one and now upon the other. At every repetition of the horrid contact each instinctively repelled it with the greater haste; and the process, natural although it was, began to tell upon the nerves of the companions. Macfarlane made some ill-favoured jest about the farmer's wife, but it came hollowly from his lips, and was allowed to drop in silence. Still their unnatural burden bumped from side to side; and now the head would be laid, as if in confidence, upon their shoulders, and now the drenching sack-cloth would flap icily about their faces. A creeping chill began to possess the soul of Fettes. He peered at the bundle, and it seemed somehow larger than at first. All over the countryside, and from every degree of distance, the farm dogs accompanied their passage with tragic ululations; and it grew and grew upon his mind that some unnatural miracle had been accomplished, that some nameless change had befallen the dead body, and that it was in fear of their unholy burden that the dogs were howling.

'For God's sake,' said he, making a great effort to arrive at speech, 'for God's sake, let's have a light!'

Seemingly Macfarlane was affected in the same direction; for, though he made no reply, he stopped the horse, passed the reins to his companion, got down, and proceeded to kindle the remaining lamp. They had by that time got no farther than the cross-road down to Auchenclinny. The rain still poured as though the deluge were returning, and it was no easy matter to make a light in such a world of wet and darkness. When at last the flickering blue flame had been transferred to the wick and began to expand and clarify, and shed a wide circle of misty brightness round the gig, it became possible for the two young men to see each other and the thing they had along with them. The rain had moulded the rough sacking to the outlines of the body underneath; the head was distinct from the trunk, the shoulders plainly modelled; something at once spectral and human riveted their eyes upon the ghastly comrade of their drive.

For some time Macfarlane stood motionless, holding up the lamp. A nameless dread was swathed, like a wet sheet, about the body, and tightened the white skin upon the face of Fettes; a fear that was meaningless, a horror of what could not be, kept mounting to his brain. Another beat of the watch, and he had spoken. But his comrade forestalled him.

'That is not a woman,' said Macfarlane, in a hushed voice.

'It was a woman when we put her in,' whispered Fettes.

'Hold that lamp,' said the other. 'I must see her face.'

And as Fettes took the lamp his companion untied the fastenings of the sack and drew down the cover from the head. The light fell very clear upon the dark, well-moulded features and smooth-shaven cheeks of a too familiar countenance, often beheld in dreams of both of these young men. A wild yell rang up into the night; each leaped from his own side into the roadway: the lamp fell, broke, and was extinguished; and the horse, terrified by this unusual commotion, bounded and went off toward Edinburgh at a gallop, bearing along with it, sole occupant of the gig, the body of the dead and long-dissected Gray.

Wilkie Collins (1824–89)

━━━━◆⦙⦙⦙⦙⦙⦙◆━━━━

The Story of a Terribly Strange Bed

Ranking closely with 'Dr Jekyll and Mr Hyde' for popularity at the time we are dealing with was the mysterious and macabre novel 'The Woman in White' by Wilkie Collins, the friend and confidant of Charles Dickens. Though in the main only mentioned in the same breath as the great English social novelist, Collins was a distinguished author in his own right and has been assigned the distinction of having written the first full length detective novel, 'The Moonstone'. He also wrote a number of outstanding short stories – many of which were based on personal knowledge or experience – and of these, the one I have reprinted here, 'The Story of a Terribly Strange Bed', is on record in a number of biographies as having sent numerous young readers 'shivering to bed so that never again did they look at their beds with quite the same eyes.' (Charles Dickens.)

SHORTLY after my education at college was finished, I happened to be staying at Paris with an English friend. We were both young men then, and lived, I am afraid, rather a wild life, in the delightful city of our sojourn. One night we were idling about the neighbourhood of the Palais Royal, doubtful to what amusement we should next betake ourselves. My friend proposed a visit to Frascati's; but his suggestion was not to my taste. I knew Frascati's, as the French saying is, by heart; had lost and won plenty of five-franc pieces there, merely for amusement's sake, until it was amusement no longer, and was thoroughly tired, in fact, of all the ghastly respectabilities of such a social anomaly as a respectable gambling-house. 'For heaven's sake,' said I to my friend, 'let us go somewhere where we can see a little genuine, blackguard, poverty-stricken gaming, with no false gingerbread glitter thrown over it at all. Let us get away from fashionable Frascati's, to a house where they don't mind letting in a man with a ragged coat, or a man with no coat, ragged or otherwise.' – 'Very well,' said my friend, 'we needn't go out of the Palais Royal to find the sort of company you want. Here's the place just before us; as blackguard a place, by all report, as you could possibly wish to see.' In another minute we arrived at the door, and entered the house.

When we got upstairs, and left our hats and sticks with the doorkeeper, we were admitted into the chief gambling-room. We did not find many people assembled there. But, few as the men were who looked up at us on our entrance, they were all types – lamentably true types – of their respective classes.

We had come to see blackguards; but these men were something worse. There is a comic side, more or less appreciable, in all blackguardism – here there was nothing but tragedy – mute, weird tragedy. The quiet in the room was horrible. The thin, haggard, long-haired young man, whose sunken eyes fiercely watched the turning up of the cards, never spoke; the flabby, fat-faced, pimply player, who pricked his piece of pasteboard perseveringly, to register how often black won, and how often red – never spoke; the dirty, wrinkled old man, with the vulture eyes and the darned greatcoat, who had lost his last *sou*, and still looked on desperately, after he could play no longer – never spoke. Even the voice of the croupier sounded as if it were strangely dulled and thickened in the atmosphere of the room. I had entered the place to laugh, but the spectacle before me was something to weep over. I soon found it necessary to take refuge in excitement from the depression of spirits which was fast stealing on me. Unfortunately I sought the nearest excitement, by going to the table, and beginning to play. Still more unfortunately, as the events will show, I won – won prodigiously; won incredibly; won at such a rate, that the regular players at the table crowded round me, and, staring at my stakes with hungry, superstitious eyes, whispered to one another that the English stranger was going to break the bank.

The game was *Rouge et Noir*. I had played at it in every city in Europe, without, however, the care or the wish to study the Theory of Chances – that philosopher's stone of all gamblers! And a gambler, in the strict sense of the word, I had never been. I was heart-whole from the corroding passion for play. My gaming was a mere idle amusement. I never resorted to it by necessity, because I never knew what it was to want money. I never practised it so incessantly as to lose more than I could afford, or to gain more than I could coolly pocket without being thrown off my balance by my good luck. In short, I had hitherto frequented gambling-tables – just as I frequented ball-rooms and opera-houses – because they amused me, and because I had nothing better to do with my leisure hours.

But on this occasion it was very different – now, for the first time in my life, I felt what the passion for play really was. My success first bewildered, and then, in the most literal meaning of the word, intoxicated me. Incredible as it may appear, it is nevertheless true, that I only lost when I attempted to estimate chances, and played according to previous calculation. If I left everything to luck, and staked without any care or consideration, I was sure to win – to win in the face of every recognized probability in favour of the bank. At first, some of the men present ventured their money safely enough on my colour; but I speedily increased my stakes to sums which they dared not risk. One after another they left off playing, and breathlessly looked on at my game.

Still, time after time, I staked higher and higher, and still won. The excitement in the room rose to fever pitch. The silence was interrupted by a deep-muted chorus of oaths and exclamations in different languages every time the gold was shovelled across to my side of the table – even the imperturbable croupier dashed his rake to the floor in a (French) fury of astonishment at my success. But one man present preserved his self-possession; and that man was my friend. He came to my side and, whispering in English, begged me to leave the place, satisfied with what I had already gained. I must do him the justice to say that he repeated his warnings and entreaties several times, and only left me and went away, after I had rejected his advice (I was to all intents and purposes gambling-drunk) in terms which rendered it impossible for him to address me again that night.

Shortly after he had gone, a horse voice behind me cried: 'Permit me, my dear sir! – permit me to restore to their proper place two Napoleons which you have dropped. Wonderful luck, sir! I pledge you my word of honour, as an old soldier, in the course of my long experience in this sort of thing, I never saw such luck as yours! – never! Go on, sir – *sacré mille bombes!* Go on boldly, and break the bank!'

I turned round and saw, nodding and smiling at me with inveterate civility, a tall man, dressed in a frogged and braided surtout.

If I had been in my senses, I should have considered him, personally, as being rather a suspicious specimen of an old soldier. He had goggling blood-shot eyes, mangy mustachios, and a broken nose. His voice betrayed a barrack-room intonation of the worst order, and he had the dirtiest pair of hands I ever saw – even in France. These little personal peculiarities exercised, however, no repelling influence on me. In the mad excitement the reckless triumph of that moment, I was ready to 'fraternize' with anybody who encouraged me in my game. I accepted the old soldier's offered pinch of snuff; clapped him on the back, and swore he was the honestest fellow in the world – the most glorious relic of the Grand Army that I had ever met with. 'Go on!' cried my military friend, snapping his fingers in ecstasy – 'Go on, and win! Break the bank – *mille tonnerres!* my gallant English comrade, break the bank!'

And I *did* go on – went on at such a rate that in another quarter of an hour the croupier called out: 'Gentlemen! the bank has discontinued for tonight.' All the notes, and all the gold in that 'bank', now lay in a heap under my hands; the whole floating capital of the gambling-house was waiting to pour into my pockets!

'Tie up the money in your pocket-handkerchief, my worthy sir,' said the old soldier, as I wildly plunged my hands into my heap of gold. 'Tie it up, as we used to tie up a bit of dinner in the Grand Army; your winnings are too heavy for any breeches pockets that ever were sewed. There! that's it! – shovel them in, notes and all! *Crediè!* what luck! – Stop! another Napoleon on the floor! *Ah! sacré petit polisson de Napoléon!* have I found thee at last? Now then, sir – two tight double knots each way with your honourable permission, and the money's safe. Feel it! Feel it, fortunate sir! hard and round as a cannon ball – *ah, bah!* if they had only fired such cannon balls at us at Austerlitz – *nom d'une pipe!* if they only had! And now, as an ancient grenadier, as an ex-brave of the French Army, what remains for me to do? I ask what? Simply this: to entreat my valued English friend to drink a bottle of champagne with me, and toast the goddess Fortune in foaming goblets before we part!'

Excellent ex-brave! Convivial ancient grenadier! Champagne by all means! An English cheer for an old soldier! Hurrah! hurrah! Another English cheer for the goddess Fortune! Hurrah! hurrah! hurrah!

'Bravo! the Englishman; the amiable, gracious Englishman, in whose veins circulates the vivacious blood of France! Another glass? *Ah, bah!* – the bottle is empty! Never mind! *Vive le vin!* I, the old soldier, order another bottle, and half a pound of *bonbons* with it!'

'No, no, ex-brave; never – ancient grenadier! *Your* bottle last time; *my* bottle this. Behold it! Toast away! The French Army! – the great Napoleon! – the present company! the croupier! the honest croupier's wife and daughters – if he has any! the Ladies generally! Everybody in the world!'

By the time the second bottle of champagne was

emptied, I felt as if I had been drinking liquid fire – my brain seemed all a-flame. No excess in wine ever had this effect on me before in my life. Was it the result of a stimulant acting upon my system when I was in a highly excited state? Was my stomach in a particularly disordered condition? Or was the champagne amazingly strong?

'Ex-brave of the French Army!' cried I, in a mad state of exhilaration, '*I* am on fire! how are *you*? You have set me on fire! Do you hear, my hero of Austerlitz? Let us have a third bottle of champagne to put the flame out!'

The old soldier wagged his head, rolled his goggle eyes, until I expected to see them slip out of their sockets; placed his dirty forefinger by the side of his broken nose; solemnly ejaculated 'Coffee!' and immediately ran off into an inner room.

The word pronounced by the eccentric veteran seemed to have a magical effect on the rest of the company present. With one accord they all rose to depart. Probably they had expected to profit by my intoxication; but finding that my new friend was benevolently bent on preventing me from getting dead drunk, had now abandoned all hope of thriving pleasantly on my winnings. Whatever their motive might be, at any rate they went away in a body. When the old soldier returned, and sat down again opposite to me at the table, we had the room to ourselves. I could see the croupier, in a sort of vestibule which opened out of it, eating his supper in solitude. The silence was now deeper than ever.

A sudden change, too, had come over the 'ex-brave'. He assumed a portentiously solemn look! and when he spoke to me again, his speech was ornamented by no oaths, enforced by no finger-snapping, enlivened by no apostrophes or exclamations.

'Listen, my dear sir,' said he, in mysteriously confidential tones – 'listen to an old soldier's advice. I have been to the mistress of the house (a very charming woman, with a genius for cookery!) to impress on her the necessity of making us some particularly strong and good coffee. You must drain this coffee in order to get rid of your little amiable exaltation of spirits before you think of going home – you *must*, my good and gracious friend! With all that money to take home to-night, it is a sacred duty to yourself to have your wits about you. You are known to be a winner to an enormous extent by several gentlemen present tonight, who, in a certain point of view, are very worthy and excellent fellows, but they are mortal men, my dear sir, and they have their amiable weaknesses! Need I say more? Ah, no, no! you understand me! Now, this is what you must do – send for a cabriolet when you feel quite well again – draw up all the windows when you get into it – and tell the driver to take you home only through the large and well-lighted thoroughfares. Do this; and you and your money will be safe. Do this; and tomorrow you will thank an old soldier for giving you a word of honest advice.'

Just as the ex-brave ended his oration in very lachrymose tones, the coffee came in, ready poured out in two cups. My attentive friend handed me one of the cups with a bow. I was parched with thirst, and drank it off at a draught. Almost instantly afterwards, I was seized with a fit of giddiness, and felt more completely intoxicated than ever. The room whirled round and round furiously; the old soldier seemed to be regularly bobbing up and down before me like the piston of a steam-engine. I was half deafened by a violent singing in my ears; a feeling of utter bewilderment, helplessness, idiocy, overcame me. I rose from my chair, holding on by the table to keep my balance, and stammered out that I felt dreadfully unwell – so unwell that I did not know how I was to get home.

'My dear friend,' answered the old soldier – and even his voice seemed to be bobbing up and down as he spoke – 'my dear friend, it would be madness to go home in *your* state; you would be sure to lose your money; you might be robbed and murdered with the greatest ease. *I* am going to sleep here: do *you* sleep here, too – they make up capital beds in this house – take one; sleep off the effects of the wine, and go home safely with your winnings tomorrow – tomorrow, in broad daylight.'

I had but two ideas left : – one, that I must never let go hold of my handkerchief full of money; the other, that I must lie down somewhere immediately, and fall off into a comfortable sleep. So I agreed to the proposal about the bed, and took the offered arm of the old soldier, carrying my money with my disengaged hand. Preceded by the croupier, we passed along some passages and up a flight of stairs into the bedroom which I was to occupy. The ex-brave shook me warmly by the hand, proposed that we should breakfast together, and then, followed by the croupier, left me for the night.

I ran to the wash-hand stand; drank some of the water in my jug; poured the rest out, and plunged my face into it; then sat down in a chair and tried to compose myself. I soon felt better. The change for my lungs, from the fetid atmosphere of the gambling-room to the cool air of the apartment I now occupied; the almost equally refreshing change for my eyes, from the glaring gas-lights of the 'salon' to the dim, quiet flicker of one bedroom candle, aided wonderfully the restorative effects of cold water. The giddiness left me, and I began to feel a little like a reasonable being again. My first thought was of the risk of sleeping all night in a gambling-house; my second, of the still greater risk of trying to get out after the house was closed, and of going home alone at night, through the streets of Paris, with a large sum of money about me. I had slept in worse places than this on my travels; so I determined to lock, bolt, and barricade my door, and take my chance till the next morning.

Accordingly, I secured myself against all intrusion; looked under the bed, and into the cupboard; tried the fastening of the window; and then, satisfied that I had taken every proper precaution, pulled off my upper clothing, put my light, which was a dim one, on the hearth among a feathery litter of wood ashes, and got into bed, with the handkerchief full of money under my pillow.

I soon felt not only that I could not go to sleep, but that I could not even close my eyes. I was wide awake, and in a high fever. Every nerve in my body trembled – every one of my senses seemed to be preternaturally sharpened. I tossed and rolled, and tried every kind of position, and perseveringly sought out the cold corners of the bed, and all to no purpose. Now, I thrust my arms over the clothes; now, I poked them under the clothes; now, I violently shot my legs straight out down to the bottom of the bed; now, I convulsively coiled them up as near my chin as they would go; now I shook out my crumpled pillow, changed it to the cool side, patted it flat, and lay down quietly on my back; now, I fiercely doubled it in two, set it up on end, thrust it against the board of the bed, and tried a sitting posture. Every effort was in vain; I groaned with vexation, as I felt that I was in for a sleepless night.

What could I do? I had no book to read. And yet, unless I found out some method of diverting my mind, I felt certain that I was in the condition to imagine all sorts of horrors; to rack my brain with forebodings of every possible and impossible danger; in short, to pass the night in suffering all conceivable varieties of nervous terror.

I raised myself on my elbow, and looked about the room – which was brightened by a lovely moonlight pouring straight through the window – to see if it contained any pictures or ornaments that I could at all clearly distinguish. While my eyes wandered from wall to wall, a remembrance of Le Maistre's delightful little book, *Voyage autour de ma Chambre*, occurred to me. I resolved to imitate the French author, and find occupation and amusement enough to relieve the tedium of my wakefulness, by making a mental inventory of every article of furniture I could see, and by following up to their sources the multitude of associations which even a chair, a table, or a wash-stand may be made to call forth.

In the nervous unsettled state of my mind at that moment, I found it much easier to make my inventory than to make my reflections, and thereupon soon gave up all hope of thinking in Le Maistre's fanciful track – or, indeed, of thinking at all. I looked about the room at the different articles of furniture, and did nothing more.

There was, first, the bed I was lying in; a four-post bed, of all things in the world to meet with in Paris! – yes, a thoroughly clumsy British four-poster, with the regular top lined with chintz – the regular fringed valance all around – the regular stifling unwholesome curtains, which I remembered having mechanically drawn back against the posts without particularly noticing the bed when I first got into the room. Then there was the marble-topped wash-hand stand, from which the water I had spilt, in my hurry to pour it out, was still dripping, slowly and more slowly, on to the brick floor. Then two small chairs, with my coat, waistcoat, and trousers flung on them. Then a large elbow-chair covered with dirty-white dimity, with my cravat and shirt-collar thrown over the back. Then a chest of drawers with two of the brass handles off, and a tawdry, broken china inkstand placed on it by way of ornament for the top. Then the dressing-table, adorned by a very small looking-glass, and a very large pincushion. Then the window – an unusually large window. Then a dark old picture, which the feeble candle dimly showed me. It was the picture of a fellow in a high Spanish hat, crowned with a plume of towering feathers. A swarthy sinister ruffian, looking upward, shading his eyes with his hand, and looking intently upward – it might be at some tall gallows at which he was going to be hanged. At any rate, he had the appearance of thoroughly deserving it.

This picture put a kind of constraint upon me to look upward too – at the top of the bed. It was a gloomy and not an interesting object, and I looked back at the picture. I counted the feathers in the man's hat – they stood out in relief – three white, two green. I observed the crown of his hat, which was of a conical shape, according to the fashion supposed to have been favoured by Guido Fawkes. I wondered what he was looking up at. It couldn't be at the stars; such a desperado was neither astrologer nor astronomer. It must be at the high gallows, and he was going to be hanged presently. Would the executioner come into possession of his conical-crowned hat and plume of feathers? I counted the feathers again – three white, two green.

While I still lingered over this very improving intellectual employment, my thoughts insensibly began to wander. The moonlight shining into the room reminded me of a certain moonlight night in England – the night after a picnic party in a Welsh valley. Every incident of the drive homeward, through lovely scenery, which the moonlight made lovelier than ever, came back to my remembrance, though I had never given the picnic a thought for years; though, if I had *tried* to recollect it, I could certainly have recalled little or nothing of that scene long past. Of all the wonderful faculties that help to tell us we are immortal, which speaks the sublime truth more eloquently than memory? Here was I, in a strange house of the most suspicious character, in a situation of uncertainty, and even of peril, which might seem to make the cool exercise of my recollection almost out of the question; nevertheless, remembering, quite involuntarily, places, people, conversations, minute circumstances of every kind, which I had thought forgotten for ever; which I could not possibly have recalled at will, even under the most favourable auspices. And what cause had produced in a moment the whole of this strange, complicated, mysterious effect? Nothing but some rays of moonlight shining in at my bedroom window.

I was still thinking of the picnic – of our merriment on the drive home – of the sentimental young lady who *would* quote *Childe Harold* because it was moonlight. I was absorbed by these past scenes and past amusements, when, in an instant, the thread on which my memories hung snapped asunder; my attention immediately came back to present things more vividly than ever, and I found myself, I neither knew why nor wherefore, looking hard at the picture again.

Looking for what?

Good God! the man had pulled his hat down on his brows! — No! the hat itself was gone! Where was the conical crown? Where the feathers — three white, two green? Not there! In place of the hat and feather, what dusky object was it that now hid his forehead, his eyes, his shading hand?

Was the bed moving?

I turned on my back and looked up. Was I mad? drunk? dreaming? giddy again? or was the top of the bed really moving down — sinking slowly, regularly, silently, horribly, right down through the whole of its length and breadth — right down upon me, as I lay underneath?

My blood semed to stand still. A deadly paralysing coldness stole all over me, as I turned my head round on the pillow, and determined to test whether the bedtop was really moving or not by keeping my eye on the man in the picture.

The next look in that direction was enough. The dull, black, frowsy outline of the valance above me was within an inch of being parallel with his waist. I still looked breathlessly. And steadily, and slowly — very slowly — I saw the figure, and the line of frame below the figure, vanish, as the valance moved down before it.

I am, constitutionally, anything but timid. I have been on more than one occasion in peril of my life, and have not lost my self-possession for an instant; but when the conviction first settled on my mind that the bed-top was really moving, was steadily and continuously sinking down upon me, I looked up shuddering, helpless, panic-stricken, beneath the hideous machinery for murder, which was advancing closer and closer to suffocate me where I lay.

I looked up, motionless, speechless, breathless. The candle, fully spent, went out; but the moonlight still brightened the room. Down and down, without pausing and without sounding, came the bed-top and still my panic-terror seemed to bind me faster and faster to the mattress on which I lay – down and down it sank, till the dusty odour from the lining of the canopy came stealing into my nostrils.

At that final moment the instinct of self-preservation startled me out of my trance, and I moved at last. There was just room for me to roll myself sideways off the bed. As I dropped noiselessly to the floor, the edge of the murderous canopy touched me on the shoulder.

Without stopping to draw my breath, without wiping the cold sweat from my face, I rose instantly on my knees to watch the bed-top. I was literally spellbound by it. If I had heard footsteps behind me, I could not have turned round; if a means of escape had been miraculously provided for me, I could not have moved to take advantage of it. The whole life in me was, at that moment, concentrated in my eyes.

It descended – the whole canopy, with the fringe round it, came down – down – close down; so close that there was not room now to squeeze my finger between the bed-top and the bed. I felt at the sides, and discovered that what had appeared to me from beneath to be the ordinary light canopy of a four-post bed, was in reality a thick, broad mattress, the substance of which was concealed by the valance and its fringe. I looked up and saw the four posts rising, hideously bare. In the middle of the bed-top was a huge wooden screw that had evidently worked it down through a hole in the ceiling, just as ordinary presses are worked down on the substance selected for compression. The frightful apparatus moved without making the faintest noise. There had been no creaking as it came down; there was now not the faintest sound from the room above. Amid a dead and awful silence I beheld before me – in the nineteenth century, and in the civilized capital of France – such a machine for secret murder by suffocation as might have existed in the worst days of the Inquisition, in the lonely inns among the Hartz Mountains, in the mysterious tribunals of Westphalia! Still, as I looked on it, I could not move, I could hardly breathe, but I began to recover the power of thinking, and in a moment I discovered the murderous conspiracy framed against me in all its horror.

My cup of coffee had been drugged, and drugged too strongly. I had been saved from being smothered by having taken an overdose of some narcotic. How I had chafed and fretted at the fever-fit which had preserved my life by keeping me awake! How recklessly I had confided myself to the two wretches who had led me into this room, determined, for the sake of my winnings, to kill me in my sleep by the surest and most horrible contrivance for secretly accomplishing my destruction! How many men, winners like me, had slept, as I had proposed to sleep, in that bed, and had never been seen or heard of more! I shuddered at the bare idea of it.

But, ere long, all thought was again suspended by the sight of the murderous canopy moving once more. After it had remained on the bed – as nearly as I could guess – about ten minutes, it began to move up again. The villains who worked it from above evidently believed that their purpose was now accomplished. Slowly and silently, as it had descended, that horrible bed-top rose towards its former place. When it reached the upper extremities of the four posts, it reached the ceiling too. Neither hole nor screw could be seen; the bed became in appearance an ordinary bed again – the canopy an ordinary canopy – even to the most suspicious eyes.

Now, for the first time, I was able to move – to rise from my knees – to dress myself in my upper clothing – and to consider of how I should escape. If I betrayed, by the smallest noise, that the attempt to suffocate me had failed, I was certain to be murdered. Had I made any noise already? I listened intently, looking towards the door.

No! no footsteps in the passage outside – no sound of a tread, light or heavy, in the room above – absolute silence everywhere. Besides locking and bolting my door, I had moved an old wooden chest against it, which I had found under the bed. To remove this chest (my blood ran cold as I thought of what its contents *might* be!) without making some disturbance was impossible; and, moreover, to think of escaping through the house, now barred up for the night, was sheer insanity. Only one chance was left me – the window. I stole to it on tiptoe.

My bedroom was on the first floor, above an *entresol*, and looked into the back street, which you have sketched in your view. I raised my hand to open the window, knowing that on that action hung, by the merest hair's-breadth, my chance of safety. They keep vigilant watch in a House of Murder. If any part of the

frame cracked, if the hinge creaked, I was a lost man!
It must have occupied me at least five minutes, reckoning by time – five *hours*, reckoning by suspense – to
open that window. I succeeded in doing it silently – in
doing it with all the dexterity of a housebreaker – and
then looked down into the street. To leap the distance
beneath me would be almost certain destruction!
Next, I looked round at the sides of the house. Down
the left side ran the thick water-pipe which you have
drawn – it passed close by the outer edge of the window. The moment I saw the pipe, I knew I was saved.
My breath came and went freely for the first time since
I had seen the canopy of the bed moving down upon
me!

To some men the means of escape which I had discovered might have seemed difficult and dangerous
enough – to *me* the prospect of slipping down the pipe
into the street did not sugggest even a thought of peril.
I had always been accustomed, by the practice of gym-
nastics, to keep up my schoolboy powers as a daring
and expert climber; and knew that my head, hands,
and feet would serve me faithfully in any hazards of
ascent or descent. I had already got one leg over the
window-sill, when I remembered the handkerchief
filled with money under my pillow. I could well have
afforded to leave it behind me, but I was revengefully
determined that the miscreants of the gambling-house
should miss their plunder as well as their victim. So I
went back to the bed and tied the heavy handkerchief
at my back by my cravat.

Just as I had made it tight and fixed it in a comfortable place, I thought I heard a sound of breathing outside the door. The chill feeling of horror ran through
me again as I listened. No! dead silence still in the

passage – I had only heard the night air blowing softly into the room. The next moment I was on the window-sill – and the next I had a firm grip on the water-pipe with my hands and knees.

I slid down into the street easily and quietly, as I thought I should, and immediately set off at the top of my speed to a branch 'Prefecture' of Police, which I knew was situated in the immediate neighbourhood. A 'Sub-prefect', and several picked men among his subordinates, happened to be up, maturing, I believe, some scheme for discovering the perpetrator of a mysterious murder which all Paris was talking of just then. When I began my story, in a breathless hurry and in very bad French, I could see the Sub-prefect suspected me of being a drunken Englishman who had robbed somebody; but he soon altered his opinion as I went on, and before I had anything like concluded, he shoved all the papers before him into a drawer, put on his hat, supplied me with another (for I was bare-headed), ordered a file of soldiers, desired his expert followers to get ready all sorts of tools for breaking open doors and ripping up brick-flooring, and took my arm, in the most friendly and familiar manner possible, to lead me with him out of the house. I will venture to say, that when the Sub-prefect was a little boy, and was taken for the first time to the play, he was not half as much pleased as he was now at the job in prospect for him at the gambling-house!

Away we went through the streets, the Sub-prefect cross-examining and congratulating me in the same breath as we marched at the head of our formidable *posse comitatus*. Sentinels were placed at the back and front of the house the moment we got to it; a tremendous battery of knocks was directed against the door; a light appeared at a window; I was told to conceal myself behind the police – then came more knocks, and a cry of 'Open in the name of the law!' At that terrible summons bolts and locks gave way before an invisible hand, and the moment after the Sub-prefect was in the passage, confronting a waiter half-dressed and ghastly pale. This was the short dialogue which immediately took place:

'We want to see the Englishman who is sleeping in this house.'

'He went away hours ago.'

'He did no such thing. His friend went away; *he* remained. Show us to his bedroom!'

'I swear to you, Monsieur le Sous-prefect, he is not here! he –'

'I swear to you, Monsieur le Garçon, he is. He slept here – he didn't find your bed comfortable – he came to us to complain of it – here he is among my men – and here am I ready to look for a flea or two in his bedstead. Renaudin!' (calling to one of the subordinates, and pointing to the waiter) 'collar that man, and tie his hands behind him. Now, then, gentlemen, let us walk upstairs!'

Every man and woman in the house was secured – the 'Old Soldier' the first. Then I identified the bed in which I had slept, and then we went into the room above.

No object that was at all extraordinary appeared in any part of it. The Sub-prefect looked round the place, commanded everybody to be silent, stamped twice on the floor, called for a candle, looked attentively at the spot he had stamped on, and ordered the flooring there to be carefully taken up. This was done in no time. Lights were produced, and we saw a deep raftered cavity between the floor of this room and the ceiling of the room beneath. Through this cavity there ran perpendicularly a sort of case of iron thickly greased; and inside the case appeared the screw, which communicated with the bed-top below. Extra lengths of screw, freshly oiled; levers covered with felt; all the complete upper works of a heavy press – constructed with infernal ingenuity so as to join the fixtures below, and when taken to pieces again to go into the smallest possible compass – were next discovered and pulled out on the floor. After some little difficulty, the Sub-prefect succeeded in putting the machinery together, and, leaving his men to work it, descended with me to the bedroom. The smothering canopy was then lowered, but not so noiselessly as I had seen it lowered. When I mentioned this to the Sub-prefect, his answer, simple as it was had a terrible significance. 'My men,' said he, 'are working down the bed-top for the first time – the men whose money you won were in better practice.'

We left the house in the sole possession of two police agents – every one of the inmates being removed to prison on the spot. The Sub-prefect, after taking down my *proces-verbal* in his office, returned with me to my hotel to get my passport. 'Do you think,' I asked, as I gave it to him, 'that any men have really been smothered in that bed, as they tried to smother *me*?'

'I have seen dozens of drowned men laid out at the Morgue,' answered the Sub-prefect, 'in whose pocketbooks were found letters, stating that they had committed suicide in the Seine, because they had lost everything at the gaming-table. Do I know how many of those men entered the same gambling-house that *you* entered? won as *you* won? took that bed as *you* took it? slept in it? were smothered in it? and were privately thrown into the river, with a letter of explanation written by the murderers and placed in their pocket-books? No man can say how many or how few have suffered the fate from which you have escaped. The people of the gambling-house kept their bedstead machinery a secret from *us* – even from the police! The dead kept the rest of the secret for them. Good night, or rather good morning, Monsieur Faulkner! Be at my office again at nine o'clock – in the meantime, *au revoir!'*

The rest of my story is soon told. I was examined and re-examined; the gambling-house was strictly searched all through from top to bottom; the prisoners were separately interrogated; and two of the less guilty among them made a confession. *I* discovered that the old soldier was the master of the gambling-house – justice discovered that he had been drummed out of the army as a vagabond years ago; that he had been guilty of all sorts of villainies since; that he was in possession of stolen property, which the owners identified; and that he, the croupier, another accomplice, and the woman who had made my cup of coffee, were all in the secret of the bedstead. There appeared some reason to doubt whether the inferior persons attached to the house knew anything of the suffocating machinery; and they received the benefit of that doubt, by being treated simply as thieves and vagabonds. As for the old soldier and his two head-myrmidons, they went to the galleys; the woman who had drugged my coffee was imprisoned for I forget how many years; the regular attendants at the gambling-house were considered 'suspicious', and placed under 'surveillance'; and I became, for one whole week (which is a long time), the head 'lion' in Parisian society. My adventure was dramatized by three illustrious playmakers, but never saw theatrical daylight; for the censorship forbade the introduction on the stage of a correct copy of the gambling-house bedstead.

One good result was produced by my adventure, which any censorship must have approved: it cured me of ever again trying *Rouge et Noir* as an amusement. The sight of a green cloth, with packs of cards and heaps of money on it, will henceforth be for ever associated in my mind with the sight of a bed-canopy descending to suffocate me in the silence and darkness of the night.

Edgar Allan Poe (1809–49)

━━━━━◁◆▷━━━━━

The Tell Tale Heart

While it is indisputably true that Wilkie Collins wrote the first full length detective novel, the genre per se was actually originated by an American, the next contributor, Edgar Allan Poe. His tale 'The Murders in the Rue Morgue' gave to literature the idea of a mystery solved by detection and it continues today to form the model of all such stories. Poe also played a major role in the evolvement of the macabre story as we now know it, and in his tales took the old-fashioned idea of the haunted Gothic castle and 'unseen terrors' and translated them into modern terms that gave the horrors a terrifying reality they had never had before. Most of Poe's stories are now rightly held as classics, many have formed the basis of successful – if not always accurate – films, and no reader who enjoys a good thrill should overlook his work. For this collection, I have selected one of the master's shortest and most effective stories which delivers a moral lesson with terrifying clarity.

TRUE! – nervous – very, very dreadfully nervous I had been and am; but why *will* you say that I am mad? The disease had sharpened my senses – not destroyed – not dulled them. Above all was the sense of hearing acute. I heard all things in the heaven and in the earth. I heard many things in hell. How, then, am I mad?

Hearken! and observe how healthily – how calmly I can tell you the whole story.

It is impossible to say how first the idea entered my brain; but once conceived, it haunted me day and night. Object there was none. Passion there was none. I loved the old man. He had never wronged me. He had never given me insult. For his gold I had no desire. I think it was his eye! yes, it was this! One of his eyes resembled that of a vulture – a pale blue eye, with a film over it. Whenever it fell upon me, my blood ran cold; and so by degrees – very gradually – I made up my mind to take the life of the old man, and thus rid myself of the eye for ever.

Now this is the point. You fancy me mad. Madmen know nothing. But you should have seen *me*. You should have seen how wisely I proceeded – with what caution – with what foresight – with what dissimulation I went to work! I was never kinder to the old man than during the whole week before I killed him. And every night, about midnight, I turned the latch of his door and opened it – oh, so gently! And then when I had made an opening sufficient for my head, I put in a dark lantern, all closed, closed, so that no light shone out, and then I thrust in my head. Oh, you would have laughed to see how cunningly I thrust it in! I moved it slowly – very, very slowly, so that I might not disturb the old man's sleep. It took me an hour to place my whole head within the opening so far that I could see him as he lay upon his bed. Ha! – would a madman have been so wise as this? And then, when my head was well in the room, I undid the lantern cautiously – oh, so cautiously – cautiously (for the hinges creaked) – I undid it just so much that a single thin ray fell upon the vulture eye. And this I did for seven long nights –

every night just at midnight – but I found the eye always closed; and so it was impossible to do the work; for it was not the old man who vexed me, but his Evil Eye. And every morning, when the day broke, I went boldly into the chamber, and spoke courageously to him, calling him by name in a hearty tone, and inquiring how he had passed the night. So you see he would have been a very profound old man, indeed, to suspect that every night, just at twelve, I looked in upon him while he slept.

Upon the eighth night I was more than usually cautious in opening the door. A watch's minute hand moves more quickly than did mine. Never before that night had I *felt* the extent of my own powers – of my sagacity. I could scarcely contain my feelings of triumph. To think that there I was, opening the door, little by little, and he not even to dream of my secret deeds or thoughts. I fairly chuckled at the idea; and perhaps he heard me; for he moved on the bed suddenly, as if startled. Now you may think that I drew back but no. His room was as black as pitch with the thick darkness (for the shutters were close fastened, through fear of robbers), and so I knew that he could not see the opening of the door, and I kept pushing it on steadily, steadily.

I had my head in, and was about to open the lantern, when my thumb slipped upon the tin fastening, and the old man sprang up in the bed, crying out – 'Who's there?'

I kept quite still and said nothing. For a whole hour I did not move a muscle, and in the meantime I did not hear him lie down. He was still sitting up in the bed, listening; – just as I have done, night after night, hearkening to the death-watches in the wall.

Presently I heard a slight groan, and I knew it was the groan of mortal terror. It was not a groan of pain or of grief – oh, no! – it was the low stifled sound that arises from the bottom of the soul when overcharged with awe. I knew the sound well. Many a night, just at midnight, when all the world slept, it has welled up from my own bosom, deepening, with its dreadful echo, the terrors that distracted me. I say I knew it well. I knew what the old man felt, and pitied him, although I chuckled at heart. I knew that he had been lying awake ever since the first slight noise, when he had turned in the bed. His fears had been ever since growing upon him. He had been trying to fancy them causeless, but could not. He had been saying to himself – 'It is nothing but the wind in the chimney – it is only a mouse crossing the floor,' or, 'it is merely a cricket which has made a single chirp.' Yes, he had been trying to comfort himself with these suppositions: but he had found all in vain. *All in vain*; because Death, in approaching him, had stalked with his black shadow before him, and enveloped the victim. And it was the mournful influence of the unperceived shadow that caused him to feel – although he neither saw nor heard – to *feel* the presence of my head within the room.

When I had waited a long time, very patiently, without hearing him lie down, I resolved to open a little – a very, very little crevice in the lantern. So I opened it – you cannot imagine how stealthily, stealthily – until, at length, a single dim ray, like the thread of the spider, shot from out of the crevice and fell upon the vulture eye.

It was open – wide, wide open – and I grew furious as I gazed upon it. I saw it with perfect distinctness – all a dull blue, with a hideous veil over it that chilled the very marrow in my bones; but I could see nothing else of the old man's face or person: for I had directed the ray, as if by instinct, precisely upon the damned spot.

And now have I not told you that what you mistake for madness is but over acuteness of the senses? – now, I say, there came to my ears a low, dull, quick sound, such as a watch makes when enveloped in cotton. I knew *that* sound well, too. It was the beating of the old man's heart. It increased my fury, as the beating of a drum stimulates the soldier into courage.

But even yet I refrained and kept still. I scarcely breathed. I held the lantern motionless. I tried how steadily I could maintain the ray upon the eye. Meantime the hellish tattoo of the heart increased. It grew quicker and quicker, and louder and louder every instant. The old man's terror *must* have been extreme! It grew louder, I say, louder every moment! – do you mark me well? I have told you that I am nervous: so I am. And now, at the dead hour of the night, amid the dreadful silence of that old house, so strange a noise as this excited me to uncontrollable terror. Yet, for some minutes longer, I refrained and stood still. But the beating grew louder, louder! I thought the heart must burst. And now a new anxiety seized me – the sound would be heard by a neighbour! The old man's hour had come! With a loud yell I threw open the lantern and leaped into the room. He shrieked once – once only. In an instant I dragged him to the floor, and pulled the heavy bed over him. I then smiled gaily, to find the deed so far done. But, for many minutes, the heart beat on with a muffled sound. This, however, did not vex me; it would not be heard through the wall. At length it ceased. The old man was dead. I removed the bed and examined the corpse. Yes, he was stone, stone dead. I placed my hand upon the heart and held it there many minutes. There was no pulsation. He was stone dead. His eye would trouble me no more.

If still you think me mad, you will think so no longer when I describe the wise precautions I took for the concealment of the body. The night waned, and I worked hastily, but in silence. First of all I dismembered the corpse. I cut off the head and the arms and the legs.

I then took up three planks from the flooring of the chamber and deposited all between the scantlings. I then replaced the boards so cleverly, so cunningly, that no human eye – not even *his* – could have detected anything wrong. There was nothing to wash out – no stain of any kind – no blood-spot whatever. I had been too wary for that. A tub had caught all – ha! ha!

When I had made an end of these labours, it was four o'clock – still dark as midnight. As the bell sounded the hour, there came a knocking at the street door. I went down to open it with a light heart – for what had I *now* to fear? There entered three men, who introduced themselves with perfect suavity, as officers of the police. A shriek had been heard by a neighbour during the night; suspicion of foul play had been aroused; information had been lodged at the police office, and they (the officers) had been deputed to search the premises.

I smiled – for *what* had I to fear? I bade the gentlemen welcome. The shriek, I said, was my own in a dream. The old man, I mentioned, was absent in the country. I took my visitors all over the house. I bade them search – search *well*. I led them, at length, to *his* chamber. I showed them his treasures, secure, undisturbed. In the enthusiasm of my confidence, I brought chairs into the room, and desired them *here* to rest from their fatigues, while I myself, in the wild audacity of my perfect triumph, placed my own seat upon the very spot beneath which reposed the corpse of the victim.

The officers were satisfied. My *manner* had convinced them. I was singularly at ease. They sat, and while I answered cheerily, they chatted of familiar things. But, ere long, I felt myself getting pale and wished them gone. My head ached, and I fancied a ringing in my ears: but still they sat and still chatted. The ringing became more distinct: – it continued and became more distinct: I talked more freely to get rid of the feeling: but it continued and gained definitiveness – until, at length, I found that the noise was *not* within my ears.

No doubt I now grew *very* pale; – but I talked more fluently, and with a heightened voice. Yet the sound increased – and what could I do? It was a *low, dull, quick sound – much such a sound as a watch makes when enveloped in cotton*. I gasped for breath – and yet the officers heard it not. I talked more quickly – more vehemently; but the noise steadily increased. I arose and argued about trifles, in a high key and with violent gesticulations; but the noise steadily increased. Why *would* they not be gone? I paced the floor to and fro with heavy strides, as if excited to fury by the observations of the men – but the noise steadily increased. Oh God! what *could* I do? I foamed – I raved – I swore! I swung the chair upon which I had been sitting, and grated it upon the boards, but the noise arose over all and continually increased. It grew louder – louder – *louder!* And still the men chatted pleasantly, and smiled. Was it possible they heard not? Almighty

God! – no, no! They heard! – they suspected! – they *knew!* – they were making a mockery of my horror! – this I thought, and this I think. But anything was better than this agony! Anything was more tolerable than this derision! I could bear those hypocritical smiles no longer! I felt that I must scream or die! – and now – again! hark! louder! louder! louder! *louder!* –

'Villains!' I shrieked, 'dissemble no more! I admit the deed! – tear up the planks! – here, here! – it is the beating of his hideous heart!'

Joseph Sheridan Le Fanu (1814–73)

Madam Crowl's Ghost

There is certainly no more widely employed figure in the horror story than the ghost, and few writers have used it with more skill than the Irishman, Joseph Sheridan Le Fanu. Several critics regard him as the first really effective ghost story writer in English and despite the passage of time his work still sets standards unreached by most modern writers. Born and brought up against the background of a decaying culture in Ireland, he was surrounded by legendary tales of the unseen and retold many of them just as he might have heard them as a child at the knee of some old nurse or serving man. Few of our grandparents as children could have resisted a shudder as they pored over this next story and put themselves in the place of the hapless little boy who crossed the path of the evil Madam Crowl...

TWENTY years have passed since we last saw Mrs Joliffe's tall slim figure. She is now past seventy, and can't have many milestones more to count on the journey that will bring her to her long home. The hair has grown white as snow, that is parted under her cap, over her shrewd, but kindly face. But her figure is still straight, and her step light and active.

She has taken of late years to the care of adult invalids, having surrendered to younger hands the little people who inhabit cradles, and crawl on all-fours.

Those who remember that good-natured face among the earliest that emerge from the darkness of nonentity, and who owe to her their first lessons in the accomplishment of walking, and a delighted appreciation of their first babblings and earliest teeth, have 'spired up' into tall lads and lasses, now. Some of them shew streaks of white by this time, in brown locks, 'the bonny gouden' hair, that she was so proud to brush and shew to admiring mothers, who are seen no more on the green of Golden Friars, and whose names are traced now on the flat grey stones in the churchyard.

So the time is ripening some, and searing others; and the saddening and tender sunset hour has come; and it is evening with the kind old north-country dame, who nursed pretty Laura Mildmay, who now stepping into the room, smiles so gladly, and throws her arms round the old woman's neck, and kisses her twice.

'Now, this is so lucky!' said Mrs Jenner, 'you have just come in time to hear a story.'

'Really! That's delightful.'

'Na, na, od wite it! no story, ouer true for that, I sid it a wi my aan eyen. But the barn here, would not like, at these hours, just goin' to her bed, to hear tell of freets and boggarts.'

'Ghosts? The very thing of all others I should most likely to hear of.'

'Well, dear,' said Mrs Jenner, 'if you are not afraid, sit ye down here, with us.'

'She was just going to tell me all about her first engagement to attend a dying old woman,' says Mrs Jenner, 'and of the ghost she saw there. Now, Mrs Jolliffe, make your tea first, and then begin.'

The good woman obeyed, and having prepared a cup of that companionable nectar, she sipped a little, drew her brows slightly together to collect her thoughts, and then looked up with a wondrous solemn face to begin.

Good Mrs Jenner, and the pretty girl, each gazed with eyes of solemn expectation in the face of the old woman, who seemed to gather awe from the recollections she was summoning.

The old room was a good scene for such a narrative, with the oak-wainscoting, quaint, and clumsy furniture, the heavy beams that crossed its ceiling, and the tall four-post bed, with dark curtains, within which you might imagine what shadows you please.

Mrs Jolliffe cleared her voice, rolled her eyes slowly round, and began her tale in these words:

MADAM CROWL'S GHOST

'I'm an ald woman now, and I was but thirteen, my last birthday, the night I came to Applewale House. My aunt was the housekeeper there, and a sort o' one-horse carriage was down at Lexhoe waitin' to take me and my box up to Applewale.

'I was a bit frightened by the time I got to Lexhoe, and when I saw the carriage and horse, I wished myself back again with my mother at Hazelden. I was crying when I got into the "shay" – that's what we used to call it – and old John Mulbery that drove it, and was a good-natured fellow, bought me a handful of apples at the Golden Lion to cheer me up a bit; and he told me that there was a currant-cake, and tea, and pork chops, waiting for me, all hot, in my aunt's room at the great house. It was a fine moonlight night, and I eat the apples, lookin' out o' the shay winda.

'It's a shame for gentlemen to frighten a poor foolish child like I was. I sometimes think it might be tricks.

72

There was two on 'em on the tap o' the coach beside me. And they began to question me after nightfall, when the moon rose, where I was going to. Well, I told them it was to wait on Dame Arabella Crowl, of Applewale House, near by Lexhoe.

'"Ho, then," says one of them, "you'll not be long there!"

'And I looked at him as much as to say "Why not?" for I had spoken out when I told them where I was goin', as if 'twas something clever I hed to say.

'"Because," says he, "and don't you for your life tell no one, only watch her and see — she's possessed by the devil, and more an half a ghost. Have you got a Bible?"

'"Yes, sir," says I. For my mother put my little Bible in my box, and I knew it was there: and by the same token, though the print's too small for my ald eyes, I have it in my press to this hour.

'As I looked up at him saying "Yes, sir," I thought I saw him winkin' at his friend; but I could not be sure.

'"Well," says he, 'be sure you put it under your bolster every night, it will keep the ald girl's claws aff ye."

'And I got such a fright when he said that, you wouldn't fancy! And I'd a liked to ask him a lot about the ald lady, but I was too shy, and he and his friend began talkin' together about their own consarns, and dowly enough I got down, as I told ye, at Lexhoe. My heart sank as I drove into the dark avenue. The trees stand very thick and big, as ald as the ald house almost, and four people, with their arms out and finger-tips touchin', barely girds round some of them.

'Well my neck was stretched out o' the winda, looking for the first view o' the great house; and all at once we pulled up in front of it.

'A great white-and-black house it is, wi' great black beams across and right up it, and gables lookin' out, as white as a sheet, to the moon, and the shadows o' the trees, two or three up and down in front, you could count the leaves on them, and all the little diamond-shaped windapanes, glimmering on the great hall winda, and great shutters, in the old fashion, hinged on the wall outside, boulted across all the rest o' the windas in front, for there was but three or four servants, and the old lady in the house, and most o' t'rooms was locked up.

'My heart was in my mouth when I sid the journey was over, and this the great house afoore me, and I sa near my aunt that I never sid till noo, and Dame Crowl, that I was come to wait upon, and was afeared on already.

'My aunt kissed me in the hall, and brought me to her room. She was tall and thin, wi' a pale face and black eyes, and long thin hands wi' black mittins on. She was past fifty, and her word was short; but her word was law. I hev no complaints to make of her; but she was a hard woman, and I think she would hev bin kinder to me if I had bin her sister's child in place of her brother's. But all that's o' no consequence noo.

The squire – his name was Mr Chevenix Crowl, he was Dame Crowl's grandson – came down there, by way of seeing that the old lady was well treated, about twice or thrice in the year. I sid him but twice all the time I was at Applewale House.

'I can't say but she was well taken care of, notwithstanding; but that was because my aunt and Meg Wyvern, that was her maid, had a conscience, and did their duty by her.

'Mrs Wyvern – Meg Wyvern my aunt called her to

herself, and Mrs Wyvern to me – was a fat, jolly lass of fifty, a good height and a good breadth, always good-humoured and walked slow. She had fine wages, but she was a bit stingy, and kept all her fine clothes under lock and key, and wore, mostly, a twilled chocolate cotton, wi' red and yellow and green sprigs and balls on it, and it lasted wonderful.

'She never gave me nout, not the vally o' a brass thimble, all the time I was there; but she was good-humoured, and always laughin', and she talked no end o' proas over her tea; and seeing me sa sackless and dowly, she roused me up wi' her laughin' and stories; and I think I liked her better than my aunt – children is so taken wi' a bit o' fun or a story – though my aunt was very good to me, but a hard woman about some things, and silent always.

'My aunt took me into her bed-chamber, that I might rest myself a bit while she was settin' the tea in her room. But first, she patted me on the shouther, and said I was a tall lass o' my years, and had spired up well, and asked me if I could do plain work and stitchin'; and she looked in my face, and said I was like my father, her brother, that was dead and gone, and she hoped I was a better Christian and wad na du a' that lids (would not do anything of that sort).

'It was a hard sayin' the first time I set foot in her room, I thought.

'When I went into the next room, the housekeeper's room – very comfortable, yak (oak) all round – there was a fine fire blazin' away, wi' coal, and peat, and wood, all in a low together, and tea on the table, and hot cake, and smokin' meat; and there was Mrs Wyvern, fat, jolly, and talkin' away, more in an hour than my aunt would in a year.

'While I was still at my tea my aunt went upstairs to see Madam Crowl.

'"She's agone up to see that old Judith Squailes is awake," says Mrs Wyvern. "Judith sits with Madam Crowl when me and Mrs Shutters" – that was my aunt's name – "is away. She's troublesome old lady. Ye'll hev to be sharp wi' her, or she'll be into the fire, or out o' t' winda. She goes on wires, she does, old though she be."

'"How old, ma'am?" says I.

'"Ninety-three her last birthday, and that's eight months gone," says she; and she laughed. "And don't be askin' questions about her before your aunt – mind, I tell ye; just take her as you find her, and that's all."

'"And what's to be my business about her, please, ma'am?" says I.

'"About the old lady? Well," says she, "your aunt, Mrs Shutters, will tell you that; but I suppose you'll hev to sit in the room with your work, and see she's at no mischief, and let her amuse herself with her things on the table, and get her food or drink as she calls for it, and keep her out o' mischief, and ring the bell hard if she's troublesome."

'"Is she deaf, ma'am?'

'"No, nor blind," says she; "as sharp as a needle, but she's gone quite aupy, and can't remember nout rightly; and Jack the Giant Killer, or Goody Twoshoes will please her as well as the king's court, or the affairs of the nation."

'"And what did the little girl go away for, ma'am, that went on Friday last? My aunt wrote to my mother she was to go."

'"Yes; she's gone."

'"What for?" says I again.

' "She didn't answer Mrs Shutters, I do suppose," says she. "I don't know. Don't be talkin'; your aunt can't abide a talkin' child."

' "And please, ma'am, is the old lady well in health?" says I.

' "It ain't no harm to ask that," says she. "She's torflin a bit lately, but better this week past, and I dare say she'll last out her hundred years yet. Hish! Here's your aunt coming down the passage."

'In comes my aunt, and begins talkin' to Mrs Wyvern, and I, beginnin' to feel more comfortable and at home like, and was walkin' about the room lookin' at this thing and at that. There was pretty old china things on the cupboard, and pictures again the wall; and there was a door open in the wainscot, and I sees a queer old leathern jacket, wi' straps and buckles to it, and sleeves as long as the bed-post hangin' up inside.

' "What's that you're at child?" says my aunt, sharp enough, turning about when I thought she least minded. "What's that in your hand?"

' "This, ma'am?" says I, turning about with the leathern jacket. 'I don't know what it is, ma'am."

'Pale as she was, the red came up in her cheeks, and her eyes flashed wi' anger, and I think only she had half a dozen steps to take, between her and me, she'd a gev me a sizzup. But she did gie me a shake by the shouther, and she plucked the thing out o' my hand, and says she, "While ever you stay here, don't ye meddle wi' nout that don't belong to ye," and she hung it up on the pin that was there, and shut the door wi' a bang and locked it fast.

'Mrs Wyvern was liftin' up her hands and laughin', all this time, quietly, in her chair, rolling herself a bit in it, as she used when she was kinkin'.

77

'The tears was in my eyes, and she winked at my aunt, and says she, dryin' her own eyes that was wet wi' the laughin', "Tut, the child meant no harm – come here to me, child. It's only a pair o' crutches for lame ducks, and ask us no questions mind, and we'll tell ye no lies; and come here and sit down, and drink a mug o' beer before ye go to your bed."

'My room, mind ye, was upstairs, next to the old lady's, and Mrs Wyvern's bed was near hers in her room, and I was to be ready at call, if need be.

'The old lady was in one of her tantrums that night and part of the day before. She used to take fits o' the sulks. Sometimes she would not let them dress her, and at other times she would not let them take her clothes off. She was a great beauty, they said, in her day. But there was no one about Applewale that remembered her in her prime. And she was dreadful fond o' dress, and had thick silks, and stiff satins, and velvets, and laces, and all sorts, enough to set up seven shops at the least. All her dresses was old-fashioned and queer, but worth a fortune.

'Well, I went to my bed. I lay for a while awake; for a' things was new to me; and I think the tea was in my nerves, too, for I wasn't used to it, except now and then on a holiday, or the like. And I heard Mrs Wyvern talkin', and I listened with my hand to my ear; but I could not hear Mrs Crowl, and I don't think she said a word.

'There was great care took of her. The people of Applewale knew that when she died they would every one get the sack; and their situations was well paid and easy.

'The doctor came twice a week to see the old lady, and you may be sure they all did as he bid them. One thing was the same every time; they were never to cross or frump her, any way, but to humour and please her in everything.

'So she lay in her clothes all that night, and next day, not a word she said, and I was at my needlework all that day, in my own room, except when I went down to my dinner.

'I would a liked to see the ald lady, and even to hear her speak. But she might as well a' bin in Lunnon a' the time for me.

'When I had my dinner my aunt sent me out for a walk for an hour. I was glad when I came back, the trees was so big, and the place so dark and lonesome, and 'twas a cloudy day, and I cried a deal, thinkin' of home, while I was walkin' alone there. That evening, the candles bein' alight, I was sittin' in my room, and the door was open into Madam Crowl's chamber, where my aunt was. It was, then, for the first time I heard what I suppose was the ald lady talking.

'It was a queer noise like, I couldn't well say which, a bird, or a beast, only it had a bleatin' sound in it, and was very small.

'I pricked my ears to hear all I could. But I could not make out one word she said. And my aunt answered:

'"The evil one can't hurt no one, ma'am, bout the Lord permits."

'Then the same queer voice from the bed says something more that I couldn't make head nor tail on.

'And my aunt med answer again: "Let them pull faces, ma'am, and say what they will; if the Lord be for us, who can be against us?"

'I kept listenin' with my ear turned to the door, holdin' my breath, but not another word or sound came in from the room. In about twenty minutes, as I was sittin' by the table, lookin' at the pictures in the old Aesop's Fables, I was aware o' something moving at the door, and lookin' up I sid my aunt's face lookin' in at the door, and her hand raised.

'"Hish!" says she, very soft, and comes over to me on tiptoe, and she says in a whisper: "Thank God, she's asleep at last, and don't ye make no noise till I come back, for I'm goin' down to take my cup o' tea, and I'll be back i' noo – me and Mrs Wyvern, and she'll be sleepin' in the room, and you can run down when we come up, and Judith will gie ye yaur supper in my room."

'And with that she goes.

'I kep' looking at the picture-book, as before, listenin' every noo and then, but there was no sound, not a breath, that I could hear; an' I began whisperin' to the pictures and talkin' to myself to keep my heart up, for I was growin' feared in that big room.

'And at last up I got, and began walkin' about the room, lookin' at this and peepin' at that, to amuse my mind, ye'll understand. And at last what sud I do but peeps into Madam Crowl's bedchamber.

'A grand chamber it was, wi' a great four-poster, wi' flowered silk curtains as tall as the ceilin', and foldin' down on the floor, and drawn close all round. There was a lookin'-glass, the biggest I ever sid before, and the room was a blaze o' light. I counted twenty-two wax candles, all alight. Such was her fancy, and no one dared say her nay.

'I listened at the door, and gaped and wondered all round. When I heard there was not a breath, and did not see so much as a stir in the curtains, I took heart, and walked into the room on tiptoe, and looked round again. Then I takes a keek at myself in the big glass;

and at last it came in my head, 'Why couldn't I ha' a keek at the ald lady herself in the bed?''

'Ye'd think me a fule if ye knew half how I longed to see Dame Crowl, and I thought to myself if I didn't peep now I might wait many a day before I got so gude a chance again.

'Well, my dear, I came to the side o' the bed, the curtains bein' close, and my heart a'most failed me. But I took courage, and I slips my finger in between the thick curtains, and then my hand. So I waits a bit, but all was still as death. So, softly, softly I draws the curtain, and there, sure enough, I sid before me, stretched out like the painted lady on the tomb-stean in Lexhoe Church, the famous Dame Crowl, of Applewale House. There she was, dressed out. You never sid the like in they days. Satin and silk, and scarlet and green, and gold and pint lace; by Jen! 'twas a sight! A big powdered wig, half as high as herself, was a-top o' her head, and, wow! – was ever such wrinkles? – and her old baggy throat all powdered white, and her cheeks rouged, and mouse-skin eyebrows, that Mrs Wyvern used to stick on, and there she lay proud and stark, wi' a pair o' clocked silk hose on, and heels to her shoon as tall as nine-pins. Lawk! But her nose was crooked and thin, and half the whites o' her eyes was open. She used to stand, dressed as she was, gigglin' and dribblin' before the lookin-' glass, wi' a fan in her hand and a big nosegay in her bodice. Her wrinkled little hands was stretched down by her sides, and such long nails, all cut into points, I never sid in my days. Could it even a bin the fashion for grit fowk to wear their fingernails so?

'Well, I think ye'd a-bin frightened yourself if ye'd a sid such a sight. I couldn't let go the curtain, nor move an inch, nor take my eyes off her; my very heart stood still. And in an instant she opens her eyes and up she sits, and spins herself round, and down wi' her, wi' a clack on her two tall heels on the floor, facin' me, ogglin' in my face wi' her two great glassy eyes, and a wicked simper wi' her wrinkled lips, and lang fause teeth.

'Well, a corpse is a natural thing: but this was the dreadfullest sight I ever sid. She had her fingers straight out pointin' at me, and her back was crooked, round again wi' age. Says she:

' "Ye little limb! what for did ye say I killed the boy? I'll tickle ye till ye're stiff!"

'If I'd a thought an instant, I'd a turned about and run. But I couldn't take my eyes off her, and I backed from her as soon as I could; and she came clatterin' after like a thing on wires, with her fingers pointing to my throat, and she makin' all the time a sound with her tongue like zizz-zizz-zizz.

'I kept backin' and backin' as quick as I could, and her fingers was only a few inches away from my throat, and I felt I'd lose my wits if she touched me.

'I went back this way, right into the corner, and I gev a yellock, ye'd think saul and body was partin', and that minute my aunt, from the door, calls out wi' a blare, and the ald lady turns round on her, and I turns about, and ran through my room, and down the stairs, as hard as my legs could carry me.

'I cried hearty, I can tell you, when I got down to the housekeeper's room. Mrs Wyvern laughed a deal when I told her what happened. But she changed her key when she heard the ald lady's words.

' "Say them again," says she.

'So I told her.

' "Ye little limb! What for did ye say I killed the boy? I'll tickle ye till ye're stiff."

' "And did ye say she killed a boy?" says she.

' "Not I, ma'am," says I.

Judith was always up with me, after that, when the two elder women was away from her. I would a jumped out at winda, rather than stay alone in the same room wi' her.

'It was about a week after, as well as I can remember, Mrs Wyvern, one day when me and her was alone, told me a thing about Madam Crowl that I did not know before.

'She being young and a great beauty, full seventy year before, had married Squire Crowl, of Applewale. But he was a widower, and had a son about nine years old.

'There never was tale or tidings of this boy after one mornin'. No one could say where he went to. He was alowed too much liberty, and used to be off in the morning, one day, to the keeper's cottage and breakfast wi' him, and away to the warren, and not home, may-hap, till evening; and another time down to the lake, and bathe there, and spend the day fishing' there, or paddlin' about in the boat. Well, no one could say what was gone wi' him; only this, that his hat was found by the lake, under a haathorn that grows thar to this day, and 'twas thought he was drowned bathin'. And the squire's son, by his second marriage, with this Madam Crowl that lived sa dreadful lang, came in far the estates. It was his son, the ald lady's grandson, Squire Chevenix Crowl, that owned the estates at the time I came to Applewale.

'There was a deal o' talk lang before my aunt's time about it; and 'twas said the stepmother knew more than she was like to let out. And she managed her husband, the ald squire, wi' her whiteheft and flatteries. And as the boy was never seen more, in course of time the thing died out of fowks' minds.

'I'm goin' to tell ye noo about what I sid wi' my own een.

'I was not there six months, and it was winter time, when the ald lady took her last sickness.

'The doctor was afeard she might a took a fit o' madness, as she did fifteen years before, and was buckled up, many a time, in a strait-waistcoat, which was the very leathern jerkin I sid in the closet, off my aunt's room.

'Well, she didn't. She pined, and windered, and went off, torflin', torflin', quiet enough, till a day or two before her flittin', and then she took to rabblin', and sometimes skirlin' in the bed, ye'd think a robber had a knife to her throat, and she used to work out o' the bed, and not being strong enough, then, to walk or stand, she'd fall on the flure, wi' her ald wizened hands stretched before her face, and skirlin' still for mercy.

'Ye may guess I didn't go into the room, and I used to be shiverin' in my bed wi' fear, at her skirlin' and scrafflin' on the flure, and blarin' out words that id make your skin turn blue.

'My aunt, and Mrs Wyvern, and Judith Squailes, and a woman from Lexhoe, was always about her. At last she took fits, and they wore her out.

'T' sir was there, and prayed for her; but she was past praying with. I suppose it was right, but none could think there was much good in it, and sa at lang last she made her flittin', and a' was over, and old Dame Crowl was shrouded and coffined, and Squire Chevenix was wrote for. But he was away in France, and the delay was sa lang, that t' sir and doctor both agreed it would not du to keep her langer out o' her place, and no one cared but just them two, and my aunt and the rest o' us, from Applewale, to go to the buryin'. So the old lady of Applewale was laid in the vault under Lexhoe Church; and we lived up at the great house till such time as the squire should come to tell his will about us, and pay off such as he chose to discharge.

'I was put into another room, two doors away from what was Dame Crowl's chamber, after her death, and this thing happened the night before Squire Chevenix came to Applewale.

'The room I was in now was a large square chamber, covered wi' yak pannels, but unfurnished except for my bed, which had no curtains to it, and a chair and a table, or so, that looked nothing at all in such a big room. And the big looking-glass, that the old lady used to keek into and admire herself from head to heel, now that there was na mair o' that wark, was put out of the way, and stood against the wall in my room, for there was shiftin' o' many things in her chamber ye may suppose, when she came to be coffined.

'The news had come that day that the squire was to be down next morning at Applewale; and not sorry was I, for I thought I was sure to be sent home again to my mother. And right glad was I, and I was thinkin' of a' at hame, and my sister Janet, and the kitten and the pymag, and Trimmer the tike, and all the rest, and I go sa fidgetty, I couldn't sleep, and the clock struck twelve, and me wide awake, and the room as dark as pick. My back was turned to the door, and my eyes towards the wall opposite.

'Well, it could na be a full quarter past twelve, when

I sees a lightin' on the wall befoore me, as if something took fire behind, and the shadas o' the bed, and the chair, and my gown, that was hangin' from the wall, was dancin' up and down on the ceilin' beams and the yak pannels; and I turns my head ower my shouther quick, thinkin' something muss a gone a' fire.

'And what sud I see, by Jen! but the likeness o' the ald beldame, bedizened out in her satins and velvets, on her dead body, simperin', wi' her eyes as wide as saucers, and her face like the fiend himself. 'Twas a red light that rose about her in a fuffin low, as if her dress round her feet was blazin'. She was drivin' on right for me, wi' her ald shrivelled hands crooked as if she was goin' to claw me. I could not stir, but she passed me straight by, wi' a blast o' cald air, and I slid her, at the wall, in the alcove as my aunt used to call it, which was a recess where the state bed used to stand in ald times wi' a door open wide, and her hands gropin' in at somethin' was there. I never sid that door befoore. And she turned round to me, like a thing on a pivot, flyrin', and all at once the room was dark, and I standin' at the far side o' the bed; I don't know how I got there, and I found my tongue at last, and if I did na blare a yellock, rennin' down the gallery and almost pulled Mrs Wyvern's door off t' hooks, and frighted her half out o' wits.

'Ye may guess I did na sleep that night; and with the first light, down wi' me to my aunt, as fast as my two legs cud carry me.

'Well my aunt did na frump or flite me, as I thought she would, but she held me by the hand, and looked hard in my face all the time. And she telt me not to be feared; and says she:

' "Hed the appearance a key in its hand?"

' "Yes," says I, bringin' it to mind, "a big key in a queer brass handle."

' "Stop a bit," says she, lettin' go ma hand, and openin' the cupboard-door. "Was it like this?" says she, takin' one out in her fingers, and showing it to me, with a dark look in my face.

' "That was it," says I, quick enough.

' "Are ye sure?" she says, turnin' it round.

' "Sart," says I, and I felt like I was gain' to faint when I sid it.

' "Well, that will do, child," says she, saftly thinkin', and she locked it up again.

' "The squire himself will be here today, before twelve o'clock, and ye must tell him all about it," says she, thinkin', "and I suppose I'll be leavin' soon, and so the best thing for the present is, that ye should go home this afternoon, and I'll look out another place for you when I can."

'Fain was I, ye may guess, at that word.

'My aunt packed up my things for me, and the three pounds that was due to me, to bring home, and Squire Crowl himself came down to Applewale that day, a handsome man, about thirty years ald. It was the second time I sid him. But this was the first time he spoke to me.

'My aunt talk wi' him in the housekeeper's room, and I don't know what they said. I was a bit feared on the squire, he bein' a great gentleman down in Lexhoe, and I darn't go near till I was called. And says he, smilin':

' "What's a' this ye a sen, child? it mun be a dream, for ye know there's na sic a thing as a bo or a freet in a' the world. But whatever it was, ma little maid, sit ye down and tell all about it from first to last."

'Well, so soon as I made an end, he thought a bit, and says he to my aunt:

'"I mind the place well. In old Sir Olivur's time lame Wyndel told me there was a door in that recess, to the left, where the lassie dreamed she saw my grandmother open it. He was past eighty when he told me that, and I but a boy. It's twenty year sen. The plate and jewels used to be kept there, long ago, before the iron closet was made in the arras chamber, and he told me the key had a brass handle, and this ye say was found in the bottom o' the kist where she kept her old fans. Now, would not it be a queer thing if we found some spoons or diamonds forgot there? Ye mun come up wi' us, lassie, and point to the very spot."

'Loth was I, and my heart in my mouth, and fast I held by my aunt's hand as I stept into that awsome room, and showed them both how she came and passed me by, and the spot where she stood, and where the door seemed to open.

'There was an ald empty press against the wall then, and shoving it aside, sure enough there was the tracing of a door in the wainscot, and a keyhole stopped with wood, and planed across as smooth as the rest, and the joining of the door all stopped wi' putty the colour o' yak, and, but for the hinges that showed a bit when the press was shoved aside, ye would not consayt there was a door there at all.

'"Ha!" says he, wi' a queer smile, "this looks like it."

'It took some minutes wi' a small chisel and hammer to pick the bit o' wood out o' the keyhole. The key fitted, sure enough, and, wi' a strang twist and a lang skreak, the boult went back and he pulled the door open.

'There was another door inside, stranger than the

first, but the lacks was gone, and it opened easy. Inside was a narrow floor and walls and vault o' brick; we could not see what was in it, for 'twas dark as pick.

'When my aunt had lighted the candle, the squire held it up and stept in.

'My aunt stood on tiptoe tryin' to look over his shouther, and I did na see nout.

' "Ha! ha!" says the squire, steppin' backward. "What's that? Gi' ma the poker – quick!" says he to my aunt. And as she went to the hearth I peeps beside his arm, and I sid squat down in the far corner a monkey or a flayin' on the chest, or else the maist shrivelled up, wizzened ald wife that ever was sen on yearth.

' "By Jen!" says my aunt, as puttin' the poker in his hand, she keeked by his shouther, and sid the ill-favoured thing, "hae a care, sir, what ye're doin'. Back wi' ye, and shut to the door!"

'But in place o' that he steps in saftly, wi' the poker pointed like a swoord, and he gies it a poke, and down it a' tumbles together, head and a', in a heap o' bayans and dust, little meyar an' a hatful.

' 'Twas the bayans o' a child; a' the rest went to dust at a touch. They said nout for a while, but he turns round the skull, as it lay on the floor.

'Young as I was, I consayted I knew well enough what they was thinkin' on.

' "A dead cat!" says he, pushin' back and blowin' out the can'le, and shuttin' to the door. "We'll come back, you and me, Mrs Shutters, and look on the shelves by-and-by. I've other matters first to speak to ye about; and this little girl's goin' hame, ye say. She has her wages, and I mun mak' her a present," says he, pattin' my shouther wi' his hand.

'And he did gimma a goud pound and I went aff to

Lexhoe about an hour after, and sa hame by the stage-coach, and fain was I to be at hame again; and I never sid Dame Crowl o' Applewale, God be thanked, either in appearance or in dream, at-efter. But when I was grown to be a woman, my aunt spent a day and night wi' me at Littleham, and she telt me there was no doubt it was the poor little boy that was missing sa lang sen, that was shut up to die thar in the dark by that wicked beldame, whar his skirls, or his prayers, or his thumpin' cud na be heard, and his hat was left by the water's edge, whoever did it, to mak' belief he was drowned. The clothes, at the first touch, a' ran into a snuff o' dust in the cell whar the bayans was found. But there was a handful o' jet buttons, and a knife with a green heft, together wi' a couple o' pennies the poor little fella had in his pocket, I suppose, when he was decoyed in thar, and sid his last o' the light. And there was, amang the squire's papers, a copy o' the notice that was prented after he was lost, when the ald squire thought he might'a run away, or bin took by gipsies, and it said he had a green-hefted knife wi' him, and that his buttons were o' cut jet. Sa that is a' I hev to say consarnin' ald Dame Crowl, o' Applewale House.'

Andrew Lang (1844–1912)

The Man in White

*After ghosts, witches and demons were the most popular
figures in contemporary terror tales. They feature in a
great variety of stories, of which not a few are familiar
entries in modern anthologies, and I have therefore chosen
a rare item which not only brings up the topic in a most
sinister and unusual manner, but also gives me the opportunity to include a piece of work by the remarkable
Andrew Lang. One of the most prolific writers of his day,
Lang was to be found on virtually every junior bookshelf
represented by his volumes of Fairy Stories culled from
around the world and each one designated by a colour –
viz., 'The Red Fairy Book', 'The Grey Fairy Book' and
so on. He also knew a great deal about folk lore and super-
stition and, combining this with his storytelling skill, was
able to produce tales as strange and uncanny as 'The Man
In White' which must almost certainly be based on fact.*

A LITTLE while ago a strange encounter took place in
Paris which has caused a great deal of talk. It all began
when the renowned surgeon, Bessé, received a note
begging him to come without fail that afternoon at
six o'clock to the Rue au Fer, near the Luxembourg
Palace. Punctually at the hour named the surgeon
arrived on the spot, where he found a man awaiting
him. This man conducted the surgeon to a house a few
steps further on, and motioning him to enter through

the open door, promptly closed it, and remained himself outside.

Bessé was surprised to find himself alone, and wondered why he had been brought there; but he had not to wait long, for the housekeeper soon appeared, who informed him that he was expected, and that he was to go up to the first storey. The surgeon did as he was told, and opened the door of an anteroom all hung with white. Here he was met by an elegant lackey, dressed also in white, frizzed and powdered, with his white hair tied in a bag wig, carrying two torches in his hand, who requested the bewildered doctor to wipe his shoes. Bessé replied that this was quite unnecessary, as he had only just stepped out of his sedan chair and was not in the least muddy, but the lackey rejoined that everything in the house was so extraordinarily clean that it was impossible to be too careful.

His shoes being wiped, Bessé was next led into another room, hung with white like the first. A second lackey, in every respect similar to the other, made his appearance; again the doctor was forced to wipe his shoes, and for the third time he was conducted into a room, where carpets, chairs, sofas, and bed were all as white as snow. A tall figure dressed in a white dressing-gown and nightcap, and having its face covered by a white mask, sat by the fire. The moment this ghostly object perceived Bessé, he observed, 'My body is possessed by the devil. I have dabbled in the darkness of witchcraft and the red fire of hell is upon me. I must be cleansed!' Then he fell silent.

For three-quarters of an hour they remained thus, the white figure occupying himself with incessantly putting on and taking off six pairs of white gloves, which were placed on a white table beside him. The strangeness of the whole affair made Bessé feel very uncomfortable, but when his eyes fell on a variety of firearms in one corner of the room he became so frightened that he was obliged to sit down, lest his legs should give way.

At last the dead silence grew more than he could bear, and he turned to the white figure and asked what he wanted of him, and begged that his orders might be given him as soon as possible, as his time belonged to the public and he was needed elsewhere. To this the white figure only answered coldly, 'What does that matter, as long as you are well paid?' and again was silent. Another quarter of an hour passed, and then the white figure suddenly pulled one of the white bell-ropes. When the summons was answered by the two white lackeys, the figure desired them to bring some bandages, and commanded Bessé to bleed him and to take from him *five pounds of blood!*

The surgeon, amazed at the quantity, inquired what doctor had ordered such extensive blood-letting. 'I myself,' replied the white figure. Bessé felt that he was too much upset by all he had gone through to trust himself to bleed in the arm without great risk of injury, so he decided to perform the operation on the foot, which is far less dangerous. Hot water was brought, and the white phantom removed a pair of white thread stockings of wonderful beauty, then another and another, up to six, and took off a slipper of beaver lined with white. The leg and foot thus left bare were the prettiest in the world; and Bessé began to think that the figure before him must be that of a woman. At the second basinful the patient showed signs of fainting, and Bessé wished to loosen the mask, in order to give him more air. This was, however, prevented by the lackeys, who stretched him out on the floor, and Bessé bandaged the foot before the patient recovered from his fainting fit.

Directly he came to himself, the white figure ordered his bed to be warmed, and as soon as it was done he lay down in it. The servants left the room, and Bessé, after feeling his pulse, walked over to the fireplace to clean his lancet, thinking all the while of his strange adventure. Suddenly he heard a noise beside him, and, turning his head, he saw reflected in the mirror the white figure coming hopping towards him. His heart sank with terror, but the figure only took five crowns from the chimney-piece, and handed them to him, asking at the same time if he would be satisfied with that payment. Trembling all over, Bessé replied that he was. 'Well, then, be off as fast as you can,' was the rejoinder. Bessé did not need to be told twice, but made the best of his way out.

As before the lackeys were awaiting him with lights, and as they walked he noticed that they looked at each other and smiled. At length Bessé, provoked at this behaviour, inquired what they were laughing at. 'Ah, Monsieur,' was their answer, 'what cause have you to complain? Has anyone done you any harm, and have you not been well paid for your services?' So saying they conducted him to his chair, and truly thankful he was to be out of the house. He rapidly made up his mind to keep silent about his adventures, but the following day someone sent to inquire how he was feeling after having bled The Man in White. Bessé felt that it was useless to make a mystery of the affair, and related exactly what had hapened, and it soon came to the ears of the King. But who was The Man in White? Echo answers 'Who?'

E. Nesbit (1858-1924)

Man-Size in Marble

One of the most significant changes to be effected in story-telling for children during the time of our grandparents was wrought by the author of the next story, E. Nesbit. It was she who, to quote one authority, 'did away with namby-pamby moralising in fiction for the young' and in so doing created two of the best known novels of the turn of the century, 'The Treasure Seekers' and 'The Railway Children', since so successfully portrayed in film and on television. My own grandparents were the first to introduce me to 'Man-Size in Marble' and there have been few more splendidy executed denouements than you will find here...

ALTHOUGH every word of this story is as true as despair, I do not expect people to believe it. Nowadays a 'rational explanation' is required before belief is possible. Let me, then, at once offer the 'rational explanation' which finds most favour among those who have heard the tale of my life's tragedy. It is held that we were 'under a delusion', Laura and I, on that 31st of October; and that this supposition places the whole matter on a satisfactory and believable basis. The reader can judge, when he, too, has heard my story, how far this is an 'explanation', and in what sense it is 'rational'. There were three who took part in this: Laura and I and another man. The other man still lives, and can speak to the truth of the least credible part of my story.

I never in my life knew what it was to have as much money as I required to supply the most ordinary needs – good colours, books, and cab-fares – and when we were married we knew quite well that we should only be able to live at all by 'strict punctuality and attention to business'. I used to paint in those days, and Laura used to write, and we felt sure we could keep the pot at least simmering. Living in town was out of the question, so we went to look for a cottage in the country, which should be at once sanitary and picturesque. So rarely do these two qualities meet in one cottage that our search was for some time quite fruitless. But when we got away from friends and house-agents, on our honeymoon, our wits grew clear again, and we knew a pretty cottage when at last we saw one.

It was at Brenzett – a litle village set on a hill over against the southern marshes. We had gone there, from the seaside village where we were staying, to see the church, and two fields from the church we found this cottage. It stood quite by itself, about two miles from the village. It was a long, low building, with rooms sticking out in unexpected places. There was a bit of stonework – ivy-covered and moss-grown, just two old rooms, all that was left of a big house that had once stood there – and round this stonework the house had grown up. Stripped of its roses and jasmine it would have been hideous. As it stood it was charming, and after a brief examination we took it. It was absurdly cheap. There was a jolly old-fashioned garden, with grass paths, and no end of hollyhocks and sunflowers, and big lilies. From the window you could see the marsh-pastures, and beyond them the blue, thin line of the sea.

We got a tall old peasant woman to do for us. Her face and figure were good, though her cooking was of the homeliest; but she understood all about gardening, and told us all the old names of the coppices and corn-fields, and the stories of the smugglers and highway-men, and, better still, of the 'things that walked', and of the 'sights' which met one in lonely glens of a star-light night. We soon came to leave all the domestic business to Mrs Dorman, and to use her legends in little magazine stories which brought in the jingling guinea.

We had three months of married happiness, and did not have a single quarrel. One October evening I had been down to smoke a pipe with the doctor – our only neighbour – a pleasant young Irishman. Laura had stayed at home to finish a comic sketch. I left her laugh-ing over her own jokes, and came in to find her a crumpled heap of pale muslin, weeping on the window seat.

'Good heavens, my darling, what's the matter?' I cried, taking her in my arms.

'What is the matter? Do speak.'

'It's Mrs Dorman,' she sobbed.

'What has she done?' I inquired, immensely relieved.

'She says she must go before the end of the month, and she says her niece is ill; she's gone down to see her now, but I don't believe that's the reason, because her niece is always ill. I believe someone has been setting her against us. Her manner was so queer –'

'Never mind, Pussy,' I said; 'whatever you do, don't

cry, or I shall have to cry too to keep you in countenance, and then you'll never respect your man again.'

'But you see,' she went on, 'it is really serious, because these village people are so sheepy, and if one won't do a thing you may be quite sure none of the others will. Aud I shall have to cook the dinners and wash up the hateful greasy plates; and you'll have to carry cans of water about and clean the boots and knives – and we shall never have any time for work or earn any money or anything.'

I represented to her that even if we had to perform these duties the day would still present some margin for other toils and recreations. But she refused to see the matter in any but the greyest light.

'I'll speak to Mrs Dorman when she comes back, and see if I can't come to terms with her,' I said. 'Perhaps she wants a rise in her screw. It will be all right. Let's walk up to the church.'

The church was a large and lonely one, and we loved to go there, especially upon bright nights. The path skirted a wood, cut through it once, and ran along the crest of the hill through two meadows, and round the churchyard wall, over which the old yews loomed in black masses of shadow.

This path, which was partly paved, was called 'the bier-walk,' for it had long been the way by which the corpses had been carried to burial. The churchyard was richly treed, and was shaded by great elms which stood just outside and stretched their majestic arms in benediction over the happy dead. A large, low porch let one into the building by a Norman doorway and a heavy oak door studded with iron. Inside, the arches rose into darkness, and between them the reticulated windows, which stood out white in the moonlight. In the chancel, the windows were of rich glass, which showed in faint light their noble colouring, and made the black oak of the choir pews hardly more solid than the shadows. But on each side of the altar lay a grey marble figure of a knight in full plate armour lying upon a low slab, with hands held up in everlasting prayer, and these figures, oddly enough, were always to be seen if there was any glimmer of light in the church. Their names were lost, but the peasants told of them that they had been fierce and wicked men, marauders by land and sea, who had been the scourge of their time, and had been guilty of deeds so foul that the house they had lived in – the big house, by the way, that had stood on the site of our cottage – had been stricken by lightning and the vengeance of Heaven. But for all that, the gold of their heirs had bought them a place in the church. Looking at the bad, hard faces reproduced in the marble, this story was easily believed.

The church looked at its best and weirdest on that night, for the shadows of the yew trees fell through the windows upon the floor of the nave and touched the pillars with tattered shade. We sat down together without speaking, and watched the solemn beauty of the old church with some of that awe which inspired its early builders. We walked to the chancel and looked at the sleeping warriors. Then we rested some time on the stone seat in the porch, looking out over the stretch of quiet moonlit meadows, feeling in every fibre of our being the peace of the night and of our happy love; and came away at last with a sense that even scrubbing and black-leading were but small troubles at their worst.

Mrs Dorman had come back from the village, and I at once invited her to a tête-à-tête.

'Now, Mrs Dorman,' I said, when I had got her into

my painting room, 'what's all this about your not staying with us?'

'I should be glad to get away, sir, before the end of the month,' she answered, with her usual placid dignity.

'Have you any fault to find, Mrs Dorman?'

'None at all, sir: you and your lady have always been most kind, I'm sure –'

'Well, what is it? Are your wages not high enough?'

'No, sir, I gets quite enough.'

'Then why not stay?'

'I'd rather not' – with some hesitation – 'my niece is ill.'

'But your niece has been ill ever since we came. Can't you stay for another month?'

'No, sir, I'm bound to go by Thursday.'

And this was Monday!

'Well, I must say, I think you might have let us know before. There's no time now to get anyone else, and your mistress is not fit to do heavy housework. Can't you stay till next week?'

'I might be able to come back next week.'

'But why must you go this week?' I persisted. 'Come, out with it.'

Mrs Dorman drew the little shawl, which she always wore, tightly across her bosom, as though she were cold. Then she said, with a sort of effort:

'They say, sir, as this was a big house in Catholic times, and there was a many deeds done here.'

The nature of the 'deeds' might be vaguely inferred from the inflection of Mrs Dorman's voice – which was enough to make one's blood run cold. I was glad that Laura was not in the room. She was always nervous, as highly-strung natures are, and I felt that these tales about our house, told by this old peasant woman, with her impressive manner and contagious credulity, might have made our home less dear to my wife.

'Tell me all about it, Mrs Dorman,' I said; 'you needn't mind about telling me. I'm not like the young people who make fun of such things.'

Which was partly true.

'Well, sir' – she sank her voice – 'you may have seen in the church, beside the altar, two shapes.'

'You mean the effigies of the knights in armour,' I said cheerfully.

'I mean them two bodies, drawed out man-size in marble,' she returned, and I had to admit that her description was a thousand times more graphic than mine, to say nothing of a certain weird force and uncanniness about the phrase 'drawed out man-size in marble.'

'They do say, as on All Saints' Eve them two bodies sits up on their slabs, and gets off of them, and then walks down the aisle, *in their marble*' – another good phrase, Mrs Dorman) – 'and as the church clock strikes eleven they walks out of the church door, and over the graves, and along the bier-walk, and if it's a wet night there's the marks of their feet in the morning.'

'And where do they go?' I asked, rather fascinated.

'They comes back here to their home, sir, and if any-one meets them –'

'Well, what then?' I asked.

But no – not another word could I get from her, save that her niece was ill and she must go.

'Whatever you do, sir, lock the door early on All Saints' Eve, and make the cross-sign over the doorstep and on the windows.'

'But has anyone ever seen these things?' I persisted. 'Who was here last year?'

'No one, sir; the lady as owned the house only stayed here in summer, and she always went to London a full month afore *the* night. And I'm sorry to inconvenience you and your lady, but my niece is ill and I must go on Thursday.'

I could have shaken her for her absurd reiteration of that obvious fiction, after she had told me her real reasons.

I did not tell Laura the legend of the shapes that 'walked in their marble,' partly because a legend concerning our house might perhaps trouble my wife, and partly, I think, from some more occult reason. This was not quite the same to me as any other story, and I did not want to talk about it till the day was over. I had very soon ceased to think of the legend, however. I was painting a portrait of Laura, against the lattice window, and I could not think of much else. I had got a splendid background of yellow and grey sunset, and was working away with enthusiasm at her face. On Thursday Mrs Dorman went. She relented, at parting, so far as to say:

'Don't you put yourself about too much, ma'am, and if there's any little thing I can do next week I'm sure I shan't mind.'

Thursday passed off pretty well. Friday came. It is about what happened on that Friday that this is written.

I got up early, I remember, and lighted the kitchen fire, and had just achieved a smoky success when my little wife came running down as sunny and sweet as the clear October morning itself. We prepared breakfast together, and found it very good fun. The housework was soon done, and when brushes and brooms and pails were quiet again the house was still indeed.

It is wonderful what a difference one makes in a house. We really missed Mrs Dorman, quite apart from considerations concerning pots and pans. We spent the day in dusting our books and putting them straight, and dined gaily on cold steak and coffee. Laura was, if possible, brighter and gayer and sweeter than usual, and I began to think that a little domestic toil was really good for her. We had never been so merry since we were married, and the walk we had that afternoon was, I think, the happiest time of all my life. When we had watched the deep scarlet clouds slowly pale into leaden grey against a pale green sky and saw the white mists curl up along the hedgerows in the distant marsh we came back to the house hand in hand.

'You are sad, my darling,' I said, half-jestingly, as we sat down together in our little parlour. I expected a disclaimer, for my own silence had been the silence of complete happiness. To my surprise she said:

'Yes, I think I am sad, or, rather, I am uneasy. I don't think I'm very well. I have shivered three or four times since we came in; and it is not cold, is it?'

'No,' I said, and hoped it was not a chill caught from the treacherous mists that roll up from the marshes in the dying night. No – she said, she did not think so. Then, after a silence, she spoke suddenly:

'Do you ever have presentiments of evil?'

'No,' I said, smiling, 'and I shouldn't believe in them if I had.'

'I do,' she went on; 'the night my father died I knew it, though he was right away in the North of Scotland.' I did not answer in words.

She sat looking at the fire for some time in silence, gently stroking my hand. At last she sprang up, came behind me, and, drawing my head back, kissed me.

'There, it's over now,' she said. 'What a baby I am! Come, light the candles, and we'll have some of these new Rubinstein duets.'

And we spent a happy hour or two at the piano.

At about half-past ten I began to long for the good-night pipe, but Laura looked so white that I felt it would be brutal of me to fill our sitting-room with the fumes of strong cavendish.

'I'll take my pipe outside,' I said.

'Let me come, too.'

'No, sweetheart, not tonight; you're much too tired. I shan't be long. Get to bed, or I shall have an invalid to nurse tomorrow as well as the boots to clean.'

I kissed her and was turning to go when she flung her arms round my neck and held me as if she would never let me go again. I stroked her hair.

'Come, Pussy, you're over-tired. The housework has been too much for you.'

She loosened her clasp a little and drew a deep breath.

'No. We've been very happy today, Jack, haven't we? Don't stay out too long.'

'I won't, my dearie.'

I strolled out of the front door, leaving it unlatched. What a night it was! The jagged masses of heavy dark cloud were rolling at intervals from horizon to horizon, and thin white wreaths covered the stars. Through all the rush of the cloud river the moon swam, breasting the waves and disappearing again in the darkness.

I walked up and down, drinking in the beauty of the quiet earth and the changing sky. The night was absolutely silent. Nothing seemed to be abroad. There was no skurrying of rabbits, or twitter of the half-asleep birds. And though the clouds went sailing across the sky, the wind that drove them never came low enough to rustle the dead leaves in the woodland paths. Across the meadows I could see the church tower standing out black and grey against the sky. I walked there thinking over our three months of happiness.

I heard a bell-beat from the church. Eleven already! I turned to go in, but the night held me. I could not go back into our little warm rooms yet. I would go up to the church.

I looked in at the low window as I went by. Laura was half-lying on her chair in front of the fire. I could not see her face, only her little head showed dark against the pale blue wall. She was quite still. Asleep, no doubt.

I walked slowly along the edge of the wood. A sound broke the stillness of the night, it was a rustling in the wood. I stopped and listened. The sound stopped too. I went on, and now distinctly heard another step than mine answer mine like an echo. It was a poacher or a wood-stealer, most likely, for these were not unknown in our Arcadian neighbourhood. But whoever it was, he was a fool not to step more lightly. I turned into the wood and now the footstep seemed to come from the path I had just left. It must be an echo, I thought. The wood looked perfect in the moonlight. The large dying ferns and the brushwood showed where through thinning foliage the pale light came down. The tree trunks stood up like Gothic columns all around me. They reminded me of the church, and I turned into the bier-walk, and passed through the corpse-gate between the graves to the low porch.

I paused for a moment on the stone seat where Laura and I had watched the fading landscape. Then I noticed that the door of the church was open, and I blamed myself for having left it unlatched the other night. We were the only people who ever cared to come to the church except on Sundays, and I was vexed to think that through our carelessness the damp autumn airs had had a chance of getting in and injuring the old fabric. I went in. It will seem strange, perhaps, that I should have gone halfway up the aisle before I remembered – with a sudden chill, followed by as sudden a rush of self-contempt – that this was the very day and hour when, according to tradition, the 'shapes drawed out man-size in marble' began to walk.

Having thus remembered the legend, and remembered it with a shiver, of which I was ashamed, I could not do otherwise than walk up towards the altar, just to look at the figures – as I said to myself; really what I wanted was to assure myself, first, that I did not believe the legend, and, secondly, that it was not true. I was rather glad that I had come. I thought now I could tell Mrs Dorman how vain her fancies were, and how peacefully the marble figures slept on through the ghastly hour. With my hands in my pockets I passed up the aisle. In the grey dim light the eastern end of the church looked larger than usual, and the arches above the two tombs looked larger too. The moon came out and showed me the reason. I stopped short, my heart gave a leap that nearly choked me, and then sank sickeningly.

The 'bodies drawed out man-size' *were gone*! and their marble slabs lay wide and bare in the vague moonlight that slanted through the east window.

Were they really gone, or was I mad? Clenching my nerves, I stooped and passed my hand over the smooth slabs, and felt their flat unbroken surface. Had someone taken the things away? Was it some vile practical joke? I would make sure, anyway. In an instant I had made a torch of a newspaper, which happened to be in my pocket, and, lighting it, held it high above my head. Its yellow glare illumined the dark arches and those slabs. The figures *were* gone. And I was alone in the church; or was I alone?

And then a horror seized me, a horror indefinable and indescribable – an overwhelming certainty of supreme and accomplished calamity. I flung down the torch and tore along the aisle and out through the porch, biting my lips as I ran to keep myself from shrieking aloud. Oh, was I mad – or what was this that possessed me? I leaped the churchyard wall and took the straight cut across the fields, led by the light from our windows. Just as I got over the first stile a dark figure seemed to spring out of the ground. Mad still with that certainty of misfortune, I made for the thing that stood in my path, shouting, 'Get out of the way, can't you!'

But my push met with a more vigorous resistance than I had expected. My arms were caught just above the elbow and held as in a vice, and the raw-boned Irish doctor actually shook me.

'Let me go, you fool,' I gasped. 'The marble figures have gone from the church; I tell you they've gone.'

He broke into a ringing laugh. 'I'll have to give ye a draught tomorrow, I see. Ye've been smoking too much and listening to old wives' tales.'

'I tell you, I've seen the bare slabs.'

'Well, come back with me. I'm going up to old Palmer's – his daughter's ill; we'll look in at the church and let me see the bare slabs.'

'You go, if you like,' I said, a little less frantic for his laughter; 'I'm going home to my wife.'

'Rubbish man,' said he; 'd'ye think I'll permit of that? Are ye to go saying all yer life that ye've seen solid marble endowed with vitality, and me to go all me life saying ye were a coward? No, sir – ye shan't do ut.'

The night air – a human voice – and I think also the physical contact with this six feet of solid common sense, brought me back a little to my ordinary self, and the word 'coward' was a mental shower-bath.

'Come on, then,' I said sullenly; 'perhaps you're right.'

He still held my arm tightly. We got over the stile and back to the church. All was still as death. The place smelt very damp and earthy. We walked up the aisle. I am not ashamed to confess that I shut my eyes: I knew the figures would not be there. I heard Kelly strike a match.

'Here they are, ye see, right enough; ye've been dreaming or drinking, asking yer pardon for the imputation.'

I opened my eyes. By Kelly's expiring vesta I saw two shapes lying 'in their marble' on their slabs. I drew a deep breath.

'I'm awfully indebted to you,' I said. 'It must have been some trick of light, or I have been working rather hard, perhaps that's it. I was quite convinced they were gone.'

'I'm aware of that,' he answered rather grimly; 'ye'll have to be careful of that brain of yours, my friend, I assure ye.'

He was leaning over and looking at the right-hand figure, whose stony face was the most villainous and deadly in expression.

'By jove,' he said, 'something has been afoot here – this hand is broken.'

And so it was. I was certain that it had been perfect the last time Laura and I had been there.

'Perhaps someone has *tried* to remove them,' said the young doctor.

'Come along,' I said, 'or my wife will be getting anxious. You'll come in and have a drop of whisky and drink confusion to ghosts and better sense to me.'

'I ought to go up to Palmer's, but it's so late now I'd best leave it till the morning,' he replied.

I think he fancied I needed him more than did Palmer's girl, so, discussing how such an illusion could have been possible, and deducing from this experience large generalities concerning ghostly apparitions, we walked up to our cottage. We saw, as we walked up the garden path, that bright light streamed out of the front door, and presently saw that the parlour door was open, too. Had she gone out?

'Come in,' I said, and Dr Kelly followed me into the parlour. It was all ablaze with candles, not only the wax ones, but at least a dozen guttering, glaring tallow dips, stuck in vases and ornaments in unlikely places. Light, I knew, was Laura's remedy for nervousness. Poor child! Why had I left her? Brute that I was.

We glanced round the room, and at first we did not see her. The window was open, and the draught set all the candles flaring one way. Her chair was empty and her handkerchief and book lay on the floor. I turned to the window. There, in the recess of the window, I saw her. Oh, my child, my love, had she gone to that window to watch for me? And what had come into the room behind her? To what had she turned with that look of frantic fear and horror? Oh, my little one, had she thought that it was I whose step she heard, and turned to meet – what?

She had fallen back across a table in the window, and her body lay half on it and half on the window-seat, and her head hung down over the table, the brown hair loosened and fallen to the carpet. Her lips were drawn back, and her eyes wide, wide open. They saw nothing now. What had they seen last?

The doctor moved towards her, but I pushed him aside and sprang to her; caught her in my arms and cried:

'It's all right, Laura! I've got you safe, wifie.'

She fell into my arms in a heap. I clasped her and kissed her, and called her by all her pet names, but I think I knew all the time that she was dead. Her hands were tightly clenched. In one of them she held something fast. When I was quite sure that she was dead, and that nothing mattered at all any more, I let him open her hand to see what she held.

It was a grey marble finger.

2

Tales That Scared Your Parents

Bram Stoker (1847–1912)

Dracula's Guest

No character figured larger in the pages of horror fiction during the childhood of our parents than the blood-drinking vampire, Count Dracula. The legendary novel of his activities by Bram Stoker enjoyed a place on the shelves of most libraries and countless children climbed the stairs trembling to bed after reading an episode or two from its pages. Today many of us perhaps know the infamous Count better through films and television plays rather than having read the original book, but this can in a measure be remedied by reading 'Dracula's Guest' which, while a complete story in itself, was written primarily by Bram Stoker as part of the main book, but then deleted at the request of the publishers as the work was too long. It has all the flavour and drama of the original and similarly has formed the basis for a successful film.

WHEN we started for our drive the sun was shining brightly on Munich, and the air was full of the joyousness of early summer. Just as we were about to depart, Herr Delbrück (the maître d'hôtel of the Quatre Saisons where I was staying) came down, bareheaded, to the carriage and, after wishing me a pleasant drive, said to the coachman, still holding his hand on the handle of the carriage door:

'Remember you are back by nightfall. The sky looks bright, but there is a shiver in the north wind that says there may be a sudden storm. But I am sure you will not be late.' Here he smiled, and added, 'For you know what night it is.'

Johann answered with an emphatic, 'Ja, mein Herr,' and, touching his hat, drove off quickly. When we had cleared the town, I said, after signalling to him to stop:

'Tell me, Johann, what is tonight?'

He crossed himself, as he answered laconically: 'Walpurgis nacht.' Then he took out his watch, a great, old-fashioned German-silver thing as big as a turnip, and looked at it, with his eyebrows gathered together and a little impatient shrug of his shoulders. I realized that this was his way of respectfully protesting against the unnecessary delay, and sank back in the carriage, merely motioning him to proceed. He started off rapidly, as if to make up for lost time. Every now and then the horses seemed to throw up their heads and sniffed the air suspiciously. On such occasions I often looked round in alarm. The road was pretty bleak, for we were traversing a sort of high, windswept plateau. As we drove, I saw a road that looked but little used, and which seemed to dip through a little winding valley. It looked so inviting that, even at the risk of offending him, I called Johann to stop. And when he had pulled up I told him I would like to drive down that road. He made all sorts of excuses, and frequently crossed himself as he spoke. This somewhat piqued my curiosity, so I asked him various questions. He answered fencingly, and repeatedly looked at his watch in protest. Finally I said:

'Well, Johann, I want to go down this road. I shall not ask you to come unless you like; but tell me why you do not like to go, that is all I ask.' For an answer he seemed to throw himself off the box, so quickly did he reach the ground. Then he stretched out his hands appealingly to me, and implored me not to go. There was just enough of English mixed with the German for me to understand the drift of his talk. He seemed always just about to tell me something – the very idea of which evidently frightened him; but each time he pulled himself up, saying, as he crossed himself: 'Walpurgis nacht! '

I tried to argue with him, but it was difficult to argue with a man when I did not know his language. The advantage certainly rested with him, for although he began to speak in English – of a very crude and broken kind – he always got excited and broke into his native tongue – and every time he did so he looked at his watch. Then the horses became restless and sniffed the air. At this he grew very pale, and, looking around in a frightened way, he suddenly jumped forward, took them by the bridles and led them on some twenty feet. I followed, and asked why he had done this. For answer he crossed himself, pointed to the spot we had left, and drew his carriage in the direction of the other road, indicating a cross, and said, first in German, then in English: 'Buried him – him what killed themselves.'

I remembered the old custom of burying suicides at crossroads: 'Ah! I see, a suicide. How interesting!' But for the life of me I could not make out why the horses were frightened.

Whilst we were talking, we heard a sort of sound between a yelp and a bark. It was far away; but the horses got very restless, and it took Johann all his time to quiet them. He was pale, and said: 'It sounds like a wolf – but yet there are no wolves here now.'

'No?' I said, questioning him; 'isn't it long since the wolves were so near the city?'

'Long, long,' he answered, 'in the spring and summer; but with the snow the wolves have been here not so long.'

Whilst he was petting the horses and trying to quiet them, dark clouds drift rapidly across the sky. The sunshine passed away, and a breath of cold wind seemed to drift past us. It was only a breath, however, and more in the nature of a warning than a fact, for the sun came out brightly again. Johann looked under his lifted hand at the horizon and said:

'The storm of snow, he comes before long time.' Then he looked at his watch again, and, straightaway, holding his reins firmly – for the horses were still pawing the ground restlessly, and shaking their heads – he climbed to his box as though the time had come for proceeding on our journey.

I felt a little obstinate, and did not at once get into the carriage.

'Tell me,' I said, 'about this place where the road leads.' And I pointed down.

Again he crossed himself and mumbled a prayer, before he answered: 'It is unholy.'

'What is unholy?' I enquired.

'The village.'

'Then there is a village?'

'No, no. No one lives there hundreds of years.'

My curiosity was piqued: 'But you said there was a village.'

'There was.'

'Where is it now?'

Whereupon he burst out into a long story in German and English, so mixed up that I could not quite understand exactly what he said, but roughly I gathered that long ago, hundreds of years, men had died

there and been buried in their graves; and sounds were
heard under the clay, and when the graves were
opened, men and women were found rosy with life,
and their mouths red with blood. And so, in haste to
save their lives (ay, and their souls! – and here he
crossed himself), those who were left fled away to other
places, where the living lived, and the dead were dead
and not – not something. He was evidently afraid to
speak the last words. As he proceeded with his narra-
tion, he grew more and more excited. It seemed as if
his imagination had got hold of him, and he ended in
a perfect paroxysm of fear – white-faced, perspiring,
trembling and looking round him, as if expecting that
some dreadful presence would manifest itself there in
the bright sunshine on the open plain. Finally, in an
agony of desperation, he cried:

'Walpurgis nacht!' and pointed to the carriage for
me to get in. All my English blood rose at this, and,
standing back, I said:

'You are afraid, Johann – you are afraid. Go home;
I shall return alone; the walk will do me good.' The
carriage door was open. I took from the seat my oak
walking-stick – which I always carry on my holiday
excursions – and closed the door, pointing back to
Munich, and said, 'Go home, Johann – Walpurgis
nacht doesn't concern Englishmen.'

The horses were now more restive than ever, and
Johann was trying to hold them in, while excitedly im-
ploring me not to do anything so foolish. I pitied the
poor fellow, he was so deeply in earnest; but all the
same I could not help laughing. His English was quite
gone now. In his anxiety he had forgotten that his only
means of making me understand was to talk my language, so he jabbered away in his native German. It

began to be a little tedious. After giving the direction, 'Home!' I turned to go down the crossroad into the valley.

With a despairing gesture, Johann turned his horses towards Munich. I leaned on my stick and looked after him. He went slowly along the road for a while: then there came over the crest of the hill a man tall and thin. I could see so much in the distance. When he drew near the horses, they began to jump and kick about, then to scream with terror. Johann could not hold them in; they bolted down the road, running away madly. I watched them out of sight, then looked for the stranger, but I found that he, too, was gone.

With a light heart I turned down the side road through the deepening valley to which Johann had objected. There was not the slightest reason, that I could see, for his objection; and I daresay I tramped for a couple of hours without thinking of time or distance, and certainly without seeing a person or a house. So far as the place was concerned, it was desolation itself. But I did not notice this particularly till, on turning a bend in the road, I came upon a scattered fringe of wood; then I recognized that I had been impressed unconsciously by the desolation of the region through which I had passed.

I sat down to rest myself, and began to look around. It struck me that it was considerably colder than it had been at the commencement of my walk – a sort of sighing sound seemed to be around me, with, now and then, high overhead, a sort of muffled roar. Looking upwards, I noticed that great thick clouds were drifting rapidly across the sky from north to south at a great height. There were signs of coming storm in some lofty stratum of the air. I was a little chilly, and, thinking that it was the sitting still after the exercise of walking, I resumed my journey.

The ground I passed over was now much more picturesque. There were no striking objects that the eye might single out; but in all there was a charm of beauty. I took little heed of time and it was only when the deepening twilight forced itself upon me that I began to think of how I should find my way home. The brightness of the day had gone. The air was cold, and the drifting of clouds high overhead was more marked. They were accompanied by a sort of far-away rushing sound, through which seemed to come at intervals that mysterious cry which the driver had said came from a wolf. For a while I hesitated. I had said I would see the deserted village, so on I went, and presently came on a wide stretch of open country shut in by hills all around. Their sides were covered with trees, which spread down to the plain, dotting, in clumps, the gentler slopes and hollows which showed here and there. I followed with my eye the winding of the road, and saw that it curved close to one of the densest of these clumps and was lost behind it.

As I looked there came a cold shiver in the air, and the snow began to fall. I thought of the miles and miles of bleak country I had passed, and then hurried on to seek the shelter of the wood in front. Darker and darker grew the sky, and faster and heavier fell the snow, till the earth before and around me was a glistening white carpet the farther edge of which was lost in misty vagueness. The road was here but crude, and, when on the level, its boundaries were not so marked as when it passed through the cuttings; and in a little while I found that I must have strayed from it, for I missed underfoot the hard surface, and my feet sank deeper in the grass and moss. Then the wind grew stronger and blew with ever increasing force, till I was fain to run before it. The air became icy-cold, and in spite of my exercise I began to suffer. The snow was now falling so thickly and whirling around me in such rapid eddies that I could hardly keep my eyes open. Every now and then the heavens were torn asunder by vivid lightning, and in the flashes I could see ahead of me a great mass of trees, chiefly yew and cypress all heavily coated with snow.

I was soon amongst the shelter of the trees, and there, in comparative silence, I could hear the rush of the wind high overhead. Presently the blackness of the storm had become merged in the darkness of the night. By and by the storm seemed to be passing away: it now only came in fierce puffs or blasts. At such moments the weird sound of the wolf appeared to be echoed by many similar sounds around me.

Now and again, through the black mass of drifting cloud, came a straggling ray of moonlight, which lit up the expanse, and showed me that I was at the edge of a dense mass of cypress and yew trees. As the snow had ceased to fall, I walked out from the shelter and began to investigate more closely. It appeared to me that, amongst so many old foundations as I had passed, there might be still standing a house in which, though in ruins, I could find some sort of shelter for a while. As I skirted the edge of the copse, I found that a low wall encircled it, and following this I presently found an opening. Here the cypresses formed an alley leading up to a square mass of some kind of building. Just as I caught sight of this, however, the drifting clouds obscured the moon, and I passed up the path in darkness. The wind must have grown colder, for I felt myself shiver as I walked; but there was hope of shelter, and I groped my way blindly on.

I stopped, for there was a sudden stillness. The storm had passed; and, perhaps in sympathy with Nature's silence, my heart seemed to cease to beat. But this was only momentarily; for suddenly the moonlight broke through the clouds, showing me that I was in a grave-yard, and that the square object before me was a great massive tomb of marble, as white as the snow that lay on and all around it. With the moonlight there came a fierce sigh of the storm, which appeared to resume its course with a long, low howl, as of many dogs or wolves. I was awed and shocked, and felt the cold perceptibly grow upon me till it seemed to grip me by the heart. Then, while the flood of moonlight still fell on the marble tomb, the storm gave further evidence of re-newing – as though it was returning on its track. Im-pelled by some sort of fascination, I approached the sepulchre to see what it was, and why such a thing stood alone in such a place. I walked around it, and read, over the Doric door, in German:

COUNTESS DOLINGER OF GRATZ
IN STYRIA
SOUGHT AND FOUND DEAD
1801

On the top of the tomb, seemingly driven through the solid marble – for the structure was composed of a few vast blocks of stone – was a great iron spike or stake. On going to the back I saw, graven in great Russian letters:

THE DEAD TRAVEL FAST

There was something so weird and uncanny about the whole thing that it gave me a turn and made me feel quite faint. I began to wish, for the first time, that I had taken Johann's advice. Here a thought struck me, which came under almost mysterious circumstances and with a terrible shock. This was Walpurgis night!

Walpurgis night, when, according to the belief of millions of people, the devil was abroad – when the graves were opened and the dead came forth and walked. When all evil things of earth and air and water held revel. This very place the driver had specially shunned. This was the depopulated village of centuries ago. This was where the suicide lay; and this was the place where I was alone – unmanned, shivering with cold in a shroud of snow with a wild storm gathering again upon me! It took all my philosophy, all the religion I had been taught, all my courage, not to collapse in a paroxysm of fright.

And now a perfect tornado burst upon me. The ground shook as though thousands of horses thundered across it; and this time the storm bore on its icy wings, not snow, but great hailstones which drove with such violence that they might have come from the thongs of Balearic slingers – hailstones that beat down leaf and branch and made the shelter of the cypresses of no more avail than though their stems were standing corn. At the first I had rushed to the nearest tree; but I was soon fain to leave it and seek the only spot that seemed to afford refuge, the deep Doric doorway of the marble tomb. There, crouching against the massive bronze door, I gained a certain amount of protection from the beating of the hailstones, for now they only drove against me as they ricochetted from the ground and the side of the marble.

As I leaned against the door it moved slightly and opened inwards. The shelter of even a tomb was welcome in that pitiless tempest, and I was about to enter it when there came a flash of forked lightning that lit up the whole expanse of the heavens. In the instant, as I am a living man, I saw, as my eyes were turned into the darkness of the tomb, a beautiful woman, with rounded cheeks and red lips, seemingly sleeping on the bier. As the thunder broke overhead, I was grasped as by the hand of a giant and hurled out into the storm. The whole thing was so sudden that, before I could realize the shock, moral as well as physical, I found the hailstones beating me down. At the same time I had a strange, dominating feeling that I was not alone. I looked towards the tomb. Just then there came another blinding flash, which seemed to strike the iron stake that surmounted the tomb and to pour through to the earth, blasting and crumbling the marble, as in a burst of flame. The dead woman rose for a moment of agony, while she was lapped in the flame, and her bitter scream of pain was drowned in the thundercrash. The last thing I heard was this mingling of dreadful sound, as again I was seized in the giant grasp and dragged away, while the hailstones beat on me, and the air around seemed reverberant with the howling of wolves. The last sight that I remembered was a vague, white, moving mass, as if all the graves around me had sent out the phantoms of their sheeted dead, and that they were closing in on me through the white cloudiness of the driving hail.

Gradually there came a sort of vague beginning of consciousness; then a sense of weariness that was dreadful. For a time I remembered nothing; but slowly my senses returned. My feet seemed positively racked with pain, yet I could not move them. They seemed to be numbed. There was an icy feeling at the back of my neck and all down my spine, and my ears, like my feet, were dead, yet in torment; but there was in my breast a sense of warmth which was, by comparison, delicious. It was as a nightmare – a physical nightmare, if one may use such an expression; for some heavy weight on my chest made it difficult for me to breathe.

This period of semi-lethargy seemed to remain a long time, and as it faded away I must have slept or swooned. Then came a sort of loathing, like the first stage of seasickness, and a wild desire to be free from something – I knew not what. A vast stillness enveloped me, as though all the world were asleep or dead – only broken by the low panting as of some animal close to me. I felt a warm rasping at my throat, then came a consciousness of the awful truth, which chilled me to the heart and sent the blood surging up through my brain. Some great animal was lying on me and now licking my throat. I feared to stir, for some instinct of prudence bade me lie still; but the brute seemed to realize that there was now some change in me, for it raised its head. Through my eyelashes I saw above me the two great flaming eyes of a gigantic wolf. Its sharp white teeth gleamed in the gaping red mouth, and I could feel its hot breath fierce and acrid upon me.

For another spell of time I remembered no more. Then I became conscious of a low growl, followed by a yelp, renewed again and again. Then, seemingly very far away, I heard a 'Holloa! Holloa!' as of many voices calling in unison. Cautiously I raised my head and looked in the direction whence the sound came; but the cemetery blocked my view. The wolf still continued to yelp in a strange way, and a red glare began to move round the grove of cypresses, as though following the sound. As the voices drew closer, the wolf yelped faster and louder. I feared to make either sound or motion. Nearer came the red glow, over the white pall which stretched into the darkness around me. Then all at once from beyond the trees there came at a trot a troop of horsemen bearing torches. The wolf rose from my breast and made for the cemetery. I saw one of the horsemen (soldiers by their caps and their long military cloaks) raise his carbine and take aim. A companion knocked up his arm, and I heard the ball whizz over my head. He had evidently taken my body for that of the wolf. Another sighted the animal as it slunk away, and a shot followed. Then, at a gallop, the troop rode forward; some towards me, others following the wolf as it disappeared amongst the snow-clad cypresses.

As they drew nearer I tried to move, but was powerless, although I could see and hear all that went on around me. Two or three of the soldiers jumped from their horses and knelt beside me. One of them raised my head, and placed his hand over my heart.

'Good news, comrades!' he cried. 'His heart still beats!'

Then some brandy was poured down my throat; it put vigour into me, and I was able to open my eyes fully and look around. Lights and shadows were moving among the trees, and I heard men call to one another. They drew together uttering frightened exclamations; and the lights flashed as the others came pouring out of the cemetery pell-mell, like men possessed. When the farther ones came close to us, those who were around me asked them eagerly:

'Well, have you found him?'

The reply rang out hurriedly:

'No! No! Come away quick – quick! This is no place to stay, and on this of all nights!'

'What was it?' was the question, asked in all manner of keys. The answer came variously and all indefinitely as though the men were moved by some common impulse to speak, yet were restrained by some common fear from giving their thoughts.

'It – it – indeed!' glibbered one, whose wits had plainly given out for the moment.

'A wolf – and yet not a wolf!' another put in shudderingly.

'No use trying for him without the sacred bullet,' a third remarked in a more ordinary manner.

'Serve us right for coming out on this night! Truly we have earned our thousand marks!' were the ejaculations of a fourth.

'There was blood on the broken marble,' another said after a pause; 'the lightning never brought that there. And for him – is he safe? Look at his throat! See, comrades, the wolf has been lying on him and keeping his blood warm.'

The officer looked at my throat and replied:

'He is all right; the skin is not pierced. What does it all mean? We should never have found him but for the yelping of the wolf.'

'What became of it?' asked the man who was holding up my head, and who seemed the least panic-stricken of the party, for his hands were steady and without tremor. On his sleeve was the chevron of a petty officer.

'It went to its home,' answered the man, whose long face was pallid, and who actually shook with terror as he glanced around him fearfully. 'There are graves enough there in which it may lie. Come, comrades – come quickly! Let us leave this cursed spot.'

The officer raised me to a sitting posture as he uttered a word of command; then several men placed me upon a horse. He sprang to the saddle behind me, took me in his arms, gave the word to advance; and, turning our faces away from the cypresses, we rode away in swift, military order.

As yet my tongue refused its office, and I was perforce silent. I must have fallen asleep; for the next thing I remembered was finding myself standing up, supported by a soldier on each side of me. It was almost broad daylight, and to the north a red streak of sunlight was reflected, like a path of blood, over the waste of snow. The officer was telling the men to say nothing of what they had seen, except that they found an English stranger, guarded by a large dog.

'Dog! That was no dog,' cut in the man who had exhibited such fear. 'I think I know a wolf when I see one.'

The young officer answered calmly: 'I said a dog.'

'Dog!' reiterated the other ironically. It was evident that his courage was rising with the sun; and, pointing to me, he said, 'Look at his throat. Is that the work of a dog, master?'   ,

Instinctively I raised my hand to my throat, and as I touched it I cried out in pain. The men crowded round to look, some stooping down from their saddles; and again there came the calm voice of the young officer:

'A dog, as I said. If aught else were said we should only be laughed at.'

I was then mounted behind a trooper, and we rode

on into the suburbs of Munich. Here we came across a stray carriage, into which I was lifted, and it was driven off to the Quatre Saisons – the young officer accompanying me, whilst a trooper followed with his horse, and the others rode off to their barracks.

When we arrived, Herr Delbrück rushed so quickly down the steps to meet me that it was apparent he had been watching within. Taking me by both hands he solicitously led me in. The officer saluted me and was turning to withdraw, when I recognized his purpose, and insisted that he should come to my rooms. Over a glass of wine I warmly thanked him and his brave comrades for saving me. He replied simply that he was more than glad, and that Herr Delbrück had at the first taken steps to make all the searching-party pleased; at which ambiguous utterance the maître d'hôtel smiled, while the officer pleaded duty and withdrew.

'But Herr Delbrück,' I inquired, 'how and why was it that the soldiers searched for me?'

He shrugged his shoulders, as if in depreciation of his own deed, as he replied:

'I was so fortunate as to obtain leave, from the commander of the regiment in which I served, to ask for volunteers.'

'But how did you know I was lost?' I asked.

'The driver came hither with the remains of his carriage, which had been upset when the horses ran away.'

'But surely you would not send a search-party of soldiers merely on this account?'

'Oh, no!' he answered; 'but even before the coachman arrived, I had this telegram from the Boyar whose guest you are,' and he took from his pocket a telegram, which he handed to me, and I read:

Bistrize.

Be careful of my guest – his safety is most precious to me. Should aught happen to him, or if he be missed, spare nothing to find him and ensure his safety. He is English and therefore adventurous. There are often dangers from snow and wolves and night. Lose not a moment if you suspect harm to him. I answer your zeal with my fortune.

Dracula.

As I held the telegram in my hand, the room seemed to whirl around me; and, if the attentive maître d'hôtel had not caught me, I think I should have fallen. There was something so strange in all this, something so weird and impossible to imagine, that there grew on me a sense of my being in some way the sport of opposite forces – the mere vague idea of which seemed in a way to paralyse me. I was certainly under some form of mysterious protection. From a distant country had come, in the very nick of time, a message that took me out of the danger of the snow-sleep and the jaws of the wolf.

H. G. Wells (1866—1946)

The Valley of the Spiders

*If it is always possible to drive away fear of ghosts and
monsters and other 'things that go bump in the night' by
the simple thought that they do not really exist anyway,
the same statement does not apply to another object of
almost universal dread, the spider. Writers of horror
stories have put this fact to great use and more than two-
thirds of the parents I consulted during the compiling of
this book requesting the story which most frightened them
in their youth, plumped for 'The Valley of the Spiders' by
H. G. Wells. It is certainly a most chilling tale (a 'real
creepy-crawly' one of my advisers called it) and demon-
strates another facet of the many and diverse talents of its
author. If your knowledge to date of Mr Wells' writing is
confined to his social novels and Science Fiction, be prepared for a real surprise.*

TOWARDS midday the three pursuers came abruptly
round a bend in the torrent bed upon the sight of a
very broad and spacious valley. The difficult and winding trench of pebbles along which they had tracked the
fugitives for so long expanded to a broad slope, and
with a common impulse the three men left the trail,
and rode to a low eminence set with olive-dun trees,
and there halted, the two others, as became them, a
little behind the man with the silver-studded bridle.

For a space they scanned the great expanse below

them with eager eyes. It spread remoter and remoter, with only a few clusters of sere thorn bushes here and there, and the dim suggestions of some now waterless ravine to break its desolation of yellow grass. Its purple distances melted at last into the bluish slopes of the further hills – hills it might be of a greener kind – and above them invisibly supported, and seeming indeed to hang in the blue, were the snow-clad summits of mountains – that grew larger and bolder to the north-westward as the sides of the valley drew together. And westward the valley opened until a distant darkness under the sky told where the forests began. But the three men looked neither east nor west, but only stead-fastly across the valley.

The gaunt man with the scarred lip was the first to speak. 'Nowhere,' he said, with a sigh of disappoint-ment in his voice. 'But after all, they had a full day's start.'

'They don't know we are after them,' said the little man on the white horse.

'*She* would know,' said the leader bitterly, as if speaking to himself.

'Even then they can't go fast. They've got no beast but the mule, and all today the girl's foot has been bleeding –'

The man with the silver bridle flashed a quick in-tensity of rage on him. 'Do you think I haven't seen that?' he snarled.

'It helps, anyhow,' whispered the little man to him-self.

The gaunt man with the scarred lip stared impas-sively. 'They can't be over the valley,' he said. 'If we ride hard –'

He glanced at the white horse and paused.

'Curse all white horses!' said the man with the silver bridle and turned to scan the beast his curse included.

The little man looked down between the melancholy ears of his steed.

'I did my best,' he said.

The two others stared again across the valley for a space. The gaunt man passed the back of his hand across the scarred lip.

'Come up!' said the man who owned the silver bridle, suddenly. The little man started and jerked his rein, and the horse hoofs of the three made a multitudinous faint pattering upon the withered grass as they turned back towards the trail. . .

They rode cautiously down the long slope before them, and so came through a waste of prickly twisted bushes and strange dry shapes of horny branches that grew amongst the rocks, into the level below. And there the trail grew faint, for the soil was scanty, and the only herbage was this scorched dead straw that lay upon the ground. Still, by hard scanning, by leaning beside the horse's neck and pausing ever and again, even these white men could contrive to follow after their prey.

There were trodden places, bent and broken blades of the coarse grass, and ever and again the sufficient intimation of a footmark. And once the leader saw a brown smear of blood where the half-caste girl may have trod. And at that under his breath he cursed her for a fool.

The gaunt man checked his leader's tracking, and the little man on the white horse rode behind, a man lost in a dream. They rode one after another, the man with the silver bridle led the way, and they spoke never a word. After a time it came to the little man on the white horse that the world was very still. He started out of his dream. Besides the minute noises of their horses and equipment, the whole great valley kept the brooding quiet of a painted scene.

Before him went his master and his fellow, each intently leaning forward to the left, each impassively moving with the paces of his horse; their shadows went before them – still, noiseless, tapering attendants; and nearer a crouched cool shape was his own. He looked about him. What was it had gone? Then he remembered the reverberation from the banks of the gorge and the perpetual accompaniment of shifting, jostling pebbles. And, moreover –? There was no breeze. That was it! What a vast, still place it was, a monotonous afternoon slumber. And the sky open and blank, except for a sombre veil of haze that had gathered in the upper valley.

He straightened his back, fretted with his bridle, puckered his lips to whistle, and simply sighed. He turned in his saddle for a time, and stared at the throat of the mountain gorge out of which they had come. Blank! Blank slopes on either side, with never a sign of a decent beast or tree – much less a man. What a land it was! What a wilderness! He dropped again into his former pose.

It filled him with a momentary pleasure to see a wry stick of purple black flash out into the form of a snake, and vanish amidst the brown. After all, the infernal valley *was* alive. And then, to rejoice him still more, came a breath across his face, a whisper that came and went, the faintest inclination of a stiff black-antlered bush upon a crest, the first intimations of a possible breeze. Idly he wetted his finger, and held it up.

He pulled up sharply to avoid a collision with the

gaunt man, who had stopped at fault upon the trail.
Just at that guilty moment he caught his master's eye
looking towards him.

For a time he forced an interest in the tracking.
Then, as they rode on again, he studied his master's
shadow and hat and shoulder appearing and disappearing behind the gaunt man's nearer contours. They had
ridden four days out of the very limits of the world
into this desolate place, short of water, with nothing
but a strip of dried meat under their saddles, over
rocks and mountains, where surely none but these
fugitives had ever been before – for *that!*

And all this was for a girl, a mere wilful child! And
the man had whole cityfuls of people to do his basest
bidding – girls, women! Why in the name of passion-
ate folly *this* one in particular? asked the little man,
and scowled at the world, and licked his parched lips
with a blackened tongue. It was the way of the master,
and that was all he knew. Just because she sought to
evade him...

His eye caught a whole row of high plumed canes
bending in unison, and then the tails of silk that hung
before his neck flapped and fell. The breeze was growing stronger. Somehow it took the stiff stillness out of
things – and that was well.

'Hullo!' said the gaunt man.

All three stopped abruptly.

'What?' asked the master. 'What?'

'Over there,' said the gaunt man, pointing up the
valley.

'What?'

'Something coming towards us.'

And as he spoke a yellow animal crested a rise and
came bearing down upon them. It was a big wild dog,

coming before the wind, tongue out, at a steady pace, and running with such an intensity of purpose that he did not seem to see the horsemen he approached. He ran with his nose up, following, it was plain, neither scent nor quarry. As he drew nearer the little man felt for his sword. 'He's mad,' said the gaunt rider.

'Shout!' said the little man and shouted.

The dog came on. Then when the little man's blade was already out, it swerved aside and went panting by them and past. The eyes of the little man followed its flight. 'There was no foam,' he said. For a space the man with the silver-studded bridle stared up the valley. 'Oh, come on!' he cried at last. 'What does it matter?' and jerked his horse into movement again.

The little man left the insoluble mystery of a dog that fled from nothing but the wind, and lapsed into profound musings on human character. 'Come on!' he whispered to himself. 'Why should it be given to one man to say "Come on!" with that stupendous violence of effect. Always, all his life, the man with the silver bridle has been saying that. If *I* said it –!' thought the little man. But people marvelled when the master was disobeyed even in the wildest things. This half-caste girl seemed to him, seemed to everyone, mad – blasphemous almost. The little man, by way of comparison, reflected on the gaunt rider with the scarred lip, as stalwart as his master, as brave and, indeed, perhaps braver, and yet for him there was obedience, nothing but to give obedience duly and stoutly...

Certain sensations of the hands and knees called the little man back to more immediate things. He became aware of something. He rode up beside his gaunt fellow. 'Do you notice the horses?' he said in an undertone.

The gaunt face looked interrogation.

'They don't like this wind,' said the little man, and dropped behind as the man with the silver bridle turned upon him.

'It's all right,' said the gaunt-faced man.

They rode on again for a space in silence. The foremost two rode downcast upon the trail, the hindmost man watched the haze that crept down the vastness of the valley, nearer and nearer, and noted how the wind grew in strength moment by moment. Far away on the left he saw a line of dark bulks – wild hog perhaps, galloping down the valley, but of that he said nothing, nor did he remark again upon the uneasiness of the horses.

And then he saw first one and then a second great white ball, a great shining white ball like a gigantic head of thistledown, that drove before the wind athwart the path. These balls soared high in the air, and dropped and rose again and caught for a moment, and hurried on and passed, but at the sight of them the restlessness of the horses increased.

Then presently he saw that more of these drifting globes – and then soon very many more – were hurrying towards him down the valley.

They became aware of a squealing. Athwart the path a huge boar rushed, turning his head but for one instant to glance at them, and then hurtling on down the valley again. And at that, all three stopped and sat in their saddles, staring into the thickening haze that was coming upon them.

'If it were not for this thistledown –' began the leader.

But now a big globe came drifting past within a score of yards of them. It was really not an even sphere at all, but a vast, soft, ragged, filmy thing, a sheet gathered by the corners, an aerial jelly-fish, as it were, but rolling over and over as it advanced, and trailing long, cobwebby threads and streamers that floated in its wake.

'It isn't thistledown,' said the little man.

'I don't like the stuff,' said the gaunt man.

And they looked at one another.

'Curse it!' cried the leader. 'The air's full of it up there. If it keeps on at this pace long, it will stop us altogether.'

An instinctive feeling, such as lines out a herd of deer at the approach of some ambiguous thing, prompted them to turn their horses to the wind, ride forwards for a few paces, and stare at that advancing multitude of floating masses. They came on before the wind with a sort of smooth swiftness, rising and falling noiselessly, sinking to earth, rebounding high, soaring – all with a perfect unanimity, with a still, deliberate assurance.

Right and left of the horsemen the pioneers of this strange army passed. At one that rolled along the ground, breaking shapelessly and trailing out reluctantly into long grappling ribbons and bands, all three horses began to shy and dance. The master was seized with a sudden, unreasonable impatience. He cursed the drifting globes roundly. 'Get on!' he cried; 'get on! What do these things matter? How *can* they matter? Back to the trail!' He fell swearing at his horse and sawed the bit across its mouth.

He shouted aloud with rage. 'I will follow that trail, I tell you,' he cried. 'Where is the trail!'

He gripped the bridle of his prancing horse and searched amidst the grass. A long and clinging thread fell across his face, a grey streamer dropped about his bridle arm, some big, active thing with many legs ran down the back of his head. He looked up to discover one of those grey masses anchored as it were above him by these things and flapping out ends as a sail flaps when a boat comes about – but noiselessly.

He had an impression of many eyes, of a dense crew of squat bodies, of long, many-jointed limbs hauling at their mooring ropes to bring the thing down upon him. For a space he stared up, reining in his prancing horse with the instinct born of years of horsemanship. Then the flat of a sword smote his back, and a blade flashed overhead and cut the drifting balloon of spider-web free, and the whole mass lifted softly and drove clear and away.

'Spiders!' cried the voice of the gaunt man. 'The things are full of big spiders! Look, my lord!'

The man with the silver bridle still followed the mass that drove away.

'Look, my lord!'

The master found himself staring down at a red smashed thing on the ground that, in spite of partial obliteration, could still wriggle unavailing legs. Then when the gaunt man pointed to another mass that bore down upon them, he drew his sword hastily. Up the valley now it was like a fog bank torn to rags. He tried to grasp the situation.

'Ride for it!' the little man was shouting. 'Ride for it down the valley.'

What happened then was like the confusion of a battle. The man with the silver bridle saw the little man go past him slashing furiously at imaginary cobwebs, saw him cannon into the horse of the gaunt man and hurl it and its rider to earth. His own horse went a dozen paces before he could rein it in. Then he looked up to avoid imaginary dangers, and then back again to see a horse rolling on the ground, the gaunt man standing and slashing over it at a rent and fluttering mass of grey that streamed and wrapped about them both. And thick and fast as thistledown on waste land on a windy day in July, the cobweb masses were coming on.

The little man had dismounted, but he dared not release his horse. He was endeavouring to lug the struggling brute back with the strength of one arm, while with the other he slashed aimlessly. The tentacles of a second grey mass had entangled themselves with the struggle, and this second grey mass came to its moorings, and slowly sank.

The master set his teeth, gripped his bridle, lowered his head, and spurred his horse forward. The horse on the ground rolled over, there was blood and moving shapes upon the flanks, and the gaunt man suddenly leaving it, ran forward towards his master, perhaps ten paces. His legs were swathed and encumbered with grey; he made ineffectual movements with his sword. Grey streamers waved from him; there was a thin veil of grey across his face. With his left hand he beat at something on his body, and suddenly he stumbled and fell. He struggled to rise, and fell again, and suddenly, horribly, began to howl, 'Oh – ohoo, ohooh!'

The master could see the great spiders upon him, and others upon the ground.

As he strove to force his horse nearer to this gesticulating screaming grey object that struggled up and down, there came a clatter of hoofs, and the little man, in act of mounting, swordless, balanced on his belly athwart the white horse, and clutching its mane, whirled past. And again a clinging thread of grey gossamer swept across the master's face. All about him and over him, it seemed this drifting, noiseless cobweb circled and drew nearer him...

To the day of his death he never knew just how the event of that moment happened. Did he, indeed, turn his horse, or did it really of its own accord stampede after its fellow? Suffice it that in another second he was galloping full tilt down the valley with his sword whirling furiously overhead. And all about him on the quickening breeze, the spiders' airships, their air bundles and air sheets, seemed to him to hurry in a conscious pursuit.

Clatter, clatter, thud, thud – the man with the silver bridle rode, heedless of his direction, with his fearful face looking up now right, now left, and his sword arm ready to slash. And a few hundred yards ahead of him, with a tail of torn cobweb trailing behind him, rode the little man on the white horse, still but imperfectly in the saddle. The reeds bent before them, the wind blew fresh and strong, over his shoulder the master could see the webs hurrying to overtake...

He was so intent to escape the spiders' webs that only as his horse gathered together for a leap did he realize the ravine ahead. And then he realized it only to misunderstand and interfere. He was leaning forward on his horse's neck and sat up and back all too late.

But if in his excitement he had failed to leap, at any rate he had not forgotten how to fall. He was horseman again in mid-air. He came off clear with a mere bruise upon his shoulder, and his horse rolled, kicking spasmodic legs, and lay still. But the master's sword drove its point into the hard soil, and snapped clean across, as though Chance refused him any longer as her Knight, and the splintered end missed his face by an inch or so.

He was on his feet in a moment, breathlessly scanning the onrushing spider-webs. For a moment he was minded to run, and then thought of the ravine, and turned back. He ran aside once to dodge one drifting terror, and then he was swiftly clambering down the precipitous sides, and out of the touch of the gale.

There under the lee of the dry torrent's steeper banks he might crouch, and watch these strange, grey masses pass and pass in safety till the wind fell, and it became possible to escape. And there for a long time he crouched, watching the strange, grey, ragged masses trail their streamers across his narrowed sky.

Once a stray spider fell into the ravine close beside him – a full foot it measured from leg to leg, and its body was half a man's hand – and after he had watched its monstrous alacrity of search and escape for a little while, and tempted it to bite his broken sword, he lifted up his iron heeled boot and smashed it into a pulp. He swore as he did so, and for a time sought up and down for another.

Then presently, when he was sure these spider swarms could not drop into the ravine, he found a place where he could sit down, and sat and fell into deep thought and began after his manner to gnaw his knuckles and bite his nails. And from this he was moved by the coming of the man with the white horse.

He heard him long before he saw him, as a clattering of hoofs, stumbling footsteps, and a reassuring voice. Then the little man appeared, a rueful figure, still with a tail of white cobweb trailing behind him. They approached each other without speaking, without a salutation. The little man was fatigued and shamed to the pitch of hopeless bitterness, and came to a stop at last, face to face with his seated master. The latter winced a little under his dependant's eye. 'Well?' he said at last, with no pretence of authority.

'You left him!'

'My horse bolted.'

'I know. So did mine.'

He laughed at his master mirthlessly.

'I say my horse bolted,' said the man who once had a silver-studded bridle.

'Cowards both,' said the little man.

The other gnawed his knuckle through some meditative movements, with his eyes on his inferior.

'Don't call me a coward,' he said at length.

'You are a coward like myself.'

'A coward possibly. There is a limit beyond which every man must fear. That I have learnt at last. But not like yourself. That is where the difference comes in.'

'I never could have dreamt you would have left him. He saved your life two minutes before. . . Why are you our lord?'

The master gnawed his knuckles again, and his countenance was dark.

'No man calls me a coward,' he said. 'No. . . A broken sword is better than none. . . One spavined white horse cannot be expected to carry two men a four days' journey. I hate white horses, but this time it cannot be helped. You begin to understand me? . . . I perceive that you are minded, on the strength of what you have seen and fancy, to taint my reputation. It is men of your sort who unmake kings. Besides which – I never liked you.'

'My lord!' said the little man.

'No,' said the master. '*No!*'

He stood up sharply as the little man moved. For a

minute perhaps they faced one another. Overhead the spiders' balls went driving. There was a quick movement among the pebbles; a running of feet, a cry of despair, a gasp and a blow...

Towards nightfall the wind fell. The sun set in a calm serenity, and the man who had once possessed the silver bridle came at last very cautiously and by an easy slope out of the ravine again; but now he led the white horse that once belonged to the little man. He would have gone back to his horse to get his silver-mounted bridle again, but he feared night and a quickening breeze might still find him in the valley, and besides he disliked greatly to think he might discover his horse all swathed in cobwebs and perhaps unpleasantly eaten.

And as he thought of those cobwebs and of all the dangers he had been through, and the manner in which he had been preserved that day, his hand sought a little reliquary that hung about his neck, and he clasped it for a moment with heartfelt gratitude. As he did so his eyes went across the valley.

'I was hot with passion,' he said, 'and now she has met her reward. They also, no doubt –'

And behold! Far away out of the wooded slopes across the valley, but in the clearness of the sunset distinct and unmistakable, he saw a little spire of smoke.

At that his expression of serene resignation changed to an amazed anger. Smoke? He turned the head of the white horse about, and hesitated. And as he did so a little rustle of air went through the grass about him. Far away upon some reeds swayed a tattered sheet of grey. He looked at the cobwebs; he looked at the smoke.

'Perhaps, after all, it is not them,' he said at last.

But he knew better.

After he had stared at the smoke for some time, he mounted the white horse.

As he rode, he picked his way amidst stranded masses of web. For some reason there were many dead spiders on the ground, and those that lived feasted guiltily on their fellow. At the sound of his horse's hoofs they fled.

Their time had passed. From the ground, without either a wind to carry them or a winding sheet ready, these things, for all their poison, could do him no evil.

He flicked with his belt at those he fancied came too near. Once, where a number ran together over a bare place, he was minded to dismount and trample them with his boots, but this impulse he overcame. Ever and again he turned in his saddle, and looked back at the smoke.

'Spiders,' he muttered over and over again. 'Spiders! Well, well. . . . The next time I must spin a web.'

M. R. James (1862–1936)

The Haunted Doll's House

*Everyday items are used in other stories in this collection,
but to my knowledge there has been no more unlikely item
to find its way into a macabre tale than that which comes
next – a doll's house. Perhaps armed with the knowledge
that the author is the greatest of modern English ghost
story writers,* M. R. James, *the surprise is lessened somewhat, but the bizarre nature of the whole episode is nonetheless the reason why so many parents remember the tale
with a shiver. This might also well be true (and I do hasten
to underline the word* might*) of the Queen, for the story
was written, the author tells us in a later preface, 'for the
library of the Queen's Dolls' House and was printed in the
book thereof'.*

'I SUPPOSE you get stuff of that kind through your
hands pretty often?' said Mr Dillet, as he pointed with
his stick to an object which shall be described when the
time comes: and when he said it, he lied in his throat,
and knew that he lied. Not once in twenty years – perhaps not once in a lifetime – could Mr Chittenden,
skilled as he was in ferreting out the forgotten
treasures of half-a-dozen counties, expect to handle
such a specimen. It was collectors' palaver, and Mr
Chittenden recognized it as such.

'Stuff of that kind, Mr Dillet! It's a museum piece,
that is.'

'Well, I suppose there are museums that'll take anything.'

'I've seen one, not as good as that, years back,' said Mr Chittenden, thoughtfully. 'But that's not likely to come into the market: and I'm told they 'ave some fine ones of the period over the water. No: I'm only telling you the truth, Mr Dillet, when I say that if you was to place an unlimited order with me for the very best that could be got – and you know I 'ave facilities for getting to know of such things, and a reputation to maintain – well, all I can say is, I should lead you straight up to that one and say, "I can't do no better for you than that, Sir." '

'Hear, hear!' said Mr Dillet, applauding ironically with the end of his stick on the floor of the shop. 'How much are you sticking the innocent American buyer for it, eh?'

'Oh, I shan't be over hard on the buyer, American or otherwise. You see, it stands this way, Mr Dillet – if I knew just a bit more about the pedigree –'

'Or just a bit less,' Mr Dillet put in.

'Ha, ha! you will have your joke, Sir. No, but as I was saying, if I knew just a little more than what I do about the piece – though anyone can see for themselves it's a genuine thing, every last corner of it, and there's not been one of my men allowed to so much as touch it since it came into the shop – there'd be another figure in the price I'm asking.'

'And what's that: five and twenty?'

'Multiply that by three and you've got it, Sir. Seventy-five's my price.'

'And fifty's mine,' said Mr Dillet.

The point of agreement was, of course, somewhere between the two, it does not matter exactly where – I think sixty guineas. But half an hour later the object was being packed, and within an hour Mr Dillet had called for it in his car and driven away. Mr Chittenden, holding the cheque in his hand, saw him off from the door with smiles, and returned, still smiling, into the parlour where his wife was making the tea. He stopped at the door.

'It's gone,' he said.

'Thank God for that!' said Mrs Chittenden, putting down the teapot. 'Mr Dillet, was it?'

'Yes, it was.'

'Well, I'd sooner it was him than another.'

'Oh, I don't know, he ain't a bad feller, my dear.'

'May be not, but in my opinion he'd be none the worse for a bit of a shake up.'

'Well, if that's your opinion, it's my opinion he's put himself into the way of getting one. Anyhow, we shan't have no more of it, and that's something to be thankful for.'

And so Mr and Mrs Chittenden sat down to tea.

And what of Mr Dillet and of his new acquisition? What it was, the title of this story will have told you. What it was like, I shall have to indicate as well as I can.

There was only just room enough for it in the car, and Mr Dillet had to sit with the driver: he had also to go slow, for though the rooms of the Doll's House had all been stuffed carefully with soft cotton-wool, jolting was to be avoided, in view of the immense number of small objects which thronged them; and the ten-mile drive was an anxious time for him, in spite of all the precautions he insisted upon. At last his front door was reached, and Collins, the butler, came out.

'Look here, Collins, you must help me with this

thing – it's a delicate job. We must get it out upright, see? It's full of little things that mustn't be displaced more than we can help. Let's see, where shall we have it? (After a pause for consideration.) Really, I think I shall have to put it in my own room, to begin with at any rate. On the big table – that's it.'

It was conveyed – with much talking – to Mr Dillet's spacious room on the first floor, looking out on the drive. The sheeting was unwound from it, and the front thrown open, and for the next hour or two Mr Dillet was fully occupied in extracting the padding and setting in order the contents of the rooms.

When this thoroughly congenial task was finished, I must say that it would have been difficult to find a more perfect and attractive specimen of a Doll's House in Strawberry Hill Gothic than that which now stood on Mr Dillet's large kneehole table, lighted up by the evening sun which came slanting through three tall sash-windows.

It was quite six feet long, including the Chapel or Oratory which flanked the front on the left as you faced it, and the stable on the right. The main block of the house was, as I have said, in the Gothic manner; that is to say, the windows had pointed arches and were sur-mounted by what are called ogival hoods, with crockets and finials such as we see on the canopies of tombs built into church walls. At the angles were absurd turrets covered with arched panels. The Chapel had pinnacles and buttresses and a bell in the turret and coloured glass in the windows. When the front of the house was open you saw four large rooms, bedroom, dining-room, drawing-room and kitchen, each with its appro-priate furniture in a very complete state.

The stable on the right was in two storeys, with

its proper complement of horses, coaches and grooms, and with its clock and Gothic cupola for the clock bell.

Pages, of course, might be written on the outfit of the mansion—how many frying pans, how many gilt chairs, what pictures, carpets, chandeliers, four-posters, table linen, glass, crockery and plate it possessed; but all this must be left to the imagination. I will only say that the base or plinth on which the house stood (for it was fitted with one of some depth which allowed of a flight of steps to the front door and a terrace, partly balustraded) contained a shallow drawer or drawers in which were neatly stored sets of embroidered curtains, changes of raiment for the inmates, and, in short, all the materials for an infinite series of variations and refittings of the most absorbing and delightful kind.

'Quintessence of Horace Walpole, that's what it is: he must have had something to do with the making of it.' Such was Mr Dillet's murmured reflection as he knelt before it in a reverent ectasy. 'Simply wonderful; this is my day and no mistake. Five hundred pound coming in this morning for that cabinet which I never cared about, and now this tumbling into my hands for a tenth, at the very most, of what it would fetch in town. Well, well! It almost makes one afraid something'll happen to counter it. Let's have a look at the population, anyhow.'

Accordingly, he set them before him in a row. Again, here is an opportunity, which some would snatch at, of making an inventory of costume: I am incapable of it.

There were a gentleman and lady, in blue satin and brocade respectively. There were two children, a boy and a girl. There was a cook, a nurse, a footman, and there were the stable servants, two postillions, a coach-man, two grooms.

'Anyone else? Yes, possibly.'

The curtains of the four-poster in the bedroom were closely drawn round four sides of it, and he put his finger in between them and felt in the bed. He drew the finger back hastily, for it almost semed to him as if something had – not stirred, perhaps, but yielded – in an odd live way as he pressed it. Then he put back the curtains, which ran on rods in the proper manner, and extracted from the bed a white-haired old gentleman in a long linen nightdress and cap, and laid him down by the rest. The tale was complete.

Dinner time was now near, so Mr Dillet spent but five minutes in putting the lady and children into the drawing-room, the gentleman into the dining-room, the servants into the kitchen and stables, and the old man back into his bed. He retired into his dressing-room next door, and we see and hear no more of him until something like eleven o'clock at night.

His whim was to sleep surrounded by some of the gems of his collection. The big room in which we have seen him contained his bed: bath, wardrobe, and all the appliances of dressing were in a commodious room adjoining: but his four-poster, which itself was a valued treasure, stood in the large room where he sometimes wrote, and often sat, and even received visitors. To-night he repaired to it in a highly complacent frame of mind.

There was no striking clock within earshot – none on the staircase, none in the stable, none in the distant church tower. Yet it is indubitable that Mr Dillet was startled out of a very pleasant slumber by a bell tolling One.

He was so much startled that he did not merely lie breathless with wide-open eyes, but actually sat up in his bed.

He never asked himself, till the morning hours, how it was that, though there was no light at all in the room, the Doll's House on the kneehole table stood out with complete clearness. But it was so. The effect was that of a bright harvest moon shining full on the front of a big white stone mansion – a quarter of a mile away it might be, and yet every detail was photographically sharp. There were trees about it, too – trees rising behind the chapel and the house. He seemed to be conscious of the scent of a cool still September night. He thought he could hear an occasional stamp and clink from the stables, as of horses stirring. And with another shock he realized that, above the house, he was looking, not at the wall of his room with its pictures, but into the profound blue of a night sky.

There were lights, more than one, in the windows, and he quickly saw that this was no four-roomed house with a movable front, but one of many rooms, and staircases – a real house, but seen as if through the wrong end of a telescope. 'You mean to show me something,' he muttered to himself, and he gazed earnestly on the lighted windows. They would in real life have been shuttered or curtained, no doubt, he thought; but, as it was, there was nothing to intercept his view of what was being transacted inside the rooms.

Two rooms were lighted – one on the ground floor to the right of the door, one upstairs, on the left – the first brightly enough, the other rather dimly. The lower room was the dining-room: a table was laid, but the meal was over, and only wine and glasses were left on the table. The man of the blue satin and the woman of the brocade were alone in the room, and they were talking very earnestly, seated close together at the table, their elbows on it: every now and again stopping to listen, as it seemed. Once *he* rose, came to the window and opened it and put his head out and his hand to his ear. There was a lighted taper in a silver candlestick on a sideboard. When the man left the window he seemed to leave the room also; and the lady, taper in hand, remained standing and listening. The expression on her face was that of one striving her utmost to keep down a fear that threatened to master her – and succeeding. It was a hateful face, too; broad, flat and sly. Now the man came back and she took some small thing from him and hurried out of the room. He, too, disappeared, but only for a moment or two. The front door slowly opened and he stepped out and stood on the top of the *perron*, looking this way and that; then turned towards the upper window that was lighted, and shook his fist.

It was time to look at that upper window. Through it was seen a four-post bed: a nurse or other servant in an armchair, evidently sound asleep; in the bed an old man lying: awake, and, one would say, anxious, from the way in which he shifted about and moved his fingers, beating tunes on the coverlet. Beyond the bed a door opened. Light was seen on the ceiling, and the lady came in: she set down her candle on a table, came to the fireside and roused the nurse. In her hand she had an old-fashioned wine bottle, ready uncorked. The nurse took it, poured some of the contents into a little silver saucepan, added some spice and sugar from casters on the table, and set it to warm on the fire. Meanwhile the old man in the bed beckoned feebly to the lady, who came to him, smiling, took his wrist as if to feel his pulse, and bit her lip as if in consternation. He looked at her anxiously, and then pointed to the window, and spoke. She nodded, and did as the man below had done; opened the casement and listened – perhaps rather ostentatiously: then drew in her head and shook it, looking at the old man, who seemed to sigh.

By this time the posset on the fire was steaming, and the nurse poured it into a small two-handled silver bowl and brought it to the bedside. The old man seemed disinclined for it and was waving it away, but the lady and the nurse together bent over him and evidently pressed it upon him. He must have yielded, for they supported him into a sitting position, and put it to his lips. He drank most of it, in several draughts, and they laid him down. The lady left the room, smiling goodnight to him, and took the bowl, the bottle and the silver saucepan with her. The nurse returned to the chair, and there was an interval of complete quiet.

Suddenly the old man started up in his bed – and he must have uttered some cry, for the nurse started out of her chair and made but one step of it to the bedside. He was a sad and terrible sight – flushed in the face, almost to blackness, the eyes glaring whitely, both hands clutching at his heart, foam at his lips.

For a moment the nurse left him, ran to the door, flung it wide open, and, one supposes, screamed aloud for help, then darted back to the bed and seemed to try feverishly to soothe him – to lay him down – anything. But as the lady, her husband, and several servants, rushed into the room with horrified faces, the old man collapsed under the nurse's hands and lay back, and the features, contorted with agony and rage, relaxed slowly into calm.

A few moments later, lights showed out to the left of

the house, and a coach with flambeaux drove up to the door. A white-wigged man in black got nimbly out and ran up the steps, carrying a small leather trunk-shaped box. He was met in the doorway by the man and his wife, she with her handkerchief clutched between her hands, he with a tragic face, but retaining his self-control. They led the newcomer into the dining-room, where he set his box of papers on the table, and, turning to them, listened with a face of consternation at what they had to tell. He nodded his head again and again, threw out his hands slightly, declined, it seemed, offers of refreshment and lodging for the night, and within a few minutes came slowly down the steps, entering the coach and driving off the way he had come. As the man in blue watched him from the top of the steps, a smile not pleasant to see stole slowly over his fat white face. Darkness fell over the whole scene as the lights of the coach disappeared.

But Mr Dillet remained sitting up in the bed: he had rightly guessed that there would be a sequel. The house front glimmered out again before long. But now there was a difference. The lights were in other windows, one at the top of the house, the other illuminating the range of coloured windows of the chapel. How he saw through these is not quite obvious, but he did. The interior was as carefully furnished as the rest of the establishment, with its minute red cushions on the desks, its Gothic stall-canopies, and its western gallery and pinnacled organ with gold pipes. On the centre of the black and white pavement was a bier: four tall candles burned at the corners. On the bier was a coffin covered with a pall of black velvet.

As he looked the folds of the pall stirred. It seemed to rise at one end: it slid downwards: it fell away, exposing the black coffin with its silver handles and name-plate. One of the tall candlesticks swayed and toppled over. Ask no more, but turn, as Mr Dillet hastily did, and look in at the lighted window at the top of the house, where a boy and girl lay in two truckle-beds, and a four-poster for the nurse rose above them. The nurse was not visible for the moment; but the father and mother were there, dressed now in mourning, but with very little sign of mourning in their demeanour. Indeed, they were laughing and talking with a good deal of animation, sometimes to each other, and sometimes throwing a remark to one or other of the children, and again laughing at the answers. Then the father was seen to go on tiptoe out of the room, taking with him as he went a white garment that hung on a peg near the door. He shut the door after him. A minute or two later it was slowly opened again, and a muffled head poked round it. A bent form of sinister shape stepped across to the truckle-beds, and suddenly stopped, threw up its arms and revealed, of course, the father, laughing. The children were in agonies of terror, the boy with the bedclothes over his head, the girl throwing herself out of bed into her mother's arms. Attempts at consolation followed – the parents took the children on their laps, patted them, picked up the white gown and showed there was no harm in it, and so forth; and at last putting the children back into bed, left the room with encouraging waves of the hand. As they left it, the nurse came in, and soon the light died down.

Still Mr Dillet watched immovable.

A new sort of light – not of lamp or candle – a pale ugly light, began to dawn around the door-case at the back of the room. The door was opening again. The seer does not like to dwell upon what he saw entering the room: he says it might be described as a frog – the size of a man – but it had scanty white hair about its head. It was busy about the truckle-beds, but not for long. The sound of cries – faint, as if coming out of a vast distance – but, even so, infinitely appalling, reached the ear.

There were signs of a hideous commotion all over the house: lights passed along and up, and doors opened and shut, and running figures passed within the windows. The clock in the stable turret tolled one, and darkness fell again.

It was only dispelled once more, to show the house front. At the bottom of the steps dark figures were drawn up in two lines, holding flaming torches. More dark figures came down the steps, bearing, first one, then another small coffin. And the lines of torch-bearers with the coffins between them moved silently onward to the left.

The hours of night passed on – never so slowly, Mr Dillet thought. Gradually he sank down from sitting to lying in his bed – but he did not close an eye: and early next morning he sent for the doctor.

The doctor found him in a disquieting state of nerves, and recommended sea air. To a quiet place on the East Coast he accordingly repaired by easy stages in his car.

One of the first people he met on the sea front was Mr Chittenden, who, it appeared, had likewise been advised to take his wife away for a bit of a change.

Mr Chittenden looked somewhat askance upon him when they met: and not without cause.

'Well, I don't wonder at you being a bit upset, Mr Dillet. What? Yes, well, I might say 'orrible upset, to be sure, seeing what me and my poor wife went through ourselves. But I put it to you, Mr Dillet, one of two things: was I going to scrap a lovely piece like that on the one 'and, or was I going to tell customers: "I'm selling you a regular picture-palace-dramar in reel life of the olden time, billed to perform regular at one o'clock a.m."? Why, what would you 'ave said yourself? And next thing you know, two Justices of the Peace in the back parlour, and pore Mr and Mrs Chittenden off in a spring cart to the County Asylum and everyone in the street saying, "Ah, I thought it 'ud come to that. Look at the way the man drank!" – and me next door, or next door but one, to a total abstainer, as you know. Well, there was my position. What? Me 'ave it back in the shop? Well, what do *you* think? No, but I'll tell you what I will do. You shall have your money back, bar the ten pound I paid for it, and you make what you can.'

Later in the day, in what is offensively called the 'smoke-room' of the hotel, a murmured conversation between the two went on for some time.

'How much do you really know about that thing, and where it came from?'

'Honest, Mr Dillet, I don't know the 'ouse. Of course, it came out of the lumber room of a country 'ouse – that anyone could guess. But I'll go as far as say this, that I believe it's not a hundred miles from this place. Which direction and how far I've no notion. I'm only judging by guesswork. The man as I actually paid the cheque to ain't one of my regular men, and I've lost sight of him; but I 'ave the idea that this part of the country was his beat, and that's every word I can tell you. But now, Mr Dillet, there's one thing that rather physics me – that old chap – I suppose you saw him drive up to the door – I thought so: now, would he have been the medical man, do you take it? My wife would have it so, but I stuck to it that was the lawyer, because he had papers with him, and one he took out was folded up.'

'I agree,' said Mr Dillet. 'Thinking it over, I came to the conclusion that was the old man's will, ready to be signed.'

'Just what I thought,' said Mr Chittenden, 'and I took it that will would have cut out the young people, eh? Well, well! It's been a lesson to me, I know that. I shan't buy no more dolls' houses, nor waste no more money on the pictures – and as to this business of poisonin' grandpa, well, if I know myself, I never 'ad much of a turn for that. Live and let live: that's bin my motto throughout life, and I ain't found it a bad one.'

Filled with these elevated sentiments, Mr Chittenden retired to his lodgings. Mr Dillet next day repaired to the local institute, where he hoped to find some clue to the riddle that absorbed him. He gazed in despair at a long file of the Canterbury and York Society's publications of the Parish Registers of the district. No print resembling the house of his nightmare was among those that hung on the staircase and in the passages. Disconsolate, he found himself at last in a derelict room, staring at a dusty model of a church in a dusty glass case: *Model of St Stephen's Church, Coxham. Presented by J. Merewether, Esq., of Ilbridge House, 1877. The work of his ancestor James Merewether, d. 1786.* There was something in the fashion of it that reminded him dimly of his horror. He retraced his steps to a wall map he had noticed, and made out that Ilbridge House was in Coxham Parish. Coxham was, as it happened, one of the parishes of which he had retained the name when he glanced over the file of printed registers, and it was not long before he found in them the record of the burial of Roger Milford, aged 76, on the 11th of September, 1757, and of Roger and Elizabeth Merewether, aged 9 and 7, on the 19th of the same month. It seemed worthwhile to follow up this clue, frail as it was; and in the afternoon he drove out to Coxham. The east end of the north aisle of the church is a Milford chapel, and on its north wall are tablets to the same persons; Roger, the elder, it seems, was distinguished by all the qualities which adorn 'the Father, the Magistrate, and the Man': the memorial was erected by his detached daughter Elizabeth, 'who did not long survive the loss of a parent ever solicitous for her welfare, and of two amiable children'. The last sentence was plainly an addition to the original inscription.

A yet later slab told of James Merewether, husband of Elizabeth, 'who in the dawn of life practised, not without success, those arts which, had he continued their exercise, might in the opinion of the most competent judges have earned for him the name of the British Vitruvius: but who, overwhelmed by the visitation which deprived him of an affectionate partner and a blooming offspring, passed his Prime and Age in a secluded yet elegant Retirement: his grateful Nephew and Heir indulges a pious sorrow by this too brief recital of his excellences.'

The children were more simply commemorated. Both died on the night of the 12th of September.

Mr Dillet felt sure that in Ilbridge House he had found the scene of his drama. In some old sketch book, possibly in some old print, he may yet find convincing evidence that he is right. But the Ilbridge House of today is not that which he sought; it is an Elizabethan erection of the forties, in red brick with stone quoins and dressings. A quarter of a mile from it, in a low part of the park, backed by ancient, stag-horned, ivy-strangled trees and thick undergrowth, are marks of a terraced platform overgrown with rough grass. A few stone balusters lie here and there, and a heap or two, covered with nettles and ivy, of wrought stones with badly carved crockets. This, someone told Mr Dillet, was the site of an older house.

As he drove out of the village, the hall clock struck four, and Mr Dillet started up and clapped his hands to his ears. It was not the first time he had heard that bell.

Awaiting an offer from the other side of the Atlantic, the doll's house still reposes, carefully sheeted, in a loft over Mr Dillet's stables, whither Collins conveyed it on the day when Mr Dillet started for the sea coast.

Ambrose Bierce (1842—1914)

The Middle Toe of the Right Foot

Before television exerted such a pull, many people were avid listeners to the radio. For those who enjoyed a real thriller, one weekly series stood out above all others – 'The Man in Black', in which the grim and distinctive voice of Valentine Dyall recounted famous ghost and horror stories. As one who was a child at the time, the broadcasts left an indelible memory on my mind and certainly no one else has ever succeeded in making the hairs on the back of my neck rise as did Mr Dyall describing some strange occurrence. The series embraced many well-known tales, but for me and a great many others one story surpassed all others and really 'put the frights' into us, 'The Middle Toe of the Right Foot'. This perfectly paced and devastatingly-climaxed story was by the strange American writer, Ambrose Bierce, a man cast in the Poe tradition, who was wild, eccentric and talented to the very verge of genius. So, in reprinting this story here I pay my tribute to Bierce for his marvellous tale (oh, how it has long haunted me!) and the storytelling skill of Valentine Dyall (will no one revive that riveting series?).

I

IT is well known that the old Manton house is haunted. In all the rural district near about, and even in the town of Marshall, a mile away, not one person of un-biased mind entertains a doubt of it; incredulity is confined to those opinionated people who will be called 'cranks' as soon as the useful word shall have penetrated the intellectual demesne of the Marshall *Advance*. The evidence that the house is haunted is of two kinds: the testimony of disinterested witnesses who have had ocular proof, and that of the house itself. The former may be disregarded and ruled out on any of the various grounds of objections which may be urged against it by the ingenious; but facts within the observation of all are fundamental and controlling.

In the first place, the Manton house has been unoccupied by mortals for more than ten years, and with its outbuildings is slowly falling into decay – a circumstance which in itself the judicious will hardly venture to ignore. It stands a little way off the loneliest reach of the Marshall and Harriston road, in an opening which was once a farm and is still disfigured with strips of rotting fence and half covered with brambles overrunning a stony and sterile soil long unacquainted with the plough. The house itself is in tolerably good condition, though badly weather-stained and in dire need of attention from the glazier, the smaller male population of the region having attested in the manner of its kind its disapproval of dwellings without dwellers. The house is two storeys in height, nearly square, its front pierced by a single doorway flanked on each side by a window boarded up to the very top. Corresponding windows above, not protected, serve to admit light and rain to the rooms of the upper floor. Grass and weeds grow pretty rankly all about, and a few shade trees, somewhat the worse for wind and leaning all in one direction, seem to be making a concerted effort to run away. In short, as the Marshall town humourist explained in the columns of the *Advance*, 'the proposition that the Manton house is badly haunted is the only logical conclusion from the premises.' The fact that in this dwelling Mr Manton thought it expedient one night some ten years ago to rise and cut the throats of his wife and two small children, removing at once to another part of the country, has no doubt done its share in directing public attention to the fitness of the place for supernatural phenomena.

To this house, one summer evening, came four men in a wagon. Three of them promptly alighted, and the one who had been driving hitched the team to the only remaining post of what had been a fence. The fourth remained seated in the wagon. 'Come,' said one of his companions, approaching him, while the others moved away, in the direction of the dwelling – 'this is the place.'

The man addressed was deathly pale and trembled visibly. 'By God!' he said harshly, 'this is a trick, and it looks to me as if you were in it.'

'Perhaps I am,' the other said, looking him straight in the face and speaking in a tone which had something of contempt in it. 'You will remember, however, that the choice of place was, with your own assent, left to the other side. Of course if you are afraid of spooks –'

'I am afraid of nothing,' the man interrupted with another oath, and sprang to the ground. The two then joined the others at the door, which one of them had already opened with some difficulty, caused by rust of lock and hinge. All entered. Inside it was dark, but the man who had unlocked the door produced a candle and matches and made a light. He then unlocked a door on their right as they stood in the passage. This gave them entrance to a large, square room, which the candle but dimly lighted. The floor had a thick carpeting of dust, which partly muffled their footfalls. Cobwebs were in the angles of the walls and depended from the ceiling like strips of rotting lace, making undulatory movements in the disturbed air. The room had two windows in adjoining sides, but from neither could anything be seen except the rough inner surfaces of boards a few inches from the glass. There was no fireplace, no furniture; there was nothing. Besides the cobwebs and the dust, the four men were the only objects there which were not a part of the architecture. Strange enough they looked in the yellow light of the candle. The one who had so reluctantly alighted was specially 'spectacular' – he might have been called sensational. He was of middle age, heavily built, deep chested and broad shouldered. Looking at his figure, one would have said that he had a giant's strength; at his face, that he would use it like a giant. He was clean shaven, his hair rather closely cropped and grey. His low forehead was seamed with wrinkles above the eyes, and over the nose these became vertical. The heavy black brows followed the same law, saved from meeting only by an upward turn at what would otherwise have been the point of contact. Deeply sunken beneath these, glowed in the obscure light a pair of eyes of uncertain colour, but, obviously enough, too small. There was something forbidding in their expression, which was not bettered by the cruel mouth and wide jaw. The nose was well enough, as noses go; one does not expect much of noses. All that was sinister in the man's face seemed accentuated by an unnatural pallor – he appeared altogether bloodless.

The appearance of the other men was sufficiently

commonplace: they were such persons as one meets and forgets that he met. All were younger than the man described, between whom and the eldest of the others, who stood apart, there was apparently no kindly feeling. They avoided looking at one another.

'Gentlemen,' said the man holding the candle and keys, 'I believe everything is right. Are you ready, Mr Rosser?'

The man standing apart from the group bowed and smiled.

'And you, Mr Grossmith?'

The heavy man bowed and scowled.

'You will please remove your outer clothing.'

Their hats, coats, waistcoats, and neckwear were soon removed and thrown outside the door, in the passage. The man with the candle now nodded, and the fourth man – he who had urged Mr Grossmith to leave the wagon – produced from the pocket of his overcoat two long, murderous-looking bowie knives, which he drew from the scabbards.

'They are exactly alike,' he said, presenting one to each of the two principals – for by this time the dullest observer would have understood the nature of this meeting. It was to be a duel to the death.

Each combatant took a knife, examined it critically near the candle and tested the strength of blade and handle across his lifted knee. Their persons were then searched in turn, each by the second of the other.

'If it is agreeable to you, Mr Grossmith,' said the man holding the light, 'you will place yourself in that corner.'

He indicated the angle of the room farthest from the door, to which Grossmith retired, his second parting from him with a grasp of the hand which had nothing of cordiality in it. In the angle nearest the door Mr Rosser stationed himself, and, after a whispered consultation, his second left him, joining the other near the door. At that moment the candle was suddenly extinguished, leaving all in profound darkness. This may have been done by draught from the open door; whatever the cause, the effect was appalling!

'Gentlemen,' said a voice which sounded strangely unfamiliar in the altered condition affecting the relations of the senses, 'gentlemen, you will not move until you hear the closing of the outer door.'

A sound of trampling ensued, the closing of the inner door; and finally the outer one closed with a concussion which shook the entire building.

A few minutes later a belated farmer's boy met a wagon which was being driven furiously towards the town of Marshall. He declared that behind the two figures on the front seat stood a third with its hands upon the bowed shoulders of the others, who appeared to struggle vainly to free themselves from its grasp. This figure, unlike the others, was clad in white, and had undoubtedly boarded the wagon as it passed the haunted house. As the lad could boast a considerable former experience with the supernatural thereabout, his word had the weight justly due to the tesimony of an expert. The story eventually appeared in the *Advance*, with some slight literary embellishments and a concluding intimation that the gentlemen referred to would be allowed the use of the paper's columns for their version of the night's adventure. But the privilege remained without a claimant.

II

The events which led up to this 'duel in the dark' were simple enough. One evening three young men of the town of Marshall were sitting in a quiet corner of the porch of the village hotel, smoking and discussing such matters as three educated young men of a Southern village would naturally find interesting. Their names were King, Sancher and Rosser. At a little distance, within easy hearing but taking no part in the conversation, sat a fourth. He was a stranger to the others. They merely knew that on his arrival by the stage coach that afternoon he had written in the hotel register the name of Robert Grossmith. He had not been observed to speak to anyone except the hotel clerk. He seemed, indeed, singularly fond of his own company – or, as the *personnel* of the *Advance* expressed it, 'grossly addicted to evil associations'. But then it should be said in justice to the stranger that the *personnel* was himself of a too convivial disposition fairly to judge one differently gifted, and had, moreover, experienced a slight rebuff in an effort of an 'interview'.

'I hate any kind of deformity in a woman,' said King, 'whether natural or – or acquired. I have a theory that any physical defect has its correlative mental and moral defect.'

'I infer, then,' said Rosser, gravely, 'that a lady lacking the advantage of a nose would find the struggle to become Mrs King an arduous enterprise.'

'Of course you may put it that way,' was the reply; 'but, seriously, I once threw over a most charming girl on learning, quite accidentally, that she had suffered amputation of a toe. My conduct was brutal, if you like, but if I had married that girl I should have been miserable and should have made her so.'

'Whereas,' said Sancher, with a light laugh, 'by marrying a gentleman of more liberal views she escaped with a cut throat.'

'Ah, you know to whom I refer! Yes, she married Manton, but I don't know about his liberality; I'm not sure but he cut her throat because he discovered that she lacked that excellent thing in woman, the middle toe of the right foot.'

'Look at that chap!' said Rosser in a low voice, his eyes fixed upon the stranger.

That person was obviously listening intently to the conversation.

'That's an easy one,' Rosser replied, rising. 'Sir,' he continued, addressing the stranger, 'I think it would be better if you would remove your chair to the other end of the veranda. The presence of gentlemen is evidently an unfamiliar situation to you.'

The man sprang to his feet and strode forward with clenched hands, his face white with rage. All were now standing. Sancher stopped between the belligerents.

'You are hasty and unjust,' he said to Rosser; 'this gentleman has done nothing to deserve such language.'

But Rosser would not withdraw a word. By the custom of the country and the time, there could be but one outcome to the quarrel.

'I demand the satisfaction due to a gentleman,' said the stranger, who had become more calm. 'I have not an acquaintance in this region. Perhaps you, sir,' bowing to Sancher, 'will be kind enough to represent me in this matter.'

Sancher accepted the trust – somewhat reluctantly, it must be confessed, for the man's appearance and manner were not at all to his liking. King, who during the colloquy had hardly removed his eyes from the stranger's face, and had not spoken a word, consented with a nod to act for Rosser, and the upshot of it was that, the principals having retired, a meeting was arranged for the next evening. The nature of the arrangements has been already disclosed. The duel with knives in a dark room was once a commoner feature of South-western life than it is likely to be again. How thin a veneering of 'chivalry' covered the essential brutality of the code under which such encounters were possible, we shall see.

III

In the blaze of a midsummer noonday, the old Manton house was hardly true to its traditions. It was of the earth, earthy. The sunshine caressed it warmly and affectionately, with evident unconsciousness of its bad reputation. The grass greening all the expanse in its front seemed to grow, not rankly, but with a natural and joyous exuberance, and the weeds blossomed quite like plants. Full of charming lights and shadows, and populous with pleasant-voiced birds, the neglected shade trees no longer struggled to run away, but bent reverently beneath their burdens of sun and song. Even in the glassless upper windows was an expression of peace and contentment, due to the light within. Over the stony fields the visible heat danced with a lively tremor incompatible with the gravity which is an attribute of the supernatural.

Such was the aspect under which the place presented itself to Sheriff Adams and two other men who had come out from Marshall to look at it. One of these men was Mr King, the sheriff's deputy; the other, whose name was Brewer, was a brother of the late Mrs Manton. Under a beneficent law of the State relating to property which has been for a certain period abandoned by its owner, whose residence cannot be ascertained, the sheriff was the legal custodian of the Manton farm and the appurtenances thereunto belonging. His present visit was in mere perfunctory compliance with some order of a court in which Mr Brewer had an action to get possession of the property as heir to his deceased sister. By a mere coincidence the visit was made on the day after the night that Deputy King had unlocked the house for another and very different purpose. His presence now was not of his own choosing: he had been ordered to accompany his superior, and at the moment could think of nothing more prudent than simulated alacrity in obedience. He had intended going anyhow, but in other company.

Carelessly opening the front door, which to his surprise was not locked, the sheriff was amazed to see, lying on the floor of the passage into which it opened, a confused heap of men's apparel. Examination showed it to consist of two hats, and the same number of coats, waistcoats, and scarves, all in a remarkably good state of preservation, albeit somewhat defiled by the dust in which they lay. Mr Brewer was equally astonished, but Mr King's emotion is not on record. With a new and lively interest in his own actions, the sheriff now unlatched and pushed open a door on the right, and the three entered. The room was apparently vacant – no; as their eyes became accustomed to the dimmer light, something was visible in the farthest angle of the wall. It was a human figure – that of a man crouching close in the corner. Something in the attitude made the intruders halt when they had barely passed the threshold. The figure more and more clearly defined itself. The man was upon one knee, his back in the angle of the wall, his shoulders elevated to the level of his ears, his hands before his face, palms outward, the fingers spread and crooked like claws; the white face turned upward on the retracted neck had an expression of unutterable fright, the mouth half open, the eyes incredibly expanded. He was stone dead – dead of terror! Yet, with the exception of a knife, which had evidently fallen from his own hand, not another object was in the room.

In the thick dust which covered the floor were some confused footprints near the door and along the wall through which it opened. Along one of the adjoining walls, too, past the boarded-up windows, was the trail made by the man himself in reaching his corner. Instinctively in approaching the body the three men now followed that trail. The sheriff grasped one of the out-thrown arms; it was as rigid as iron, and the application of a gentle force rocked the entire body without altering the relation of its parts. Brewer, pale with terror, gazed intently into the distorted face. 'God of mercy!' he suddenly cried, 'it is Manton!'

'You are right,' said King, with an evident attempt at calmness: 'I knew Manton. He then wore a full beard and his hair long, but this is he.'

He might have added: 'I recognized him when he challenged Rosser. I told Rosser and Sancher who he was before we played him this horrible trick. When Rosser left this dark room at our heels, forgetting his clothes in the excitement, and driving away with us in his shirt – all through the discreditable proceedings we knew whom we were dealing with, murderer and coward that he was!'

But nothing of this did Mr King say. With his better light he was trying to penetrate the mystery of the man's death. That he had not once moved from the corner where he had been stationed, that his posture was that of neither attack nor defence, that he had dropped his weapon, that he had obviously perished of sheer terror of something that he *saw* – these were circumstances which Mr King's disturbed intelligence could not rightly comprehend.

Groping in intellectual darkness for a clue to his maze of doubt, his gaze, directed mechanically downward, as is the way of one who ponders momentous matters, fell upon something which, there, in the light of day, and in the presence of living companions, struck him with an invincible terror. In the dust of years that lay thick upon the floor – leading from the door by which they had entered, straight across the room to within a yard of Manton's crouching corpse – were three parallel lines of footprints – light but definite impressions of bare feet, the outer ones those of small children, the inner a woman's. From the point at which they ended they did not return; they pointed all one way. Brewer, who had observed them at the same moment, was leaning forward in an attitude of rapt attention, horribly pale.

'Look at that!' he cried, pointing with both hands at the nearest print of the woman's right foot, where she had apparently stopped and stood. 'The middle toe is missing – it was Gertrude!'

Gertrude was the late Mrs Manton, sister to Mr Brewer.

Algernon Blackwood (1869—1951)

The Transfer

*One of the thriller writers to figure most prominently dur-
ing the heyday of radio, both as a provider of material and
a broadcaster himself, was Algernon Blackwood, another
master of the supernatural tale. A great many of his stories,
particularly those which were based on his experiences as a
world traveller and worker at unusual trades, were particularly suited to reading aloud and it is gratifying to see
his material still so widely used on both radio and television. Blackwood seems to have enjoyed more 'brushes
with the unknown' than most other writers (he claimed to
have seen several ghosts, for instance, and recounted a
most bizarre encounter with a corpse on a small off-shore
island in Canada) and consequently his stories are both
vivid and imaginative – like 'The Transfer', as unusual a
tale as you will find in this or any other anthology of horror stories. Remember, you have been warned!*

THE child first began to cry in the early afternoon –
about three o'clock, to be exact. I remember the hour,
because I had been listening with secret relief to the
sound of the departing carriage. Those wheels fading
into distance down the gravel drive with Mrs Frene,
and her daughter Gladys to whom I was governess,
meant for me some hours' welcome rest, and the June
day was oppressively hot. Moreover, there was this
excitement in the little country household that had

173

told upon us all, but especially upon myself. This excitement, running delicately behind all the events of the morning, was due to some mystery, and the mystery was of course kept concealed from the governess. I had exhausted myself with guessing and keeping on the watch. For some deep and unexplained anxiety possessed me, so that I kept thinking of my sister's dictum that I was really much too sensitive to make a good governess, and that I should have done far better as a professional clairvoyante.

Mr Frene, senior, 'Uncle Frank', was expected for an unusual visit from town about teatime. That I knew. I also knew that his visit was concerned somehow with the future welfare of little Jamie, Gladys' seven-year-old brother. More than this, indeed, I never knew, and this missing link makes my story in a fashion incoherent – an important bit of the strange puzzle left out. I only gathered that the visit of Uncle Frank was of a condescending nature, that Jamie was told he must be upon his very best behaviour to make a good impression, and that Jamie, who had never seen his uncle, dreaded him horribly already in advance. Then, trailing thinly through the dying crunch of the carriage wheels this sultry afternoon, I heard the curious little wail of the child's crying, with the effect, wholly unaccountable, that every nerve in my body shot its bolt electrically, bringing me to my feet with a tingling of unequivocal alarm. Positively, the water ran into my eyes. I recalled his white distress that morning when told that Uncle Frank was motoring down for tea and that he was to be 'very nice indeed' to him. It had gone into me like a knife. All through the day, indeed, had run this nightmare quality of terror and vision.

'The man with the 'normous face?' he had asked in a

little voice of awe, and then gone speechless from the room in tears that no amount of soothing management could calm. That was all I saw; and what he meant by 'the 'normous face' gave me only a sense of vague presentiment. But it came as an anti-climax somehow – a sudden revelation of the mystery and excitement that pulsed beneath the quiet of the stifling summer day. I feared for him. For of all that commonplace household I loved Jamie best, though professionally I had nothing to do with him. He was a high-strung, ultra-sensitive child, and it seemed to me that no one understood him, least of all his honest, tender-hearted parents; so that his little wailing voice brought me from my bed to the window in a moment like a call for help.

The haze of June lay over that big garden like a blanket; the wonderful flowers, which were Mr Frene's delight, hung motionless; the lawns, so soft and thick, cushioned all other sounds; only the limes and huge clumps of guelder roses hummed with bees. Through this muted atmosphere of heat and haze the sound of the child's crying floated faintly to my ears – from a distance. Indeed, I wonder now that I heard it at all, for the next moment I saw him down beyond the garden, standing in his white sailor suit alone, two hundred yards away. He was down by the ugly patch where nothing grew – the Forbidden Corner. A faintness then came over me at once, a faintness as of death, when I saw him *there* of all places – where he never was allowed to go, and where, moreover, he was usually too terrified to go. To see him standing solitary in that singular spot, above all to hear him crying there, bereft me momentarily of the power to act. Then, before I could recover my composure sufficiently to call him in,

Mr Frene came round the corner from the Lower Farm with the dogs, and, seeing his son, performed that office for me. In his loud, good natured, hearty voice he called him, and Jamie turned and ran as though some spell had broken just in time – ran into the open arms of his fond but uncomprehending father, who carried him indoors on his shoulder, while asking 'what all this hubbub was about?' And, at their heels, the tail-less sheep-dogs followed, barking loudly, and performing what Jamie called their 'Gravel Dance', because they ploughed up the moist, rolled gravel with their feet.

I stepped back swiftly from the window lest I should be seen. Had I witnessed the saving of the child from fire or drowning the relief could hardly have been greater. Only Mr Frene, I felt sure, would not say and do the right thing quite. He would protect the boy from his own vain imaginings, yet not with the explanation that could really heal. They disappeared behind the rose trees, making for the house. I saw no more till later, when Mr Frene, senior, arrived.

To describe the ugly patch as 'singular' is hard to justify, perhaps, yet some such word is what the entire family sought, though never – oh, never! – used. To Jamie and myself, though equally we never mentioned it, that treeless, flowerless spot was more than singular. It stood at the far end of the magnificent rose garden, a bald, sore place, where the black earth showed uglily in winter, almost like a piece of dangerous bog, and in summer baked and cracked with fissures where green lizards shot their fire in passing. In contrast to the rich luxuriance of the whole amazing garden it was like a glimpse of death amid life, a centre of disease that cried for healing lest it spread. But it never did spread. Behind it stood the thick wood of silver birches and, glimmering beyond, the orchard meadow, where the lambs played.

The gardeners had a very simple explanation of its barrenness – that the water all drained off it owing to the lie of the slopes immediately about it, holding no remnant to keep the soil alive. I cannot say. It was Jamie – Jamie who felt its spell and haunted it, who spent whole hours there, even while afraid, and for whom it was finally labelled 'strictly out of bounds' because it stimulated his already big imagination, not wisely but too darkly – it was Jamie who buried ogres there and heard it crying in an earthy voice, swore that it shook its surface sometimes while he watched it, and secretly gave it food in the form of birds or mice or rabbits he found dead upon his wanderings. And it was Jamie who put so extraordinarily into words the *feeling* that the horrid spot had given me from the moment I first saw it.

'It's bad, Miss Gould,' he told me.

'But, Jamie, nothing in Nature is bad – exactly; only different from the rest sometimes.'

'Miss Gould, if you please, then it's empty. It's not fed. It's dying because it can't get the food it wants.'

And when I stared into the little pale face where the eyes shone so dark and wonderful, seeking within myself for the right thing to say to him, he added, with an emphasis and conviction that made me suddenly turn cold: 'Miss Gould' – he always used my name like this in all his sentences – 'it's hungry, don't you see? But *I* know what would make it feel all right.'

Only the conviction of an earnest child, perhaps, could have made so outrageous a suggestion worth listening to for an instant; but for me, who felt that things an imaginative child believed were important, it came with a vast disquieting shock of reality. Jamie, in this exaggerated way, had caught at the edge of a shocking fact – a hint of dark, undiscovered truth had leaped into that sensitive imagination. Why there lay horror in the words I cannot say, but I think some power of darkness trooped across the suggestion of that sentence at the end, 'I know what would make it feel all right.' I remember that I shrank from asking explanation. Small groups of other words, veiled fortunately by his silence, gave life to an unspeakable possibility that hitherto had lain at the back of my own consciousness. The way it sprang to life proves, I think, that my mind already contained it. The blood rushed from my heart as I listened. I remember that my knees shook. Jamie's idea was – had been all along – my own as well.

And now, as I lay down on my bed and thought about it all, I understood why the coming of his uncle involved somehow an experience that wrapped terror at its heart. With a sense of nightmare certainty that left me too weak to resist the preposterous idea, too shocked, indeed, to argue or reason it away, this certainty came with its full, black blast of conviction; and the only way I can put it into words, since nightmare horror really is not properly tellable at all, seems this: that there *was* something missing in that dying patch of garden; something lacking that it ever searched for; something, once found and taken, that would turn it rich and living as the rest; more – that there *was* some living person who could do this for it. Mr Frene, senior, in a word, 'Uncle Frank', was this person who out of his abundant life could supply the lack – unwittingly.

For this connection between the dying, empty patch and the person of this vigorous, wealthy, and successful man had already lodged itself in my subconsciousness

before I was aware of it. Clearly it must have lain
there all along, though hidden. Jamie's words, his sudden pallor, his vibrating emotion of fearful anticipa-
tion had developed the plate, but it was his weeping
alone there in the Forbidden Corner that had printed
it. The photograph shone framed before me in the air.
I hid my eyes. But for the redness – the charm of my
face goes to pieces unless my eyes are clear – I could
have cried. Jamie's words that morning about the
''normous face' came back upon me like a battering-
ram.

Mr Frene, senior, had been so frequently the subject
of conversation in the family since I came, I had so
often heard him discussed, and had then read so much
about him in the papers – his energy, his philanthropy,
his success with everything he laid his hand to – that a
picture of the man had grown complete within me. I
knew him as he was – within; or, as my sister would
have said – clairvoyantly. And the only time I saw him
(when I took Gladys to a meeting where he was chair-
man, and later *felt* his atmosphere and presence while
for a moment he patronizingly spoke with her) had
justified the portrait I had drawn. The rest, you may
say, was a woman's wild imagining; but I think rather
it was that kind of divining intuition which women
share with children. If souls could be made visible, I
would stake my life upon the truth and accuracy of my
portrait.

For this Mr Frene was a man who drooped alone, but
grew vital in a crowd – because he used their vitality.
He was a supreme, unconscious artist in the science of
taking the fruits of others' work and living – for his
own advantage. He vampired, unknowingly no doubt,
every one with whom he came in contact; left them

exhausted, tired, listless. Others fed him, so that while in a full room he shone, alone by himself and with no life to draw upon he languished and declined. In the man's immediate neighbourhood you felt his presence draining you; he took your ideas, your strength, your very words, and later used them for his own benefit and aggrandisement. Not evilly, of course; the man was good enough; but you felt that he was dangerous owing to the facile way he absorbed into himself all loose vitality that was to be had. His eyes and voice and presence devitalized you. Life, it seemed, not highly organized enough to resist, must shrink from his too near approach, and hide away for fear of being appropriated, for fear, that is, of – death.

Jamie, unknowingly, put in the finishing touch to my unconscious portrait. The man carried about with him some silent, compelling trick of drawing out all your reserves – then swiftly pocketing them. At first you would be conscious of taut resistance; this would slowly shade off into weariness; the will would become flaccid; then you either moved away or yielded – agreed to all he said with a sense of weakness pressing ever closer upon the edges of collapse. With a male antagonist it might be different, but even then the effort of resistance would generate force that *he* absorbed and not the other. He never gave out. Some instinct taught him how to protect himself from that. To human beings, I mean, he never gave out. This time it was a very different matter. He had no more chance than a fly before the wheels of a huge – what Jamie used to call – 'attraction' engine.

So this was how I saw him – a great human sponge, crammed and soaked with the life, or proceeds of life, absorbed from others – stolen. My idea of a human vampire was satisfied. He went about carrying these accumulations of the life of others. In this sense his 'life' was not really his own. For the same reason, I think, it was not so fully under his control as he imagined.

And in another hour this man would be here. I went to the window. My eye wandered to the empty patch, dull black there amid the rich luxuriance of the garden flowers. It struck me as a hideous bit of emptiness yawning to be filled and nourished. The idea of Jamie playing round its bare edge was loathsome. I watched the big summer clouds above, the stillness of the afternoon, the haze. The silence of the overheated garden was oppressive. I had never felt a day so stifling, motionless. It lay there waiting. The household, too, was waiting – waiting for the coming of Mr Frene from London in his big motor-car.

And I shall never forget the sensation of icy shrinking and distress with which I heard the rumble of the car. He had arrived. Tea was all ready on the lawn beneath the lime trees, and Mrs Frene and Gladys, back from their drive, were sitting in wicker chairs. Mr Frene, junior, was in the hall to meet his brother, but Jamie, as I learned afterwards, had shown such hysterical alarm, offered such bold resistance, that it had been deemed wiser to keep him in his room. Perhaps, after all, his presence might not be necessary. The visit clearly had to do with something on the uglier side of life – money, settlements, or what not; I never knew exactly; only that his parents were anxious, and that Uncle Frank had to be propitiated. It does not matter. That has nothing to do with the affair. What has to do with it – or I should not be telling the story – is that

Mrs Frene sent for me to come down 'in my nice white dress, if I didn't mind', and that I was terrified, yet pleased, because it meant that a pretty face would be considered a welcome addition to the visitor's landscape. Also, most odd it was, I felt my presence was somehow inevitable, that in some way it was intended that I should witness what I did witness. And the instant I came upon the lawn – I hesitate to set it down, it sounds so foolish, disconnected – I could have sworn, as my eyes met his, that a kind of sudden darkness came, taking the summer brilliance out of everything, and that it was caused by troops of small black horses that raced about us from his person – to attack.

After a first momentary approving glance he took no further notice of me. The tea and talk went smoothly; I helped to pass the plates and cups, filling in pauses with little under-talk to Gladys. Jamie was never mentioned. Outwardly all seemed well, but inwardly everything was awful – skirting the edge of things unspeakable, and so charged with danger that I could not keep my voice from trembling when I spoke.'

I watched his hard, bleak face; I noticed how thin he was, and the curious, oily brightness of his steady eyes. They did not glitter, but they drew you with a sort of soft, creamy shine like Eastern eyes. And everything he said or did announced what I may dare to call the *suction* of his presence. His nature achieved this result automatically. He dominated us all, yet so gently that until it was accomplished no one noticed it.

Before five minutes had passed, however, I was aware of one thing only. My mind focused exclusively upon it, and so vividly that I marvelled the others did not scream, or run, or do something violent to prevent it. And it was this: that, separated merely by some dozen yards or so, this man, vibrating with the acquired vitality of others, stood within easy reach of that spot of yawning emptiness, waiting and eager to be filled. Earth scented her prey.

These two active 'centres' were within fighting distance; he so thin, so hard, so keen, yet really spreading large with the loose 'surround' of others' life he had appropriated, so practised and triumphant; that other so patient, deep, with so mighty a draw of the whole earth behind it, and – ugh! – so obviously aware that its opportunity at last had come.

I saw it all as plainly as though I watched two great animals prepare for battle, both unconsciously; yet in some inexplicable way I saw it, of course, within me, and not externally. The conflict would be hideously unequal. Each side had already sent out emissaries, how long before I could not tell, for the first evidence *he* gave that something was going wrong with him was when his voice grew suddenly confused, he missed his words, and his lips trembled a moment and turned flabby. The next second his face betrayed that singular and horrid change, growing somehow loose about the bones of the cheek, and larger, so that I remembered Jamie's miserable phrase. The emissaries of the two kingdoms, the human and the vegetable, had met, I make it out, in that very second. For the first time in his long career of battening on others, Mr Frene found himself pitted against a vaster kingdom than he knew and, so finding, shook inwardly in that little part that was his definite actual self. He felt the huge disaster coming.

'Yes, John,' he was saying, in his drawling, self-congratulating voice, 'Sir George gave me the car – gave it to me as a present. Wasn't it char –?' and then broke off abruptly, stammered, drew breath, stood up, and looked uneasily about him. For a second there was a gaping pause. It was like the clock which starts some huge machinery moving – that instant's pause before it actually starts. The whole thing, indeed, then went with the rapidity of machinery running down and beyond control. I thought of a giant dynamo working silently and invisibly.

'What's that?' he cried, in a soft voice charged with alarm. 'What's that horrid place? And someone's crying there – who is it?'

He pointed to the empty patch. Then, before any one could answer, he started across the lawn towards it, going every minute faster. Before anyone could move he stood upon the edge. He leaned over – peering down into it.

It seemed a few hours passed, but really they were seconds, for time is measured by the quality and not the quantity of sensations it contains. I saw it all with merciless photographic detail, sharply etched amid the general confusion. Each side was intensely active, but only one side, the human, exerted *all* its force – in resistance. The other merely stretched out a feeler, as it were, from its vast, potential strength; no more was necessary. It was such a soft and easy victory. Oh, it was rather pitiful! There was no bluster or great effort, on one side at least. Close by his side I witnessed it, for I, it seemed, alone had moved and followed him. No one else stirred, though Mrs Frene clattered noisily with the cups, making some sudden impulsive gesture with her hands, and Gladys, I remember, gave a cry – it was like a little scream – 'Oh, mother, it's the heat, isn't it?' Mr Frene, her father, was speechless, pale as ashes.

But the instant I reached his side, it became clear

what had drawn me there thus instinctively. Upon the other side, among the silver birches, stood little Jamie. He was watching. I experienced – for him – one of those moments that shake the heart; a liquid fear ran all over me, the more effective because unintelligible really. Yet I felt that if I could know all, what lay actually behind, my fear would be more than justified; that the thing *was* awful, full of awe.

And then it happened – a truly wicked sight – like watching a universe in action, yet all contained within a small square foot of space. I think he understood vaguely that if someone could only take his place he might be saved, and that was why, discerning instinctively the easiest substitute within reach, he saw the child and called aloud to him across the empty patch, 'James, my boy, come here!'

His voice was like a thin report, but somehow flat and lifeless, as when a rifle misfires, sharp, yet weak; it had no 'crack' in it. It was really supplication. And, with amazement, I heard my own ring out imperious and strong, though I was not conscious of saying it, 'Jamie, don't move. Stay where you are!' But Jamie, the little child, obeyed neither of us. Moving up nearer to the edge, he stood there – laughing! I heard that laughter, but could have sworn it did not come from him. The empty, yawning patch gave out that sound.

Mr Frene turned sideways, throwing up his arms. I saw his hard, bleak face grow somehow wider, spread through the air, and downwards. A similar thing, I saw, was happening at the same time to his entire person, for it drew out into the atmosphere in a stream of movement. The face for a second made me think of those toys of green indiarubber that children pull. It grew enormous. But this was an external impression only.

What actually happened, I clearly understood, was that all this vitality and life he had transferred from others to himself for years was now in turn being taken from him and transferred – elsewhere.

One moment on the edge he wobbled horribly, then with that queer sideways motion, rapid yet ungainly, he stepped forward into the middle of the patch and fell heavily upon his face. His eyes, as he dropped, faded shockingly, and across the countenance was written plainly what I can only call an expression of destruction. He looked utterly destroyed. I caught a sound – from Jamie? – but this time not of laughter. It was like a gulp; it was deep and muffled and it dipped away into the earth. Again I thought of a troop of small black horses galloping away down a subterranean passage beneath my feet – plunging into the depths – their tramping growing fainter and fainter into buried distance. In my nostrils was a pungent smell of earth.

And then – all passed. I came back into myself. Mr Frene, junior, was lifting his brother's head from the lawn where he had fallen from the heat, close beside the tea-table. He had never really moved from there. And Jamie, I learned afterwards, had been the whole time asleep upon his bed upstairs, worn out with his crying and unreasoning alarm. Gladys came running out with cold water, sponge and towel, brandy too – all kinds of things. 'Mother, it *was* the heat, wasn't it?' I heard her whisper, but I did not catch Mrs Frene's reply. From her face it struck me that she was bordering on collapse herself. Then the butler followed, and they just picked him up and carried him into the house. He recovered even before the doctor came.

But the queer thing to me is that I was convinced the

others all had seen what I saw, only that no one said a word about it; and to this day no one *has* said a word. And that was, perhaps, the most horrid part of all.

From that day to this I have scarcely heard a mention of Mr Frene, senior. It seemed as if he dropped suddenly out of life. The papers never mentioned him. His activities ceased, as it were. His after-life, at any rate, became singularly ineffective. Certainly he achieved nothing worth public mention. But it may be only that, having left the employ of Mrs Frene, there was no particular occasion for me to hear anything.

The after-life of that empty patch of garden, however, was quite otherwise. Nothing, so far as I know, was done to it by gardeners, or in the way of draining it or bringing in new earth, but even before I left in the following summer it had changed. It lay untouched, full of great, luscious, driving weeds and creepers, very strong, full-fed, and bursting thick with life.

Agatha Christie (1891–   )

The Lamp

Of all the writers in this collection, few need less introduction than Agatha Christie, 'Queen of the Thriller Writers', and avidly read by devoted millions of fans around the world. Perhaps not a traditional horror story writer in the strictest sense of the word, she has nonetheless caused enough shivers among both the young and the old of at least two generations to be a must for these pages. No story by this remarkable lady has ever quite impressed me as much as 'The Lamp' and as it was mentioned to me by several other anthologists who recalled it as 'under-the-bedclothes-with-a-torch-reading' from their youth it makes a most fitting climax to this second section of the book...

It was undoubtedly an old house. The whole square was old, with that disapproving dignified old age often met with in a cathedral town. But No. 19 gave the impression of an elder among elders; it had a veritable patriarchal solemnity; it towered greyest of the grey, haughtiest of the haughty, chillest of the chill. Austere, forbidding, and stamped with that particular desolation attaching to all houses that have been long untenanted, it reigned above the other dwellings.

In any other town it would have been freely labelled 'haunted', but Weyminster was averse from ghosts and considered them hardly respectable except as the appanage of a 'county family'. So No. 19 was never alluded to as a haunted house; but nevertheless, it remained, year after year, 'To be Let or Sold.'

Mrs Lancaster looked at the house with approval as she drove up with the talkative house agent, who was in an unusually hilarious mood at the idea of getting No. 19 off his books. He inserted the key in the door without ceasing his appreciative comments.

'How long has the house been empty?' inquired Mrs Lancaster, cutting short his flow of language rather brusquely.

Mr Raddish (of Raddish and Foplow) became slightly confused.

'Er – er – some time,' he remarked blandly.

'So I should think,' said Mrs Lancaster dryly.

The dimly lighted hall was chill with a sinister chill. A more imaginative woman might have shivered, but this woman happened to be eminently practical. She was tall with much dark brown hair just tinged with grey and rather cold blue eyes.

She went over the house from attic to cellar, asking a pertinent question from time to time. The inspection over, she came back into one of the front rooms looking out on the square and faced the agent with a resolute mien.

'What is the matter with the house?'

Mr Raddish was taken by surprise.

'Of course, an unfurnished house is always a little gloomy,' he parried feebly.

'Nonsense,' said Mrs Lancaster. 'The rent is ridiculously low for such a house – purely nominal. There must be some reason for it. I suppose the house is haunted?'

Mr Raddish gave a nervous little start but said nothing.

Mrs Lancaster eyed him keenly. After a few moments she spoke again.

'Of course that is all nonsense, I don't believe in ghosts or anything of that sort, and personally it is no deterrent to my taking the house; but servants, unfortunately, are very credulous and easily frightened. It would be kind of you to tell me exactly what – what thing *is* supposed to haunt this place.'

'I – er – really don't know,' stammered the house agent.

'I am sure you must,' said the lady quietly. 'I cannot take the house without knowing. What was it? A murder?'

'Oh! no,' cried Mr Raddish, shocked by the idea of anything so alien to the respectability of the square. 'It's – it's – only a child.'

'A child?'

'Yes.'

'I don't know the story exactly,' he continued reluctantly. 'Of course, there are all kinds of different versions, but I believe that about thirty years ago a man going by the name of Williams took No. 19. Nothing was known of him; he kept no servants; he had no friends; he seldom went out in the daytime. He had one child, a little boy. After he had been there about two months, he went up to London, and had barely set foot in the metropolis before he was recognized as being a man "wanted" by the police on some charge – exactly what, I do not know. But it must have been a grave one, because, sooner than give himself up, he shot himself. Meanwhile, the child lived on here, alone in the house. He had food for a little time, and he waited day after day for his father's return. Unfortunately, it had been impressed upon him that he was never under any circumstances to go out of the house or to speak to anyone. He was a weak, ailing, little creature, and did not dream of disobeying this command. In the night, the neighbours, not knowing that his father had gone away, often heard him sobbing in the awful loneliness and desolation of the empty house.'

Mr Raddish paused.

'And – er – the child starved to death,' he concluded, in the same tones as he might have announced that it had just begun to rain.

'And it is the child's ghost that is supposed to haunt the place?' asked Mrs Lancaster.

'It is nothing of consequence really,' Mr Raddish hastened to assure her. 'There's nothing *seen*, not *seen*, only people say, ridiculous, of course, but they do say they hear – the child – crying, you know.'

Mrs Lancaster moved towards the front door.

'I like the house very much,' she said. 'I shall get nothing as good for the price. I will think it over and let you know.'

'It really looks very cheerful, doesn't it, Papa?'

Mrs Lancaster surveyed her new domain with approval. Gay rugs, well-polished furniture, and many knick-knacks, had quite transformed the gloomy aspect of No. 19.

She spoke to a thin, bent old man with stooping shoulders and a delicate mystical face. Mr Winburn did not resemble his daughter; indeed no greater contrast could be imagined than that presented by her resolute practicalness and his dreamy abstraction.

'Yes,' he answered with a smile, 'no one would dream the house was haunted.'

'Papa, don't talk nonsense! On our first day too.'

Mr Winburn smiled.

'Very well, my dear, we will agree that there are no such things as ghosts.'

'And please,' continued Mrs Lancaster, 'don't say a word before Geoff. He's so imaginative.'

Geoff was Mrs Lancaster's little boy. The family consisted of Mr Winburn, his widowed daughter, and Geoffrey.

Rain had begun to beat against the window – pitter-patter, pitter-patter.

'Listen,' said Mr Winburn. 'Is it not like little footsteps?'

'It's more like rain,' said Mrs Lancaster, with a smile.

'But *that, that* is a footstep,' cried her father, bending forward to listen.

Mrs Lancaster laughed outright.

'That's Geoff coming downstairs.'

Mr Winburn was obliged to laugh too. They were having tea in the hall, and he had been sitting with his back to the staircase. He now turned his chair round to face it.

Little Geoffrey was coming down, rather slowly and sedately, with a child's awe of a strange place. The stairs were of polished oak, uncarpeted. He came across and stood by his mother. Mr Winburn gave a slight start. As the child was crossing the floor, he distinctly heard another pair of footsteps on the stairs, as of someone following Geoffrey. Dragging footsteps, curiously painful they were. Then he shrugged his shoulders incredulously. 'The rain, no doubt,' he thought.

'I'm looking at the sponge cakes,' remarked Geoff

with the admirably detached air of one who points out an interesting fact.

His mother hastened to comply with the hint.

'Well, Sonny, how do you like your new home?' she asked.

'Lots,' replied Geoffrey with his mouth generously filled. 'Pounds and pounds and pounds.' After this last assertion, which was evidently expressive of the deepest contentment, he relapsed into silence, only anxious to remove the sponge-cake from the sight of man in the least time possible.

Having bolted the last mouthful, he burst forth into speech.

'Oh! Mummy, there's attics here, Jane says; and can I go at once and *eggz*plore them? And there might be a secret door, Jane says there isn't, but I think there must be, and, anyhow, I know there'll be *pipes, water pipes* (with a full face of ecstasy) and can I play with them, and, oh! can I go and see the Boi-i-ler?' He spun out the last word with such evident rapture that his grandfather felt ashamed to reflect that this peerless delight of childhood only conjured up to his imagination the picture of hot water that wasn't hot, and heavy and numerous plumber's bills.

'We'll see about the attics tomorrow, darling,' said Mrs Lancaster. 'Suppose you fetch your bricks and build a nice house, or an engine.'

'Don't want to build an 'ouse.'

'House.'

'House, or h'engine h'either.'

'Build a boiler,' suggested his grandfather.

'With pipes?'

'Yes, lots of pipes.'

Geoffrey ran away happily to fetch his bricks.

The rain was still falling. Mr Winburn listened. Yes, it must have been the rain he had heard; but it did sound like footsteps.

He had a queer dream that night.

He dreamt that he was walking through a town, a great city it seemed to him. But it was a children's city; there were no grown-up people there, nothing but children, crowds of them. In his dream they all rushed to the stranger crying: 'Have you brought him?' It seemed that he understood what they meant and shook his head sadly. When they saw this, the children turned away and began to cry, sobbing bitterly.

The city and the children faded away and he awoke to find himself in bed, but the sobbing was still in his ears. Though wide awake, he heard it distinctly; and he remembered that Geoffrey slept on the floor below, while this sound of a child's sorrow descended from above. He sat up and struck a match. Instantly the sobbing ceased.

Mr Winburn did not tell his daughter of the dream or its sequel. That it was no trick of his imagination, he was convinced; indeed soon afterwards he heard it again in the day time. The wind was howling in the chimney but *this* was a separate sound – distinct, unmistakable: pitiful little heartbroken sobs.

He found out too, that he was not the only one to hear them. He overheard the housemaid saying to the parlourmaid that she 'didn't think as that there nurse was kind to Master Geoffrey, she'd 'eard 'im crying 'is little 'eart out only that very morning.' Geoffrey had come down to breakfast and lunch beaming with health and happiness; and Mr Winburn knew that it was not Geoff who had been crying, but that other child whose dragging footsteps had startled him more than once.

Mrs Lancaster alone never heard anything. Her ears were not perhaps attuned to catch sounds from another world.

Yet one day she also received a shock.

'Mummy,' said Geoff plaintively. 'I wish you'd let me play with that little boy.'

Mrs Lancaster looked up from her writing-table with a smile.

'What little boy, dear?'

'I don't know his name. He was in an attic, sitting on the floor crying. But he ran away when he saw me. I suppose he was *shy* (with slight contempt), not like a *big* boy, and then, when I was in the nursery building, I saw him standing in the door watching me build, and he looked so awful lonely and as though he wanted to play wiv me. I said: "Come and build a h'engine," but he didn't say nothing, just looked as – as though he saw a lot of chocolates, and his Mummy had told him not to touch them.' Geoff sighed, sad personal reminiscences evidently recurring to him. 'But when I asked Jane who he was and told her I wanted to play wiv him, she said there wasn't no little boy in the 'ouse and not to tell naughty stories. I don't love Jane at all.'

Mrs Lancaster got up.

'Jane was right. There was no little boy.'

'But I saw him. Oh! Mummy, do let me play wiv him, he did look so awful lonely and unhappy. I *do* want to do something to "make him better".'

Mrs Lancaster was about to speak again, but her father shook his head.

'Geoff,' he said very gently, 'that poor little boy *is* lonely, and perhaps you may do something to comfort him; but you must find out how by yourself – like a puzzle – do you see?'

'Is it because I am getting *big* I must do it all my lone?'

'Yes, because you are getting big.'

As the boy left the room, Mrs Lancaster turned to her father impatiently.

'Papa, this is absurd. To encourage the boy to believe the servants' idle tales!'

'No servant has told the child anything,' said the old man gently. 'He's seen – what I *hear*, what I could see perhaps if I were his age.'

'But it's such nonsense! Why don't I see it or hear it?'

Mr Winburn smiled, a curiously tired smile, but did not reply.

'Why?' repeated his daughter. 'And why did you tell him he could help the – the – thing. It's – it's all so impossible.'

The old man looked at her with his thoughtful glance.

'Why not?' he said. 'Do you remember these words:

> *'What Lamp has Destiny to guide*
> *Her little Children stumbling in the Dark?*
> *"A Blind Understanding," Heaven replied.*

'Geoffrey has that – a blind understanding. All children possess it. It is only as we grow older that we lose it, that we cast it away from us. Sometimes, when we are quite old, a faint gleam comes back to us, but the Lamp burns brightest in childhood. That is why I think Geoffrey may help.'

'I don't understand,' murmured Mrs Lancaster feebly.

'No more do I. That – that child is in trouble and wants – to be set free. But how? I do not know, but – it's awful to think of it – sobbing its heart out – a *child*.'

A month after this conversation Geoffrey fell very ill. The east wind had been severe, and he was not a strong child. The doctor shook his head and said that it was a grave case. To Mr Winburn he divulged more and confessed that the case was quite hopeless. 'The child would never have lived to grow up, under any circumstances,' he added. 'There has been serious lung trouble for a long time.'

It was when nursing Geoff that Mrs Lancaster became aware of that – other child. At first the sobs were an indistinguishable part of the wind, but gradually they became more distinct, more unmistakable. Finally she heard them in moments of dead calm: a child's sobs – dull, hopeless, heartbroken.

Geoff grew steadily worse and in his delirium he spoke of the 'little boy' again and again. 'I do want to help him get away, I do!' he cried.

Succeeding the delirium there came a state of lethargy. Geoffrey lay very still, hardly breathing, sunk in oblivion. There was nothing to do but wait and watch. Then there came a still night, clear and calm, without one breath of wind.

Suddenly the child stirred. His eyes opened. He looked past his mother towards the open door. He tried to speak and she bent down to catch the half-breathed words.

'All right, I'm comin',' he whispered; then he sank back.

The mother felt suddenly terrified, she crossed the room to her father. Somewhere near them the other child was laughing. Joyful, contented, triumphant, the silvery laughter echoed through the room.

'I'm frightened; I'm frightened,' she moaned.

He put his arm round her protectingly. A sudden gust of wind made them both start, but it passed swiftly and left the air quiet as before.

The laughter had ceased and there crept to them a faint sound, so faint as hardly to be heard, but growing louder till they could distinguish it. Footsteps – light footsteps, swiftly departing.

Pitter-patter, pitter-patter, they ran – those well-known halting little feet. Yet – surely – now *other* footsteps suddenly mingled with them, moving with a quicker and a lighter tread.

With one accord they hastened to the door.

Down, down, down, past the door, close to them, pitter-patter, pitter-patter, went the unseen feet of the little children *together*.

Mrs Lancaster looked up wildly.

'There are two of them – *two!*'

Grey with sudden fear, she turned towards the cot in the corner, but her father restrained her gently, and pointed away.

'There,' he said simply.

Pitter-patter, pitter-patter – fainter and fainter.

And then – silence.

3

Tales That Will Horrify You

August Derleth (1909—71)

The Lonesome Place

So to the third and final section of the collection – to the stories which I hope will send a shiver up your spine. Among them I hope you are going to find some which will leave the same kind of indelible mark on your memory that the previous tales have done on your parents' and grandparents'. We have already met some of the traditional figures of horror such as ghosts, vampires and 'spirits of the unseen' and it is now time to meet the remainder of the unholy assembly. Here you are going to find monsters, werewolves and other evil beings but, I hasten to add, not of the old fashioned fairy-tale kind. In the stories which follow there are some very unusual 'denizens of the dark' which might, just might, rub shoulders with you on any night of the week and just about anywhere you could be. Take, for instance, our first contributor, August Derleth, a master of the modern American horror story. He's got a very pertinent little tale to tell of what goes on in that 'Lonesome Place' which we all have in our neighbourhood...*

You who sit in your houses of nights, you who sit in the theatres, you who are gay at dances and parties – all you who are enclosed by four walls – you have no conception of what goes on outside in the dark. In the lonesome places. And there are so many of them, all over – in the country, in the small towns, in the cities. If you were out in the evenings, in the night, you would know about them, you would pass them and wonder, perhaps, and if you were a small boy you might be frightened. Frightened the way Johnny Newell and I were frightened, the way thousands of small boys from one end of the country to the other are being frightened when they have to go out alone at night, past lonesome places, dark and lightless, sombre and haunted. . .

I want you to understand that if it had not been for the lonesome place at the grain elevator, the place with the big old trees and the sheds up close to the pavement, and the piles of lumber – if it had not been for that place Johnny Newell and I would never have been guilty of murder. I say it even if there is nothing the law can do about it. They cannot touch us, but it is true, and I know, and Johnny knows, but we never talk about it, we never say anything. It is just something we keep here, behind our eyes, deep in our thoughts where it is a fact which is lost among thousands of others, but no less there, something we know beyond cavil.

It goes back a long way. But as time goes, perhaps it is not long. We were young, we were little boys in a small town. Johnny lived three houses away and across the street from me, and both of us lived in the block west of the grain elevator. We were never afraid to go past the lonesome place together. But we were not often together. Sometimes one of us had to go that way alone, sometimes the other. I went that way most of the time – there was no other, except to go far around, because that was the straight way down town, and I had to walk there, when my father was too tired to go.

In the evenings it would happen like this. My mother would discover that she had no sugar or salt or bologna, and she would say, 'Steve, you go down town and get it. Your father's too tired.'

I would say, 'I don't wanna.'

She would say, 'You go.'

I would say, 'I can go in the morning before school.'

She would say, 'You go now. I don't want to hear another word out of you. Here's the money.'

And I would have to go.

Going down was never quite so bad, because most of the time there was still some afterglow in the west, and a kind of pale light lay there, a luminousness, like part of the day lingering there, and all around town you could hear the kids hollering in the last hour they had to play, and you felt somehow not alone. You could go down into that dark place under the trees and you would never think of being lonesome. But when you came back – that was different. When you came back the afterglow was gone; if the stars were out, you could never see them for the trees, and though the street lights were on – the old-fashioned lights arched over the crossroads – not a ray of them penetrated the lonesome place near to the elevator. There it was, half a block long, black as black could be, dark as the deepest night, with the shadows of the trees making it a solid place of darkness, with the faint glow of light where a street light pooled at the end of the street. Far away it seemed, and that other glow behind, where the other corner light lay.

And when you came that way you walked slower and slower. Behind you lay the brightly lit stores; all along the way there had been houses, with lights in the windows and music playing and voices of people sitting to talk on their porches. But up there, ahead of you, there was the lonesome place, with no house nearby, and up beyond it the tall, dark grain elevator, gaunt and forbidding. The lonesome place of trees and sheds and lumber, in which anything might be lurking, anything at all. The lonesome place where you were sure that something haunted the darkness waiting for the moment and the hour and the night when you came through to burst forth from its secret place and leap upon you, tearing you and rending you and doing the unmentionable things before it had done for you.

That was the lonesome place. By day it was oak and maple trees over a hundred years old, low enough so that you could almost touch the big spreading limbs; it was sheds and lumber piles which were seldom disturbed; it was a pavement and long grass, never mowed or kept down until late autumn, when somebody burned it off; it was a shady place in the hot summer days where some cool air always lingered. You were never afraid of it by day, but by night it was a different place.

For, then, it was lonesome, away from sight or sound, a place of darkness and strangeness, a place of terror for little boys haunted by a thousand fears.

And every night, coming home from town, it happened like this. I would walk slower and slower, the closer I got to the lonesome place. I would think of every way around it. I would keep hoping somebody would come along, so that I could walk with him, Mr Newell, maybe, or old Mrs Potter, who lived farther up the street, or Reverend Bislor, who lived at the end of the block beyond the grain elevator. But nobody ever came. At this hour it was too soon after supper for them to go out, or, already out, too soon for them to return. So I walked slower and slower, until I got to the edge of the lonesome place – and then I ran as fast as I could, sometimes with my eyes closed.

Oh, I knew what was there, all right. I knew there was something in that dark, lonesome place. Perhaps it was the bogey-man. Sometimes my grandmother spoke of him, of how he waited in dark places for bad boys and girls. Perhaps it was an ogre. I knew about ogres in the books of fairy tales. Perhaps it was something else, something worse. I ran. I ran hard. Every blade of grass, every leaf, every twig that touched me was *its* hand reaching for me. The sound of my footsteps slapping the pavement were *its* steps pursuing. The hard breathing which was my own became *its* breathing in its frantic struggle to reach me, to rend and tear me, to imbue my soul with terror.

I would burst out of that place like a flurry of wind, fly past the gaunt elevator, and not pause until I was safe in the yellow glow of the familiar street light. And then, in a few steps, I was home.

And mother would say, 'For the Lord's sake, have you been running on a hot night like this?'

I would say, 'I hurried.'

'You didn't have to hurry that much. I don't need it till breakfast time.'

And I would say, 'I coulda got it in the morning. I coulda run down before breakfast. Next time, that's what I'm gonna do.'

Nobody would pay any attention.

Some nights Johnny had to go down town, too. Things then weren't the way they are today, when every woman makes a ritual of afternoon shopping and seldom forgets anything.

In those days, they didn't go down town so often, and when they did, they had such lists they usually forgot something. And after Johnny and I had been through the lonesome place on the same night, we compared notes next day.

'Did you see anything?' he would ask.

'No, but I heard it,' I would say.

'I felt it,' he would whisper tensely. 'It's got big, flat clawed feet. You know what has got the ugliest feet around?'

'Sure, one of those stinking yellow soft-shell turtles.'

'It's got feet like that. Oh, ugly and soft, and sharp claws! I saw one out of the corner of my eye,' he would say.

'Did you see its face?' I would ask.

'It ain't got no face. Cross my heart an' hope to die, there ain't no face. That's worse'n if there was one.'

Oh, it was a horrible beast – not an animal, not a man – that lurked in the lonesome place and came forth predatorily at night, waiting there for us to pass. It grew like this, out of our mutual experiences. We discovered that it had scales, and a great long tail, like a dragon. It breathed from somewhere, hot as fire, but it had no face and no mouth in it, just a horrible opening in its throat. It was as big as an elephant, but it did not look like anything so friendly. It belonged there in the lonesome place; it would never go away; that was its home, and it had to wait for its food to come to it – the unwary boys and girls who had to pass through the lonesome place at night.

How I tried to keep from going near the lonesome place after dark!

'Why can't Mady go?' I would ask.

'Mady's too little,' mother would answer.

'I'm not so big.'

'Oh, shush! You're a big boy now. You're going to be seven years old. Just think of it.'

'I don't think seven is old,' I would say. I didn't either. Seven wasn't nearly old enough to stand up against what was in the lonesome place.

'Your Sears-Roebuck pants are long ones,' she would say.

'I don't care about any old Sears-Roebuck pants. I don't wanna go.'

'I want you to go. You never get up early enough in the morning.'

'But I will. I promise I will. I promise, Ma!' I would cry out.

'Tomorrow morning it will be a different story. No, you go.'

That was the way it went every time. I had to go. And Mady was the only one who guessed. 'Fraidycat,' she would whisper. Even she never really knew. She never had to go through the lonesome place after dark. They kept her at home. She never knew how something could lie up in those old trees, lie right along those old limbs across the pavement and drop down without a sound, clawing and tearing, something without a face, with ugly clawed feet like a soft shell turtle's, with scales and a tail like a dragon, something as big as a house, all black, like the darkness in that place.

But Johnny and I knew.

'It almost got me last night,' he would say, his voice low, looking anxiously out of the woodshed where we sat, as if *it* might hear us.

'Gee, I'm glad it didn't,' I would say. 'What was it like?'

'Big and black. Awful black. I looked around when I was running, and all of a sudden there wasn't any light way back at the other end. Then I knew it was coming. I ran like everything to get out of there. It was almost on me when I got away. Look there!'

And he would show me a rip in his shirt where a claw had come down.

'And you?' he would ask excitedly, big-eyed. 'What about you?'

'It was back behind the lumber piles when I came through,' I said. 'I could just feel it waiting. I was running, but it got right up – you look, there's a pile of lumber tipped over there.'

And we would walk down into the lonesome place at midday and look. Sure enough, there would be a pile of lumber tipped over, and we would look to where something had been lying down, the grass all pressed down. Sometimes we would find a handkerchief and wonder whether *it* had caught somebody.

Then we would go home and wait to hear if anyone was missing, speculating apprehensively all the way home whether *it* had got Mady or Christine or Helen, or any one of the girls in our class or Sunday School. Or, whether maybe *it* had got Miss Doyle, the younger primary grades teacher who had to walk that way sometimes after supper. But no one was ever reported missing, and the mystery grew. Maybe *it* had got some stranger who happened to be passing by and didn't know about the Thing that lived there in the lonesome place. We were sure *it* had got somebody.

'Some night I won't come back, you'll see,' I would say.

'Oh, don't be silly,' my mother would say.

What do grown-up people know about the things boys are afraid of? Oh, hickory switches and such like, they know that. But what about what goes on in their minds when they have to come home alone at night through the lonesome places? What do they know about lonesome places, where no light from the street corner ever comes? What do they know about a place and time when a boy is very small and very alone, and the night is as big as the town, and the darkness is the whole world? When grown-ups are big, old people who cannot understand anything, no matter how plain?

A boy looks up and out, but he can't look very far when the trees bend down over and press close, when the sheds rear up along one side and the trees on the other, when the darkness lies like a cloud along the pavement and the arc-lights are far, far away. No wonder, then, that Things grow in the darkness of lonesome places the way *it* grew in that dark place near the grain elevator. No wonder a boy runs like the wind until his heartbeats sound like a drum and push up to suffocate him.

'You're white as a sheet,' Mother would say sometimes. 'You've been running again.'

'You don't have to run,' my father would say. 'Take it easy.'

'I ran,' I would say. I wanted the worst way to say I had to run and to tell them why I had to. But I knew they wouldn't believe me any more than Johnny's parents believed him when he told them, as he did once.

He got a licking with a strap and had to go to bed.

I never got licked. I never told them.

But now it must be told, now it must be set down.

For a long time we forgot about the lonesome place. We grew older and we grew bigger. We went on through school into high school, and somehow we forgot about the Thing in the lonesome place. That place never changed. The trees grew older. Sometimes the lumber piles were bigger or smaller. Once the sheds were painted – red, like blood. Seeing them that way the first time, I remembered. Then I forgot again. We took to playing baseball and basketball and football. We began to swim in the river and to date the girls. We never talked about the Thing in the lonesome place any more, and when we went through there at night it was like something forgotten that lurked back in a corner of the mind. We thought of something we ought to remember, but never could quite remember; that was the way it seemed – like a memory locked away, far away in childhood. We never ran through that place, and sometimes it was even a good place to walk through with a girl, because she always snuggled up close and said how spooky it was there under the overhanging trees. But even then we never lingered there, not exactly lingered; we didn't run through there, but we walked without faltering or loitering, no matter how pretty a girl she was.

The years went past, and we never thought about the lonesome place again.

We never thought how there would be other little boys going through it at night, running with fast-beating hearts, breathless terror, anxious for the safety of the arc-light beyond the margin of the shadow which confined the dweller in that place, the light-fearing creature that haunted the dark, like so many terrors dwelling in similar lonesome places in the cities and small towns and countrysides all over the world, waiting to frighten little boys and girls, waiting to invade them with horror and unshakable fear – waiting for something more...

Three nights ago little Bobby Jeffers was killed in the lonesome place. He was all mauled and torn and partly crushed, as if something big had fallen on him. Johnny, who was on the Village Board, went to look at the place, and after he had been there, he telephoned me to go, too, before other people walked there.

I went down and saw the marks, too. It was just as the coroner said, only not an 'animal of some kind', as he put it. Something with a dragging tail, with scales, with great clawed feet – and I knew it had no face.

I knew, too, that Johnny and I were guilty. We had murdered Bobby Jeffers because the thing that killed him was the thing Johnny and I had created out of our childhood fears and left in that lonesome place to wait for some scared little boy at some minute in some hour during some dark night, a little boy who, like fat Bobby Jeffers, couldn't run as fast as Johnny and I could run.

And the worst is not that there is nothing to do, but that the lonesome place is being changed. The village is cutting down some of the trees now, removing the sheds, and putting up a street light in the middle of that place; it will not be dark and lonesome any longer, and the Thing that lives there will have to go somewhere else, where people are unsuspecting, to some other lonesome place in some other small town or city or countryside, where it will wait as it did here, for some frightened little boy or girl to come along, waiting in the dark and the lonesomeness. . .

John Wyndham (1903–69)

Close Behind Him

John Wyndham, *who has written some of the finest and most widely known horror novels (if you have not yet discovered 'The Day of the Triffids' and 'When the Kraken Wakes' do so immediately!), takes the theme of 'danger in the dark' begun by August Derleth a step further in this next story. Even if one likes to pretend that the advent of the electric bulb and neon lighting has driven the 'shades' into oblivion, the little voices which whisper in our minds of ancient superstititions cannot be stilled. Mr Wyndham employs this premise in 'Close Behind Him' with remarkable effect to provide what may well be the most off-beat story in the book.*

'You didn't ought to of croaked him,' Smudger said resentfully. 'What in hell did you want to do a fool thing like that for?'

Spotty turned to look at the house, a black spectre against the night sky. He shuddered.

'It was him or me,' he muttered. 'I wouldn't of done it if he didn't come for me – and I wouldn't even then, not if he'd come ordinary...'

'What do you mean ordinary?'

'Like anybody else. But he was queer... He wasn't – well, I guess he was crazy – dangerous crazy...'

'All he needed was a tap to keep him quiet,' Smudger persisted. 'There wasn't no call to bash his loaf in.'

'You didn't see him. I tell you, he didn't act human.'
Spotty shuddered again at the recollection, and bent
down to rub the calf of his right leg tenderly.

The man had come into the room while Spotty was
sifting rapidly through the contents of a desk. He'd
made no sound. It had been just a feeling, a natural
alertness, that had brought Spotty round to see him
standing there. In that very first glimpse Spotty had
felt there was something queer about him. The expression on his face – his attitude – they were wrong. In his
biscuit-coloured pyjamas, he should have looked just
an ordinary citizen awakened from sleep, too anxious
to have delayed with dressing-gown and slippers. But
some way he didn't. An ordinary citizen would have
shown nervousness, at least wariness; he would most
likely have picked up something to use as a weapon.
This man stood crouching, arms a little raised, as
though he were about to spring.

Moreover, any citizen whose lips curled back as this
man's did to show his tongue licking hungrily between
his teeth, should have been considered sufficiently un-
ordinary to be locked away safely. In the course of his
profession Spotty had developed reliable nerves, but
the look of this man rocked them. Nobody should be
pleased by the discovery of a burglar at large in his
house. Yet, there could be no doubt that this victim was
looking at Spotty with satisfaction. An unpleasant
gloating kind of satisfaction, like that which might
appear on a fox's face at the sight of a plump chicken.
Spotty hadn't liked the look of him at all, so he had
pulled out the convenient piece of pipe that he carried
for emergencies.

*

Far from showing alarm, the man took a step closer. He poised, sprung on his toes like a wrestler.

'You keep off me, mate,' said Spotty, holding up his nine inches of lead pipe as a warning.

Either the man did not hear – or the words held no interest for him. His long, bony face snarled. He shifted a little closer. Spotty backed against the edge of the desk. 'I don't want no trouble. You just keep off me,' he said again.

The man crouched a little lower. Spotty watched him through narrowed eyes. An extra tensing of the man's muscles gave him a fractional warning before the attack.

The man came without feinting or rushing: he simply sprang, like an animal.

In mid-leap he encountered Spotty's boot suddenly erected like a stanchion in his way. It took him in the middle and felled him. He sprawled on the floor doubled up, with one arm hugging his belly. The other hand threatened, with fingers bent into hooks. His head turned in jerks, his jaws with their curiously sharp teeth were apart, like a dog's about to snap.

Spotty knew just as well as Smudger that what was required was a quietening tap. He had been about to deliver it with professional skill and quality when the man, by an extraordinary wriggle, had succeeded in fastening his teeth into Spotty's leg. It was unexpected, excruciating enough to ruin Spotty's aim and make the blow ineffectual. So he had hit again; harder this time. Too hard. And even then he had more or less had to pry the man's teeth out of his leg...

But it was not so much his aching leg – nor even the fact that he had killed the man – that was the chief cause of Spotty's concern. It was the kind of man he had killed.

'Like an animal he was,' he said, and the recollection made him sweat. 'Like a bloody wild animal. And the way he looked! His eyes! Christ, they wasn't human.'

That aspect of the affair held little interest for Smudger. He'd not seen the man until he was already dead and looking like any other corpse. His present concern was that a mere matter of burglary had been abruptly transferred to the murder category – a class of work he had always kept clear of until now.

The job had looked easy enough. There shouldn't have been any trouble. A man living alone in a large house – a pretty queer customer with a pretty queer temper. On Fridays, Sundays, and sometimes on Wednesdays, there were meetings at which about twenty people came to the house and did not leave until the small hours of the following morning. All this information was according to Smudger's sister, who learned it third hand from the woman who cleaned the house. The woman was darkly speculative, but unspecific, about what went on at these gatherings. But from Smudger's point of view the important thing was that on other nights the man was alone in the house.

He seemed to be a dealer of some kind. People brought odd curios to the house to sell to him. Smudger had been greatly interested to hear that they were paid for – and paid for well – in cash. That was a solid, practical consideration. Beside it, the vaguely ill reputation of the place, the queerness of its furnishings, and the rumours of strange goings-on at the gatherings, were unimportant. The only things worthy of attention were the facts that the man lived alone and had items of value in his possession.

Smudger had thought of it as a one-man job at first, and with a little more information he might have tackled it on his own. He had discovered that there was a telephone, but no dog. He was fairly sure of the room in which the money must be kept, but unfortunately his sister's source of information had its limitations. He did not know whether there were burglar alarms or similar precautions, and he was too uncertain of the cleaning woman to attempt to get into the house by a subterfuge for a preliminary investigation. So he had taken Spotty in with him on a fifty-fifty basis.

The reluctance with which he had taken that step had now become an active regret – not only because Spotty had been foolish enough to kill the man, but because the way things had been he could easily have made a hundred per cent haul on his own – and not be fool enough to kill the man had he been detected.

The attaché case which he carried was now well-filled with bundles of notes, along with an assortment of precious-looking objects in gold and silver, probably eminently traceable, but useful if melted down. It was irritating to think that the whole load, instead of merely half of it, might have been his.

The two men stood quietly in the bushes for some minutes and listened. Satisfied, they pushed through a hole in the hedge, then moved cautiously down the length of the neighbouring field in its shadow.

Spotty's chief sensation was relief at being out of the house. He hadn't liked the place from the moment they had entered. For one thing, the furnishings weren't like those he was used to. Unpleasant idols or carved figures of some kind stood about in unexpected places, looking suddenly out of the darkness into his flashlight's beam with hideous expressions on their faces. There were pictures and pieces of tapestry that were macabre and shocking to a simple burglar. Spotty was not particularly sensitive, but these seemed to him highly unsuitable to have about the home.

The same quality extended to more practical objects. The legs of a large oak table had been carved into mythical miscegenates of repulsive appearance. The two bowls which stood upon the table were either genuine or extremely good representations of polished human skulls. Spotty could not imagine why, in one room, anybody should want to mount a crucifix on the wall upside down and place on a shelf beneath it a row of sconces holding nine black candles – then flank the whole with two pictures of an indecency so revolting it almost took his breath away. All these things had somehow combined to rattle his usual hard-headedness.

But even though he was out of the place now, he didn't feel quite free of its influence. He decided he wouldn't feel properly himself again until they were in the car and several miles away.

After working around two fields they came to the dusty white lane off which they had parked the car. They prospected carefully. By now the sky had cleared of clouds and the moonlight showed the road empty in both directions. Spotty scrambled through the hedge, across the ditch, and stood on the road in a quietness broken only by Smudger's progress through the hedge. Then he started to walk towards the car.

He had gone about a dozen paces when Smudger's voice stopped him. 'Hey, Spotty. What've you got on your feet?'

Spotty stopped and looked down. There was nothing

remarkable about his feet; his boots looked just as they had always looked.

'What –?' he began.

'No! Behind you!'

Spotty looked back. From the point where he had stepped on to the road to another some five feet behind where he now stood was a series of footprints, dark in the white dust. He lifted his foot and examined the sole of his boot; the dust was clinging to it. He turned his eyes back to the footmarks once more. They looked back, and seemed to glisten.

Smudger bent down to peer more closely. When he looked up again there was a bewildered expression on his face. He gazed at Spotty's boots, and then back to the glistening marks. The prints of bare feet. . .

'There's something funny going on here,' he said inadequately.

Spotty, looking back over his shoulder, took another step forward. Five feet behind him a new mark of a bare foot appeared from nowhere.

A watery feeling swept over Spotty. He took another experimental step. As mysteriously as before, another footmark appeared. He turned widened eyes on Smudger. Smudger looked back at him. Neither said anything for a moment. Then Smudger bent down, touched one of the marks with his finger, then shone his flashlight on the finger.

'Red,' he said. 'Like blood. . .'

The words broke the trance that had settled on Spotty. Panic seized him. He stared around wildly, then began to run. After him followed the footprints. Smudger ran too. He noticed that the marks were no longer the print of a full foot but only its forepart, as if whatever made them were also running.

Spotty was frightened, but not badly enough to forget the turn where they had parked the car beneath some trees. He made for it, and clambered in. Smudger, breathing heavily, got in on the other side and dropped the attaché case in the back.

'Going to get out of this lot quick,' Spotty said, pressing the starter.

'Take it easy,' advised Smudger. 'We got to think.'

But Spotty was in no thinking mood. He got into gear, jolted out of hiding, and turned down the lane.

A mile or so farther on Smudger turned back from craning out of the window.

'Not a sign,' he said, relieved. 'Reckon we've ditched it – whatever it was.' He thought for some moments, then he said: 'Look here, if those marks were behind us all the way from the house, they'll be able to follow them by daylight to where we parked the car.'

'They'd've found the car marks anyway,' Spotty replied.

'But what if they're *still* following?' Smudger suggested.

'You just said they weren't.'

'Maybe they couldn't keep up with us. But suppose they're coming along somewhere behind us, leaving a trail?'

Spotty had greatly recovered, he was almost his old practical self again. He stopped the car. 'All right. We'll see,' he said grimly. 'And if they are – what then?'

He lit a cigarette with a hand that was almost steady. Then he leaned out of the car, studying the road behind them. The moonlight was strong enough to show up any dark marks.

'What do you reckon it was?' he said, over his shoulder. 'We can't both've been seeing things.'

'They were real enough,' Smudger looked at the stain still on his finger.

On a sudden idea, Spotty pulled up his right trouser leg. The marks of the teeth were there, and there was a little blood, too, soaked into his sock, but he couldn't make that account for anything.

The minutes passed. Still there was no manifestation of footprints. Smudger got out and walked a few yards back along the road to make sure. After a moment's hesitation Spotty followed him.

'Not a sign,' Smudger said. 'I reckon – hey!' He broke off, looking beyond Spotty.

Spotty turned around. Behind him was a trail of dark, naked footprints leading *from* the car.

Spotty stared. He walked back to the car; the footmarks followed. It was a chastened Spotty who sat down in the car.

'Well?'

Smudger had nothing to offer. Smudger, in fact, was considerably confused. Several aspects of the situation were competing for his attention. The footsteps were not following *him*, so he found himself less afraid of them than of their possible consequences. They were laying a noticeable trail for anyone to follow to Spotty, and the trouble was that the trail would lead to him, too, if he and Spotty kept together.

The immediate solution that occurred to him was that they split up, and Spotty take care of his own troubles. The best way would be to divide the haul right here and now. If Spotty could succeed in shaking off the footprints, good for him. After all, the killing was none of Smudger's affair.

He was about to make the suggestion when another aspect occurred to him. If Spotty were picked up with part of the stuff on him, the case would be clinched. It were also possible that Spotty, in a bad jam with nothing to lose, might spill. A far safer way would be for him to hold the stuff. Then Spotty could come for his share when, and if, he succeeded in losing the telltale prints.

It was obviously the only safe and reasonable course. The trouble was that Spotty, when it was suggested to him, did not see it that way.

They drove a few more miles, each occupied with his own thoughts. In a quiet lane they stopped once more. Again Spotty got out of the car and walked a few yards away from it. The moon was lower, but it still gave enough light to show the footprints following him. He came back looking more worried than frightened. Smudger decided to cut a possible loss and go back to his former plan.

'Look here,' he suggested, 'what say we share out the takings now, and you drop me off a bit up the road?'

Spotty looked doubtful, but Smudger pressed: 'If you can shake that trail off, well and good. If you can't – well, there's no sense in us both getting pinched, is there? Anyway, it was you as croaked him. And one has a better chance of getting away than two.'

Spotty was still not keen, but he had no alternative to offer.

Smudger pulled the attaché case out of the back and opened it between them. Spotty began to separate the bundles of notes into two piles. It had been a good haul. As Smudger watched, he felt a great sadness that half of it was going to benefit nobody when Spotty was picked up. Sheer waste, it seemed to him.

Spotty, with his head bent over his work, did not notice Smudger draw the piece of lead pipe out of his pocket. Smudger brought it down on the back of his head with such force and neatness that it is doubtful whether Spotty ever knew anything about it.

Smudger stopped the car at the next bridge and pushed Spotty's body over the low wall. He watched as the ripples widened out across the canal below. Then he drove on.

It was three days later that Smudger got home. He arrived in the kitchen soaked to the skin, and clutching his attaché case. He was looking worn, white, and ready to drop. He dragged a chair away from the table and slumped into it.

'Bill!' his wife whispered. 'What is it? Are they after you?'

'No, Liz – at least, it ain't the cops. But something is.'

He pointed to a mark close inside the door. At first she thought it was his own wet footprint.

'Get a wet cloth, Liz, and clean up the front step and the passage before anyone sees it,' he said.

She hesitated, puzzled.

'For God's sake, do it quick, Liz,' he urged her.

Still half bewildered, she went through the dark passage and opened the door. The rain was pelting down, seeming to bounce up from the road as it hit. The gutters were running like torrents. Everything streamed with wetness save the doorstep protected by the small jutting porch. And on the step was the blood-red print of a naked foot. . .

In a kind of trance she went down on her knees and swabbed it clean with the wet cloth. Closing the door, she switched on the lights and saw the prints leading towards the kitchen. When she had cleaned them up, she went back to her husband.

'You been hit, Bill?'

He looked at her, elbows on the table, his head supported between his hands.

'No,' he said. 'It ain't me what's making them marks, Liz – it's what's followin' me.'

'Following you? You mean they been following you all the way from your job?' she said incredulously. 'How did you get back?'

Smudger explained. His immediate anxiety, after pitching Spotty into the canal, had been to rid himself of the car. It had been a pinch for the job, and the number and description would have been circulated. He had parked it in a quiet spot and got out to walk, maybe pick up a lift. When he had gone a few yards he had looked back and seen the line of prints behind him. They had frightened him a good deal more than he now admitted. Until that moment he had assumed that since they had been following Spotty they would have followed him into the canal. Now, it seemed, they had transferred their attentions to himself. He tried a few more steps: they followed. With a great effort he got a grip on himself, and refrained from running. He perceived that unless he wanted to leave a clear trail he must go back to the car. He did.

Farther on he tried again, and with a sinking, hopeless feeling observed the same result. Back in the car, he lit a cigarette and considered plans with as much calmness as he could collect.

The thing to do was to find something that would not show tracks – or would not hold them. A flash of inspiration came to him, and he headed the car towards the river.

The sky was barely grey yet. He fancied that he managed to get the car down to the towpath without being seen. At any rate, no one had hailed him as he cut through the long grass to the water's edge. From there he had made his way downstream, plodding along through a few inches of water until he found a rowboat. It was a venerable and decrepit affair, but it served his purpose.

From then on his long journey had been unexciting, but also uncomfortable. During the day he had become extremely hungry, but he did not dare to leave the boat until after dark, and then he moved only in the darkest streets where the marks might not be seen. Both that day and the next two he had spent hoping for rain. This morning, in a drenching downpour that looked like it might continue for hours, he had sunk the boat and made his way home, trusting that the trail would be washed away. As far as he knew, it had been.

Liz was less impressed than she ought to have been.

'I reckon it must be something on your boots,' she said practically. 'Why didn't you buy some new ones?'

He looked at her with a dull resentment. 'It ain't nothing on my boots,' he said. 'Didn't I tell you it was following me? You seen the marks. How could they come off my boots? Use your head.'

'But it don't make sense. Not the way you say it. *What's* following you?'

'How do I know?' he said bitterly. 'All I know is that it makes them marks – and they're getting closer, too.'

'How do you mean closer?'

'Just what I say. The first day they was about five feet behind me. Now they're between three and four.'

It was not the kind of thing that Liz could take in too easily.

'It don't make sense,' she repeated.

It made no more sense during the days that followed, but she ceased to doubt. Smudger stayed in the house; whatever was following stayed with him. The marks of it were everywhere: on the stairs, upstairs, downstairs. Half Liz's time was spent in cleaning them up lest someone should come in and see them. They got on her nerves. But not as badly as they got on Smudger's...

Even Liz could not deny that the feet were stepping a little more closely behind him – a little more closely each day.

'And what happens when they catch up?' Smudger demanded fearfully. 'Tell me that. What can I do? What the hell can I do?'

But Liz had no suggestions. Nor was there anyone else they dared ask about it.

Smudger began to dream at night. He'd whimper and she'd wake him up asking what was the matter. The first time he could not remember, but the dream was repeated, growing a little clearer with each recurrence. A black shape appeared to hang over him as he lay. It was vaguely manlike in form, but it hovered in the air as if suspended. Gradually it sank lower and lower until it rested upon him – but weightlessly, like a pattern of fog. It seemed to flow up towards his head, and he was in panic lest it should cover his face and smother him, but at his throat it stopped. There was a prickling at the side of his neck. He felt strangely weak, as though tiredness suddenly invaded him. At the same time the shadow appeared to grow denser. He could feel, too, that there began to be some weight in it as it lay upon him. Then, mercifully, Liz would wake him.

So real was the sensation that he inspected his neck carefully in the mirror when he shaved. But there was no mark there.

Gradually the glistening red prints closed in behind him. A foot behind his heels, six inches, three inches. . .

Then came a morning when he woke tired and list-less. He had to force himself to get up, and when he looked in the mirror, there *was* a mark on his throat. He called Liz, in a panic. But it was only a very small mark, and she made nothing of it.

But the next morning his lassitude was greater. It needed all his willpower to drag himself up. The pal-lor of his face shocked Liz – and himself, too, when he saw it in the shaving mirror. The red mark on his neck stood out more vividly. . .

The next day he did not get up.

Two days later Liz became frightened enough to call in the doctor. It was a confession of desperation. Neither of them cared for the doctor, who knew or guessed uncomfortably much about the occupations of his patients. One called a doctor for remedies, not for homilies on one's way of life.

He came, he hummed, he ha'ed. He prescribed a tonic, and had a talk with Liz.

'He's seriously anaemic,' he said. 'But there's more to it than that. Something on his mind.' He looked at her. 'Have you any idea what it is?'

Liz's denial was unconvincing. He did not even pretend to believe it.

'I'm no magician,' he said. 'If you don't help me, I can't help him. Some kinds of worry can go on pressing and nagging like an abscess.'

Liz continued to deny. For a moment she had been tempted to tell about the footmarks, but caution warned her that once she began she would likely be trapped into saying more than was healthy.

'Think it over,' the doctor advised. 'And let me know tomorrow how he is.'

The next morning there was no doubt that Smudger was doing very badly. The tonic had done him no good at all. He lay in bed with his eyes, when they were open, looking unnaturally large in a drawn white face. He was so weak that she had to feed him with a spoon. He was frightened, too, that he was going to die. So was Liz. The alarm in her voice when she telephoned the doctor was unmistakably genuine.

'All right, I'll be round within an hour,' he told her. 'Have you found out what's on his mind yet?' he added.

'N-no,' Liz told him.

When he came he told her to stay downstairs while he went up to see the patient. It seemed to her that an intolerably long time passed before she heard his feet on the stairs and she went out to meet him in the hall. She looked up into his face with mute anxiety. His expression was serious, and puzzled, so that she was afraid to hear him speak.

But at last she asked: 'Is – is he going to die, Doctor?'

'He's very weak – very weak indeed,' the doctor said. After a pause, he added: 'Why didn't you tell me about those footprints he thought were following him?'

She looked up at him in alarm.

'It's all right. He's told me all about it now. I knew there was something on his mind. It's not very surprising, either.'

Liz stared at him. 'Not –?'

'In the circumstances, no,' the doctor said. 'A mind oppressed by a sense of sin can play a lot of nasty tricks. Nowadays they talk of guilt complexes and inhibitions. Names change. When I was a boy the same sort of thing was known as a bad conscience.

'When one has the main facts, these things become obvious to anyone of experience. Your husband was engaged in – well, to put it bluntly, burgling the house of a man whose interests were mystic and occult. Something that happened there gave him a shock and unbalanced his judgment.

'As a result, he has difficulty in distinguishing between the real things he sees and the imaginary ones his uneasy conscience shows him. It isn't very complicated. He feels he is being dogged. Somewhere in his subconscious lie the lines from *The Ancient Mariner*:

> *Because he knows a frightful fiend*
> *Doth close behind him tread*

and the two come together. And in addition to that, he appears to have developed a primitive, vampiric type of phobia.

'Now, once we are able to help him dispel this obsession, he –' He broke off, suddenly aware of the look on his listener's face. 'What is it?' he asked.

'But, Doctor,' Liz said. 'Those footmarks. I –' She was cut short abruptly by a sound from above that was half groan and half scream.

The doctor was up the stairs before she could move. When she followed him, it was with a heavy certainty in her heart.

She stood in the doorway watching as he bent over the bed. In a moment he turned, grave-eyed, and gave a slight shake of his head. He put his hand on her shoulder, then went quietly past her out of the room.

For some seconds Liz stood without moving. Then her eyes dropped from the bed to the floor. She trembled. Laughter, a high-pitched, frightening laughter shook her as she looked at the red naked footprints which led away from the bedside, across the floor and down the stairs, after the doctor...

Robert Bloch (1917–   )

Enoch

Most people have a pet of some kind, I am sure, a dog or cat, perhaps, or even a rabbit, hamster or some little mice. They make up our home lives and give endless hours of pleasure and delight. As the subject matter for a horror story, however, a pet may seem a most unlikely choice – but there are few more inventive writers than Robert Bloch (*he wrote that outstanding Hitchcock film 'Psycho'*) *and there has certainly never been a 'pet' like 'Enoch' before. After reading of his activities I was more than relieved to look into the bright, trusting eyes of my dog and heave a big sigh of relief...*

It always starts the same way.

First, there's the feeling.

Have you ever felt the tread of little feet walking across the top of your skull? Footsteps on your skull, back and forth, back and forth?

It starts like that.

You can't see who does the walking. After all, it's on top of your head. If you're clever, you wait for a chance and suddenly brush a hand through your hair. But you can't catch the walker that way. He knows. Even if you clamp both hands flat to your head, he manages to wriggle through, somehow. Or maybe he jumps.

He is terribly swift. And you can't ignore him. If you don't pay any attention to the footsteps, he tries the next step. He wriggles down the back of your neck and whispers in your ear.

You can feel his body, so tiny and cold, pressed tightly against the base of your brain. There must be something numbing in his claws, because they don't hurt – although later you'll find little scratches on your neck that bleed and bleed. But at the time, all you know is that something tiny and cold is pressing there. Pressing and whispering.

That's when you try to fight him. You try not to hear what he says. Because when you listen, you're lost. You have to obey him then.

Oh, he's wicked and wise!

He knows how to frighten and threaten, if you dare to resist. But I seldom try, any more. It's better for me if I do listen and then obey.

As long as I'm willing to listen, things don't seem so bad. Because he can be soothing and persuasive, too. Tempting. The things he has promised me, in that little silken whisper!

He keeps his promises, too.

Folks think I'm poor because I never have any money and live in that old shack on the edge of the swamp. But he has given me riches.

After I do what he wants, he takes me away – out of myself – for days. There are other places besides this world, you know; places where I am king.

People laugh at me and say I have no friends; the girls in town used to call me 'scarecrow'. Yet sometimes – after I've done his bidding – he brings queens to share my bed.

Just dreams? I don't think so. It's the other life that's just a dream; the life in the shack at the edge of the swamp. That part doesn't seem real any more.

Not even the killing...

Yes, I kill people.

That's what Enoch wants, you know.

That's what he whispers about. He asks me to kill people, for him.

I don't like that. I used to fight against it – I told you that before, didn't I? – but I can't any more.

He wants me to kill people for him. Enoch. The thing that lives on the top of my head. I can't see him. I can't catch him. I can only feel him, and hear him, and obey him.

Sometimes he leaves me alone for days. Then, suddenly, I feel him there, scratching away at the roof of my brain. I hear his whisper ever so plainly, and he'll be telling me about someone who is coming through the swamp.

I don't know how he knows about them. He couldn't have seen them, yet he describes them perfectly.

'There's a tramp walking down the Aylesworthy Road. A short, fat man, with a bald head. His name is Mike. He's wearing a brown sweater and blue overalls. He's going to turn into the swamp in about ten minutes when the sun goes down. He'll stop under the big tree next to the dump.

'Better hide behind that tree. Wait until he starts to look for firewood. Then you know what to do. Get the hatchet, now. Hurry.'

Sometimes I ask Enoch what he will give me. Usually, I just trust him. I know I'm going to have to do it, anyway. So I might as well go ahead at once. Enoch is never wrong about things, and he keeps me out of trouble.

That is, he always did – until the last time.

One night I was sitting in the shack eating supper when he told me about this girl.

'She's coming to visit you,' he whispered. 'A beautiful girl, all in black. She has a wonderful quality to her head – fine bones. Fine.'

At first I thought he was telling me about one of my rewards. But Enoch was talking about a real person.

'She will come to the door and ask you to help her fix her car. She has taken the side road, planning to go into town by a shorter route. Now the car is well into the swamp, and one of the tyres needs changing.'

It sounded funny, hearing Enoch talk about things like motor-car tyres. But he knows about them. Enoch knows everything.

'You will go out to help her when she asks you. Don't take anything. She has a wrench in the car. Use that.'

This time I tried to fight him. I kept whimpering, 'I won't do it, I won't do it.'

He just laughed. And then he told me what he'd do if I refused. He told me over and over again.

'Better that I do it to her and not to you,' Enoch reminded me. 'Or would you rather I –'

'No!' I said. 'No. I'll do it.'

'After all,' Enoch whispered, 'I can't help it. I must be served every so often. To keep me alive. To keep me strong. So I can serve you. So I can give you things. That is why you have to obey me. If not, I'll just stay right here and –'

'No,' I said. 'I'll do it.'

And I did it.

She knocked on my door just a few minutes later, and it was just as Enoch had whispered it. She was a pretty girl – with blonde hair. I like blonde hair. I was glad, when I went out into the swamp with her, that I didn't have to harm her hair. I hit her behind the neck with the wrench.

Enoch told me what to do, step by step.

After I used the hatchet, I put the body in the quicksand. Enoch was with me, and he cautioned me about heelmarks. I got rid of them.

I was worried about the car, but he showed me how to use the end of a rotten log and pitch it over. I wasn't sure it would sink, too, but it did. And much faster than I would have believed.

It was a relief to see the car go. I threw the wrench in after it. Then Enoch told me to go home, and I did, and at once I felt the dreamy feeling stealing over me.

Enoch had promised me something extra special for this one, and I sank down into sleep right away. I could barely feel the pressure leave my head as Enoch left me, scampering off back into the swamp for his reward. . .

I don't know how long I slept. It must have been a long time. All I remember is that I finally started to wake up, knowing somehow that Enoch was back with me again, and feeling that something was wrong.

Then I woke up all the way, because I heard the banging on my door.

I waited a moment. I waited for Enoch to whisper to me, tell me what I should do.

But Enoch was asleep now. He always sleeps – afterwards. Nothing wakes him for days on end; and during that time I am free. Usually I enjoy such freedom, but not now. I needed his help.

The pounding on my door grew louder, and I couldn't wait any longer.

I got up and answered.

Old Sheriff Shelby came through the doorway.

'Come on, Seth,' he said, 'I'm taking you up to the jail.'

I didn't say anything. His beady little black eyes were peeping everywhere inside my shack. When he looked at me, I wanted to hide, I felt so scared.

He couldn't see Enoch, of course. Nobody can. But Enoch was there; I felt him resting very lightly on top of my skull, burrowed down under a blanket of hair, clinging to my curls and sleeping as peaceful as a baby.

'Emily Robbins' folks said she was planning on cutting through the swamp,' the Sheriff told me. 'We followed the tyre tracks up to the old quicksand.'

Enoch had forgotten about the tracks. So what could I say? Besides,

'Anything you say can be used agin you,' said Sheriff Shelby. 'Come on, Seth.'

I went with him. There was nothing else for me to do. I went with him into town, and all the loafers were out trying to rush the car. There were women in the crowd too. They kept yelling for the men to 'get' me.

But Sheriff Shelby held them off, and at last I was tucked away safe and sound in back of the gaol house. He locked me up in the middle cell. The two cells on each side of mine were vacant, so I was all alone. All alone except for Enoch, and he slept through everything.

It was still pretty early in the morning, and Sheriff Shelby went out again with some other men. I guess he was going to try and get the body out of the quicksand, if he could. He didn't try to ask any questions, and I wondered about that.

Charley Potter, now, he was different. He wanted to know everything. Sheriff Shelby had left him in charge of the jail while he was away. He brought me my breakfast after a while, and hung around asking questions.

I just kept still. I knew better than to talk to a fool like Charley Potter. He thought I was crazy. Just like the mob outside. Most people in that town thought I was crazy – because of my mother, I suppose, and because of the way I lived all alone out in the swamp.

What could I say to Charley Potter? If I told him about Enoch he'd never believe me anyway.

So I didn't talk.

I listened.

Then Charley Potter told me about the search for Emily Robbins, and about how Sheriff Shelby got to wondering over some other disappearances a while back. He said that there would be a big trial, and the District Attorney was coming down from the County Seat. And he'd heard they were sending out a doctor to see me right away.

Sure enough, just as I finished breakfast, the doctor came. Charley Potter saw him drive up and let him in. He had to work fast to keep some of the oafs from breaking in with him. They wanted to lynch me, I suppose. But the doctor came in all right – a little man with one of those funny beards on his chin – and he made Charley Potter go up front into the office while he sat down outside the cell and talked to me.

His name was Dr Silversmith.

Now up to this time, I wasn't really feeling anything. It had all happened so fast I didn't get a chance to think.

It was like part of a dream; the Sheriff and the mob and all this talk about a trial and lynching and the body in the swamp.

But somehow the sight of this Dr Silversmith changed things.

He was real, all right. You could tell he was a doctor who wanted to send me to the Institution after they found my mother.

That was one of the first things Dr Silversmith asked me – what had happened to my mother?

He seemed to know quite a lot about me, and that made it easier for me to talk.

Pretty soon I found myself telling him all sorts of things. How my mother and I lived in the shack. How she made the philtres and sold them. About the big pot and the way we gathered herbs at night. About the nights when she went off alone and I would hear the queer noises from far away.

I didn't want to say much more, but he knew, anyway. He knew they had called her a witch. He even knew the way she died – when Santo Dinorelli came to our door that evening and stabbed her because she had made the potion for his daughter who ran away with that trapper. He knew about me living in the swamp alone after that, too.

But he didn't know about Enoch.

Enoch, up on top of my head all the time, still sleeping, not knowing or caring what was happening to me...

Somehow, I was talking to Dr Silversmith about Enoch. I wanted to explain that it wasn't really I who had killed this girl. So I had to mention Enoch, and how my mother had made the bargain in the woods. She hadn't let me come with her – I was only twelve – but she took some of my blood in a little bottle.

Then, when she came back, Enoch was with her. And he was to be mine forever, she said, and look after me and help me in all ways.

I told this very carefully and explained why it was I

couldn't help myself when I did anything now, because ever since my mother died Enoch had guided me.

Yes, all these years Enoch had protected me, just as my mother planned. She knew I couldn't get along alone. I admitted this to Dr Silversmith because I thought he was a wise man and would understand.

That was wrong.

I knew it at once. Because while Dr Silversmith leaned forward and stroked his little beard and said, 'Yes, yes,' over and over again, I could feel his eyes watching me. The same kind as the people in the mob. Mean eyes. Eyes that don't trust you when they see you. Prying, peeping eyes.

Then he began to ask me all sorts of ridiculous questions. About Enoch, at first – although I knew he was only pretending to believe in Enoch. He asked me how I could hear Enoch if I couldn't see him. He asked me if I ever heard any other voices. He asked me how I felt when I killed Emily Robbins and whether I – but I won't even think about that question. Why, he talked to me as if I were some kind of – crazy person!

He had only been fooling me all along about not knowing Enoch. He proved that now by asking me how many other people I had killed. And then he wanted to know, where were their heads?

He couldn't fool me any longer.

I just laughed at him, then, and shut up tighter than a clam.

After a while he gave up and went away, shaking his head. I laughed after him because I knew he hadn't found out what he wanted to find out. He wanted to know all my mother's secrets, and my secrets, and Enoch's secrets too.

But he didn't, and I laughed. And then I went to sleep. I slept almost all afternoon.

When I woke up, there was a new man standing in front of my cell. He had a big, fat smiling face, and nice eyes.

'Hello, Seth,' he said, very friendly. 'Having a little snooze?'

I reached up to the top of my head. I couldn't feel Enoch, but I knew he was there, and still asleep. He moves fast, even when he's sleeping.

'Don't be alarmed,' said the man. 'I won't hurt you.'

'Did that doctor send you?' I asked.

The man laughed. 'Of course not,' he told me. 'My name's Cassidy. Edwin Cassidy. I'm the District Attorney, and I'm in charge here. Can I come in and sit down, do you suppose?'

'I'm locked in,' I said.

'I've got the keys from the Sheriff,' said Mr Cassidy. He took them out and opened my cell; walked right in and sat down next to me on the bench.

'Aren't you afraid?' I asked him. 'You know, I'm supposed to be a murderer.'

'Why, Seth,' Mr Cassidy laughed, 'I'm not afraid of you. I know you didn't mean to kill anybody.'

He put his hand on my shoulder, and I didn't draw away. It was a nice fat, soft hand. He had a big diamond ring on his finger that just twinkled away in the sunshine.

'How's Enoch?' he said.

I jumped.

'Oh, that's all right. That fool doctor told me when I met him down the street. He doesn't understand about Enoch, does he, Seth? But you and I do.'

'That doctor thinks I'm crazy,' I whispered.

'Well, just between us, Seth, it did sound a little hard to believe, at first. But I've just come from the swamp. Sheriff Shelby and some of his men are still working down there.

'They found Emily Robbins' body just a little while ago. And other bodies, too. A fat man's body, and a small boy, and some Indian. The quicksand preserves them, you know.'

I watched his eyes, and they were still smiling, so I knew I could trust this man.

'They'll find other bodies too, if they keep on, won't they, Seth?'

I nodded.

'But I didn't wait any longer. I saw enough to understand that you were telling the truth. Enoch must have made you do these things, didn't he?'

I nodded again.

'Fine,' said Mr Cassidy, pressing my shoulder. 'You see, we do understand each other now. So I won't blame you for anything you tell me.'

'What do you want to know?' I asked.

'Oh, lots of things. I'm interested in Enoch, you see. Just how many people did he ask you to kill – all together, that is?'

'Nine,' I said.

'And they're all buried in the quicksand?'

'Yes.'

'Do you know their names?'

'Only a few.' I told him the names of the ones I knew. 'Sometimes Enoch just describes them for me and I go out to meet them,' I explained.

Mr Cassidy sort of chuckled and took out a cigar. I frowned.

'Don't want me to smoke, eh?'

'Please – I don't like it. My mother didn't believe in smoking; she never let me.'

Mr Cassidy laughed out loud now, but he put the cigar away and leaned forward.

'You can be a big help to me, Seth,' he whispered. 'I suppose you know what a District Attorney must do.'

'He's a sort of lawyer, isn't he – at trials and things?'

'That's right. I'm going to be at your trial, Seth. Now you don't want to have to get up in front of all those people and tell them about – what happened. Right?'

'No, I don't, Mr Cassidy. Not those mean people here in town. They hate me.'

'Then here's what you do. You tell me all about it, and I'll talk for you. That's friendly enough, isn't it?'

I wished Enoch was there to help me, but he was asleep. I looked at Mr Cassidy and made up my own mind.

'Yes,' I said. 'I can tell you.'

So I told him everything I knew.

After a while he stopped chuckling, but he was just getting so interested he couldn't bother to laugh or do anything but listen.

'One thing more,' he said. 'We found some bodies in the swamp. Emily Robbins' body we could identify, and several of the others. But it will be easier if we knew something else. You can tell me this, Seth.'

'Where are the heads?'

I stood up and turned away. 'I won't tell you that,' I said, 'because I don't know.'

'Don't know?'

'I give them to Enoch,' I explained. 'Don't you understand – that's why I must kill people for him. Because he wants their heads.'

Mr Cassidy looked puzzled.

'He always makes me cut the heads off and leave them,' I went on. 'I put the bodies in the quicksand, and then go home. He puts me to sleep and rewards me. After that he goes away – back to the heads. That's what he wants.'

'Why does he want them, Seth?'

I told him. 'You see, it wouldn't do you any good if you could find them. Because you probably wouldn't recognize anything anyway.'

Mr Cassidy sat up and sighed. 'But why do you let Enoch do such things?'

'I must. Or else he'll do it to me. That's what he always threatens. He has to have it. So I obey him.'

Mr Cassidy watched me while I walked the floor, but he didn't say a word. He seemed to be very nervous, all of a sudden, and when I came close, he sort of leaned away.

'You'll explain all that at the trial, of course,' I said. 'About Enoch and everything.'

He shook his head.

'I'm not going to tell about Enoch at the trial, and neither are you,' Mr Cassidy said. 'Nobody is even going to know that Enoch exists.'

'Why?'

'I'm trying to help you, Seth. Don't you know what the people will say if you mention Enoch to them? They'll say you're crazy! And you don't want that to happen.'

'No. But what can you do? How can you help me?'

Mr Cassidy smiled at me.

'You're afraid of Enoch, aren't you? Well, I was just thinking out loud. Suppose you gave Enoch to me?'

I gulped.

'Yes. Suppose you gave Enoch to me, right now? Let me take care of him for you during the trial. Then he wouldn't be yours, and you wouldn't have to say anything about him. He probably doesn't want people to know what he does, anyway.'

'That's right,' I said. 'Enoch would be very angry. He's a secret, you know. But I hate to give him to you without asking – and he's asleep now.'

'Asleep?'

'Yes. On the top of my skull. Only you can't see him, of course.'

Mr Cassidy gazed at my head and then he chuckled again.

'Oh, I can explain everything when he wakes up,' he told me. 'When he knows it's all for the best, I'm sure he'll be happy.'

'Well – I guess it's all right, then,' I sighed. 'But you must promise to take good care of him.'

'Sure,' said Mr Cassidy.

'And you'll give him what he wants? What he needs?'

'Of course.'

'And you won't tell a soul?'

'Not a soul.'

'Of course you know what will happen to you if you refuse to give Enoch what he wants,' I warned Mr Cassidy. 'He will take it – from you – by force?'

'Don't you worry, Seth.'

I stood still for a minute. Because all at once I could feel something move towards my ear.

'Enoch,' I whispered. 'Can you hear me?'

He heard.

Then I explained everything to him. How I was giving him to Mr Cassidy.

Enoch didn't say a word.

Mr Cassidy didn't say a word. He just sat there and grinned. I suppose it must have looked a little strange to see me talking to – nothing.

'Go to Mr Cassidy,' I whispered. 'Go to him, now.'

And Enoch went.

I felt the weight lift from my head. That was all, but I knew he was gone.

'Can you feel him, Mr Cassidy?' I asked.

'What – oh sure!' he said, and stood up.

'Take good care of Enoch,' I told him.

'The best.'

'Don't put your hat on,' I warned. 'Enoch doesn't like hats.'

'Sorry, I forgot. Well, Seth, I'll say goodbye now. You've been a mighty great help to me – and from now on we can just forget about Enoch, as far as telling anybody else is concerned.

'I'll come back again and talk about the trial. That Doctor Silversmith, he's going to try and tell the folks you're crazy. Maybe it would be best if you just denied everything you told him – now that I have Enoch.'

That sounded like a fine idea, but then I knew Mr Cassidy was a smart man.

'Whatever you say, Mr Cassidy. Just be good to Enoch, and he'll be good to you.'

Mr Cassidy shook my hand and then he and Enoch went away. I felt tired again. Maybe it was the strain, and maybe it was just that I felt a little queer, knowing that Enoch was gone. Anyway, I went back to sleep for a long time.

It was night time when I woke up. Old Charley Potter was banging on the cell door, bringing me my supper.

He jumped when I said hello to him, and backed away.

'Murderer!' he yelled. 'They got nine bodies out'n the swamp. You crazy fiend!'

'Why, Charley,' I said. 'I always thought you were a friend of mine.'

'Loony! I'm gonna get out of here right now – leave you locked up for the night. Sheriff'll see that nobuddy breaks in to lynch you – if you ask me, he's wasting his time.'

Then Charley turned out all the lights and went away. I heard him go out of the front door and put the padlock on, and I was all alone in the jail house.

All alone! It was strange to be all alone for the first time in years – all alone, without Enoch.

I ran my fingers across the top of my head. It felt bare and queer.

The moon was shining through the window and I stood there looking out at the empty street. Enoch always loved the moon. It made him lively. Made him restless and greedy. I wondered how he felt now, with Mr Cassidy.

I must have stood there for a long time. My legs were numb when I turned around and listened to the fumbling at the door.

The lock clicked open, and then Mr Cassidy came running in.

'Take him off me!' he yelled. 'Take him away!'

'What's the matter?' I asked.

'Enoch – that thing of yours – I thought you were crazy – maybe I'm the crazy one – but take him off!'

'Why, Mr Cassidy! I told you what Enoch was like.'

'He's crawling around up there now. I can feel him. And I can hear him. The things he whispers!'

'But I explained all that, Mr Cassidy. Enoch wants something, doesn't he? You know what it is. And you'll have to give it to him. You promised.'

'I can't. I won't kill for him – he can't make me –'

'He can. And he will.'

Mr Cassidy gripped the bars of the cell door. 'Seth, you must help me. Call Enoch. Take him back. Make him go back to you. Hurry.'

'All right, Mr Cassidy,' I said.

I called Enoch. He didn't answer. I called again. Silence.

Mr Cassidy started to cry. It shocked me, and then I felt kind of sorry for him. He just didn't understand, after all. I know what Enoch can do to you when he whispers that way. First he coaxes you, and then he pleads, and then he threatens –

'You'd better obey him,' I told Mr Cassidy. 'Has he told you who to kill?'

Mr Cassidy didn't pay any attention to me. He just cried. And then he took out the jail keys and opened up the cell next to mine. He went in and locked the door.

'I won't,' he sobbed. 'I won't, I won't!'

'You won't what?' I asked.

'I won't kill Doctor Silversmith at the hotel and give Enoch his head. I'll stay here, in the cell, where I'm safe! Oh you fiend, you devil –'

He slumped down sideways and I could see him through the bars dividing our cells, sitting all hunched over while his hands tore at his hair.

'You'd better,' I called out. 'Or else Enoch will do something. Please, Mr Cassidy – oh, hurry –'

Then Mr Cassidy gave a little moan and I guess he fainted. Because he didn't say anything more and he stopped clawing. I called him once but he wouldn't answer.

So what could I do? I sat down in the dark corner of my cell and watched the moonlight. Moonlight always makes Enoch wild.

Then Mr Cassidy started to scream. Not loud, but deep down in his throat. He didn't move at all, just screamed.

I knew it was Enoch, taking what he wanted – from him.

What was the use of looking? You can't stop him, and I had warned Mr Cassidy.

I just sat there and held my hands to my ears until it was all over.

When I turned around again, Mr Cassidy still sat slumped up against the bars. There wasn't a sound to be heard.

Oh yes, there was! A purring. A soft, faraway purring. The purring of Enoch, after he has eaten. Then I heard a scratching. The scratching of Enoch's claws, when he frisks because he's been fed.

The purring and the scratching came from inside Mr Cassidy's head.

That would be Enoch, all right, and he was happy now.

I was happy, too.

I reached my hand through the bars and pulled the gaol keys from Mr Cassidy's pocket. I opened my cell door and I was free again.

There was no need for me stay now, with Mr Cassidy gone. And Enoch wouldn't be staying, either. I called to him.

'Here, Enoch!'

That was as close as I've ever come to really seeing

Enoch – a sort of white streak that came flashing out of the big red hole he had eaten in the back of Mr Cassidy's skull.

Then I felt the soft, cold, flabby weight landing on my own head once more, and I knew Enoch had come home.

I walked through the corridor and opened the outer door of the jail.

Enoch's tiny feet began to patter on the roof of my brain.

Together we walked out into the night. The moon was shining, everything was still, and I could hear, ever so softly, Enoch's happy chuckling in my ear.

Mervyn Peake (1911—68)

Same Time, Same Place

*In the realms of modern fantasy literature two 'titles' have,
more than any others, caught the imagination of younger
readers: Tolkien's 'Lord of the Rings' and the 'Gormenghast' trilogy written by Mervyn Peake. Speaking for myself, the Gormenghast novels have a richness of character,
a vividness of prose and a scope of events that surpasses all
others and it is for this reason that I have selected a rare
short story by Peake for inclusion here. (Do not be deterred from discovering Tolkien, however. It would have
been impossible to include him here as he has written no
short fiction available for anthologizing.) The recent sad
death of Mervyn Peake after his lingering illness robbed
us of a writer of great talent as this amazingly versatile
horror story will amply demonstrate.*

THAT night, I hated father. He smelt of cabbage.
There was cigarette ash all over his trousers. His un-
tidy moustache was yellower and viler than ever with
nicotine, and he took no notice of me. He simply sat
there in his ugly armchair, his eyes half closed, brooding on the Lord knows what. I hated him. I hated his
moustache. I even hated the smoke that drifted from
his mouth and hung in the stale air above his head.

And when my mother came through the door and
asked me whether I had seen her spectacles, I hated
her too. I hated the clothes she wore; tasteless and

fussy. I hated them deeply. I hated something I had never noticed before; it was the way the heels of her shoes were worn away on their outside edges – not badly, but appreciably. It looked mean to me, slatternly, and horribly human, I hated her for being human – like father.

She began to nag me about her glasses and the threadbare condition of the elbows of my jacket, and suddenly I threw my book down. The room was unbearable. I felt suffocated. I suddenly realized that I must get away. I had lived with these two people for nearly twenty-three years. I had been born in the room immediately overhead. Was this the life for a young man? To spend his evenings watching the smoke drift out of his father's mouth and stain that decrepit old moustache, year after year – to watch the worn away edges of my mother's heels – the dark brown furniture and the familiar stains on the chocolate-coloured carpet? I would go away; I would shake off the dark, smug mortality of the place. I would forego my birthright. What of my father's business into which I would step at his death? What of it? To hell with it.

I began to make my way to the door but at the third step I caught my foot in a ruck of the chocolate-coloured carpet and in reaching out my hand for support, I sent a pink vase flying.

Suddenly I felt very small and very angry. I saw my mother's mouth opening and it reminded me of the front door and the front door reminded me of my urge to escape – to where? To where?

I did not wait to find an answer to my own question, but hardly knowing what I was doing, ran from the house.

The accumulated boredom of the last twenty-three years was at my back and it seemed that I was propelled through the garden gate from its pressure against my shoulder blades.

The road was wet with rain, black and shiny like oilskin. The reflection of the street lamps wallowed like yellow jellyfish. A bus was approaching – a bus to Piccadilly, a bus to the never-never land – a bus to death or glory.

I found neither. I found something which haunts me still.

The great bus swayed as it sped. The black street gleamed. Through the window a hundred faces fluttered by as though the leaves of a dark book were being flicked over. And I sat there, with a sixpenny ticket in my hand. What was I doing! Where was I going?

To the centre of the world, I told myself. To Piccadilly Circus, where anything might happen. What did I *want* to happen?

I wanted life to happen! I wanted adventure; but already I was afraid. I wanted to find a beautiful woman. Bending my elbow I felt for the swelling of my biceps. There wasn't much to feel. 'O hell,' I said to myself, 'O damnable hell: this is *awful*.'

I stared out of the window, and there before me was the Circus. The lights were like a challenge. When the bus had curved its way from Regent Street and into Shaftesbury Avenue, I alighted. Here was the jungle all about me and I was lonely. The wild beasts prowled around me. The wolf packs surged and shuffled. Where was I to go? How wonderful it would have been to have known of some apartment, dimly lighted; of a door that opened to the secret knock, three short ones and one long one – where a strawberry blonde was waiting – or perhaps, better still, some wise old lady with a cup of tea, an old lady, august and hallowed, and whose heels were not worn down on their outside edges.

But I knew nowhere to go either for glamour or sympathy. Nowhere except The Corner House.

I made my way there. It was less congested than usual. I had only to queue for a few minutes before being allowed into the great eating-place on the first floor. Oh, the marble and the gold of it all! The waiters coming and going, the band in the distance – how different all this was from an hour ago, when I stared at my father's moustache.

For some while I could find no table and it was only when moving down the third of the long corridors between tables that I saw an old man leaving a table for two. The lady who had been sitting opposite him remained where she was. Had she left, I would have had no tale to tell. Unsuspectingly I took the place of the old man and in reaching for the menu lifted my head and found myself gazing into the midnight pools of her eyes.

My hand hung poised over the menu. I could not move for the head in front of me was magnificent. It was big and pale and indescribably proud – and what I would now call a greedy look, seemed to me then to be an expression of rich assurance; of majestic beauty.

I knew at once that it was not the strawberry blonde of my callow fancy that I desired for glamour's sake, nor the comfort of the tea-tray lady – but this glorious creature before me who combined the mystery and exoticism of the former with the latter's mellow wisdom.

Was this not love at first sight? Why else should my heart have hammered like a foundry? Why should my hand have trembled above the menu? Why should my mouth have gone dry?

Words were quite impossible. It was clear to me that she knew everything that was going on in my breast and in my brain. The look of love which flooded from her eyes all but unhinged me. Taking my hand in hers she returned it to my side of the table where it lay like a dead thing on a plate. Then she passed me the menu. It meant nothing to me. The hors d'oeuvres and the sweets were all mixed together in a dance of letters.

What I told the waiter when he came, I cannot remember, nor what he brought me. I know that I could not eat it. For an hour we sat there. We spoke with our eyes, with the pulse and stress of our excited breathing – and towards the end of this, our first meeting, with the tips of our fingers that in touching each other in the shadow of the teapot, seemed to speak a language richer, subtler and more vibrant than words.

At last we were asked to go – and as I rose I spoke for the first time. 'Tomorrow?' I whispered. 'Tomorrow?' She nodded her magnificent head slowly. 'Same place? Same time?' She nodded again.

I waited for her to rise, but with a gentle yet authoritative gesture she signalled me away.

It seemed strange, but I knew I must go. I turned at the door and saw her sitting there, very still, very upright. Then I descended to the street and made my way to Shaftesbury Avenue, my head in a whirl of stars, my legs weak and trembling, my heart on fire.

I had not decided to return home, but found nevertheless that I was on my way back – back to the choco-late-coloured carpet, to my father in the ugly armchair – to my mother with her worn shoe heels.

When at last I turned the key it was near midnight. My mother had been crying. My father was angry. There were words, threats and entreaties on all sides. At last I got to bed.

The next day seemed endless but at long last my excited fretting found some relief in action. Soon after tea I boarded the west-bound bus. It was already dark but I was far too early when I arrived at the Circus.

I wandered restlessly here and there, adjusting my tie at shop windows and filing my nails for the hun-dredth time.

At last, when waking from a day-dream as I sat for the fifth time in Leicester Square, I glanced at my watch and found I was three minutes late for our tryst.

I ran all the way panting with anxiety but when I arrived at the table on the first floor I found my fear was baseless. She was there, more regal than ever, a monument of womanhood. Her large, pale face re-laxed into an expression of such deep pleasure at the sight of me that I almost shouted for joy.

I will not speak of the tenderness of that evening. It was magic. It is enough to say that we determined that our destinies were inextricably joined.

When the time came for us to go I was surprised to find that the procedure of the previous night was once more expected of me. I could in no way make out the reason for it. Again I left her sitting alone at the table by the marble pillar. Again I vanished into the night alone, with those intoxicating words still on my lips. 'Tomorrow ... tomorrow ... same time ... same place.'

The certainty of my love for her and hers for me was quite intoxicating. I slept little that night and my restlessness on the following day was an agony both for me and my parents.

Before I left that night for our third meeting, I crept into my mother's bedroom and opening her jewel box I chose a ring from among her few trinkets. God knows it was not worthy to sit upon my loved-one's finger, but it would symbolize our love.

Again she was waiting for me although on this occasion I arrived a full quarter of an hour before our appointed time. It was as though, when we were together, we were hidden in a veil of love – as though we were alone. We heard nothing else but the sound of our voices, we saw nothing else but one another's eyes.

She put the ring upon her finger as soon as I had given it to her. Her hand that was holding mine tightened its grip. I was surprised at its power. My whole body trembled. I moved my foot beneath the table to touch hers. I could find it nowhere.

When once more the dreaded moment arrived, I left her sitting upright, the strong and tender smile of her farewell remaining in my mind like some fantastic sunrise.

For eight days we met thus, and parted thus, and with every meeting we knew more firmly than ever, that whatever the difficulties that would result, whatever the forces against us, yet it was now that we must marry, now, while the magic was upon us.

On the eighth evening it was all decided. She knew that for my part it must be a secret wedding. My parents would never countenance so rapid an arrangement. She understood perfectly. For her part she wished a few of her friends to be present at the ceremony.

'I have a few colleagues,' she had said. I did not know what she meant, but her instructions as to where we should meet on the following afternoon put the remark out of my mind.

There was a registry office in Cambridge Circus, she told me, on the first floor of a certain building. I was to be there at four o'clock. She would arrange everything.

'Ah, my love,' she had murmured, shaking her large head slowly from side to side, 'how can I wait until then?' And with a smile unutterably bewitching, she gestured for me to go, for the great memorial hall was all but empty.

For the eighth time I left her there. I knew that women must have their secrets and must be in no way thwarted in regard to them, and so, once again I swallowed the question that I so longed to put to her. Why, O why had I always to leave her there – and why, when I arrived to meet her – was she always there to meet me?

On the following day, after a careful search, I found a gold ring in a box in my father's dressing-table. Soon after three, having brushed my hair until it shone like seal-skin I set forth with a flower in my buttonhole and a suitcase of belongings. It was a beautiful day with no wind and a clear sky.

The bus fled on like a fabulous beast, bearing me with it to a magic land.

But alas, as we approached Mayfair we were held up more than once for long stretches of time. I began to get restless. By the time the bus had reached Shaftesbury Avenue I had but three minutes in which to reach the Office.

It seemed strange that when the sunlight shone in sympathy with my marriage, the traffic should choose to frustrate me. I was on the top of the bus and having been given a very clear description of the building, was able, as we rounded at last in Cambridge Circus, to recognize it at once. When we came alongside my destination the traffic was held up again and I was offered a perfect opportunity of disembarking immediately beneath the building.

My suitcase was at my feet and as I stooped to pick it up I glanced at the windows on the first floor – for it was in one of those rooms that I was so soon to become a husband.

I was exactly on a level with the windows in question and commanded an unbroken view of the interior of a first floor room. It could not have been more than a dozen feet away from where I sat.

I remember that our bus was hooting away, but there was no movement in the traffic ahead. The hooting came to me as through a dream for I had become lost in another world.

My hand clenched upon the handle of the suitcase. Through my eyes and into my brain an image was pouring. The image of the first floor room.

I knew at once that it was in that particular room that I was expected. I cannot tell you why, for during those first few moments I had not seen her.

To the right of the stage (for I had the sensation of being in a theatre) was a table loaded with flowers. Behind the flowers sat a small pin-striped registrar. There were four others in the room, three of whom kept walking to and fro. The fourth, an enormous bearded lady, sat on a chair by the window. As I stared, one of the men bent over to speak to her. He had the longest neck on earth. His starched collar was the length of a walking-stick, and his small bony head protruded from its extremity like the skull of a bird. The other two gentlemen who kept crossing and re-crossing were very different. One was bald. His face and cranium were blue with the most intricate tattoo-ing. His teeth were gold and they shone like fire in his mouth. The other was a well-dressed young man, and seemed normal enough until, as he came for a moment closer to the window I saw that instead of a hand, the cloven hoof of a goat protruded from the left sleeve.

And then suddenly it all happened. A door of their room must have opened for all at once all the heads in the room were turned in one direction and a moment later a something in white trotted like a dog across the room.

But it was no dog. It was vertical as it ran. I thought at first that it was a mechanical doll, so close was it to the floor. I could not observe its face, but I was amazed to see the long train of satin that was being dragged along the carpet behind it.

It stopped when it reached the flower-laden table and there was a good deal of smiling and bowing and then the man with the longest neck in the world placed a high stool in front of the table and, with the help of the young man with the goat-foot, lifted the white thing so that it stood upon the high stool. The long satin dress was carefully draped over the stool so that it reached to the floor on every side. It seemed as though a tall dignified woman was standing at the civic altar.

And still I had not seen its face, although I knew what it would be like. A sense of nausea overwhelmed me and I sank back on the seat, hiding my face in my hands.

I cannot remember when the bus began to move. I know that I went on and on and on and that finally I was told that I had reached the terminus. There was nothing for it but to board another bus of the same number and make the return journey. A strange sense of relief had by now begun to blunt the edge of my disappointment. That this bus would take me to the door of the house where I was born gave me a twinge of homesick pleasure. But stronger was my sense of fear, I prayed that there would be no reason for the bus to be held up again in Cambridge Circus.

I had taken one of the downstairs seats for I had no wish to be on an eyelevel with someone I had deserted. I had no sense of having wronged her but she had been deserted nevertheless.

When at last the bus approached the Circus, I peered into the half darkness. A street lamp stood immediately below the registry office. I saw at once that there was no light in the office and as the bus moved past I turned my eyes to a group beneath the street lamp. My heart went cold in my breast.

Standing there, ossified as it were into a malignant mass – standing there as though they never intended to move until justice was done – were the five. It was only for a second that I saw them but every lamp-lit head is for ever with me – the long-necked man with his bird skull head, his eyes glinting like chips of glass; to his right the small bald man, his tattooed scalp thrust forward, the lamplight gloating on the blue markings. To the left of the long-necked man stood the youth, his elegant body relaxed, but a snarl on his face that I still sweat to remember. His hands were in his pockets but I could see the shape of the hoof through the cloth. A little ahead of these three stood the bearded woman, a bulk of evil – and in the shadow that she cast before her I saw in that last fraction of a second, as the bus rolled me past, a big whitish head, very close to the ground.

In the dusk it appeared to be suspended above the kerb like a pale balloon with a red mouth painted upon it – a mouth that, taking a single diabolical curve, was more like the mouth of a wild beast than that of a woman.

Long after I had left the group behind me – set as it were for ever under the lamp, like something made of wax, like something monstrous, long after I had left it I yet saw it all. It filled the bus. They filled my brain. They fill it still.

When at last I arrived home I fell weeping upon my bed. My father and mother had no idea what it was all about but they did not ask me. They never asked me.

That evening, after supper, I sat there, I remember, six years ago in my own chair on the chocolate-coloured carpet. I remember how I stared with love at the ash on my father's waistcoat, at his stained moustache, at my mother's worn away shoe heels. I stared at it all and I loved it all. I needed it all.

Since then I have never left the house. I know what is best for me.

Ray Bradbury (1920–   )

The Small Assassin

All anthologists should admit to a personal favourite writer, and those who have over the years read my collections will know of my predilection for the work of Ray Bradbury. *No other author, in my opinion, can create such excitement in the mind with his verbal imagery, no other writer can build such atmosphere or see so clearly into the emotions of people. One of the enduring themes of his writing has been the inherent talents for good and evil to be found in children (strange in a way, for he is happily married with four delightful daughters) and there has been no more sinister story from his pen than 'The Small Assassin'. I can't believe it can really be possible, but if it should be I suppose 'they' will be after me next for letting the cat out of the bag...*

JUST when the idea occurred to her that she was being murdered she could not tell. There had been little subtle signs, little suspicions for the past month; things as deep as sea tides in her, like looking at a perfectly calm stretch of tropic water, wanting to bathe in it and finding, just as the tide takes your body, that monsters dwell just under the surface, things unseen, bloated, many-armed, sharp-finned, malignant and inescapable.

A room floated around her in an effluvium of hysteria. Sharp instruments hovered and there were voices, and people in sterile white masks.

My name, she thought, what is it?

Alice Leiber. It came to her. David Leiber's wife. But it gave her no comfort. She was alone with these silent, whispering white people and there was great pain and nausea and death-fear in her.

I am being murdered before their eyes. These doctors, these nurses don't realize what hidden thing has happened to me. David doesn't know. Nobody knows except me and – the killer, the little murderer, the small assassin.

I am dying and I can't tell them now. They'd laugh and call me one in delirium. They'll see the murderer and hold him and never think him responsible for my death. But here I am, in front of God and man, dying, no one to believe my story, everyone to doubt me, comfort me with lies, bury me in ignorance, mourn me and salvage my destroyer.

Where is David? she wondered. In the waiting-room, smoking one cigarette after another, listening to the long tickings of the very slow clock?

Sweat exploded from all of her body at once, and with it an agonized cry. Now. Now! Try and kill me, she screamed. Try, try, but I won't die! I won't!

There was a hollowness. A vacuum. Suddenly the pain fell away. Exhaustion, and dusk came around. It was over. Oh, God! She plummeted down and struck a black nothingness which gave way to nothingness and nothingness and another and still another. . .

Footsteps. Gentle, approaching footsteps.

Far away, a voice said, 'She's asleep. Don't disturb her.'

An odour of tweeds, a pipe, a certain shaving lotion. David was standing over her. And beyond him the immaculate smell of Dr Jeffers.

She did not open her eyes. 'I'm awake,' she said, quietly. It was a surprise, a relief to be able to speak, to not be dead.

'Alice,' someone said, and it was David beyond her closed eyes, holding her tired hands.

Would you like to meet the murderer, David? she thought. I hear your voice asking to see him, so there's nothing but for me to point him out to you.

David stood over her. She opened her eyes. The room came into focus. Moving a weak hand, she pulled aside a coverlet.

The murderer looked up at David Leiber with a small, red-faced, blue-eyed calm. Its eyes were deep and sparkling.

'Why!' cried David Leiber, smiling. 'He's a *fine* baby!'

Dr Jeffers was waiting for David Leiber the day he came to take his wife and new child home. He motioned Leiber to a chair in his office, gave him a cigar, lit one for himself, sat on the edge of his desk, puffing solemnly for a long moment. Then he cleared his throat, looked David Leiber straight on and said, 'Your wife doesn't like her child, Dave.'

'What!'

'It's been a hard thing for her. She'll need a lot of love this next year. I didn't say much at the time, but she was hysterical in the delivery room. The strange things she said – I won't repeat them. All I'll say is that she feels alien to the child. Now, this may simply be a thing we can clear up with one or two questions.' He sucked on his cigar another moment, then said, 'Is this child a "wanted" child, Dave?'

'Why do you ask?'

'It's vital.'

'Yes. Yes, it is a "wanted" child. We planned it together. Alice was so happy, a year ago, when –'

'Mmmm – That makes it more difficult. Because if the child was unplanned, it would be a simple case of a woman hating the idea of motherhood. That doesn't fit Alice.' Dr Jeffers took his cigar from his lips, rubbed his hands across his jaw. 'It must be something else, then. Perhaps something buried in her childhood that's coming out now. Or it might be the simple temporary doubt and distrust of any mother who's gone through the unusual pain and near-death that Alice has. If so, then a little time should heal that. I thought I'd tell you, though, Dave. It'll help you be easy and tolerant with her if she says anything about – well – about wishing the child had been born dead. And if things don't go well, the three of you drop in on me. I'm always glad to see old friends, eh? Here, take another cigar along for – ah – for the baby.'

It was a bright spring afternoon. Their car hummed along wide, tree-lined boulevards. Blue sky, flowers, a warm wind. Dave talked a lot, lit his cigar, talked some more. Alice answered directly, softly, relaxing a bit more as the trip progressed. But she held the baby not tightly or warmly or motherly enough to satisfy the queer ache in Dave's mind. She seemed to be merely carrying a porcelain figurine.

'Well,' he said, at last, smiling. 'What'll we name him?'

Alice Leiber watched green trees slide by. 'Let's not decide yet. I'd rather wait until we get an exceptional name for him. Don't blow smoke in his face.' Her sentences ran together with no change of tone. The last statement held no motherly reproof, no interest, no irritation. She just mouthed it and it was said.

The husband, disquieted, dropped his cigar from the window. 'Sorry,' he said.

The baby rested in the crook of his mother's arm, shadows of sun and tree changing his face. His blue eyes opened like fresh blue spring flowers. Moist noises came from the tiny, pink, elastic mouth.

Alice gave her baby a quick glance. Her husband felt her shiver against him.

'Cold?' he asked.

'A chill. Better raise the window, David.'

It was more than a chill. He rolled the window slowly up.

Suppertime.

Dave had brought the child from the nursery, propped him at a tiny, bewildered angle, supported by many pillows, in a newly purchased high chair.

Alice watched her knife and fork move. 'He's not high-chair size,' she said.

'Fun having him here, anyway,' said Dave, feeling fine. 'Everything's fun. At the office, too. Orders up to my nose. If I don't watch myself I'll make another fifteen thousand this year. Hey, look at Junior, will you? Drooling all down his chin!' He reached over to wipe the baby's mouth with his napkin. From the corner of his eye he realized that Alice wasn't even watching. He finished the job.

'I guess it wasn't very interesting,' he said, back again at his food. 'But one would think a mother'd take some interest in her own child!'

Alice jerked her chin up. 'Don't speak that way! Not in front of him! Later, if you must.'

'Later?' he cried. 'In front of, in back of, what's the difference?' He quieted suddenly, swallowed, was sorry. 'All right. Okay. I know how it is.'

After dinner she let him carry the baby upstairs. She didn't tell him to; she *let* him.

Coming down, he found her standing by the radio, listening to music she didn't hear. Her eyes were closed, her whole attitude one of wondering, self-questioning. She started when he appeared.

Suddenly, she was at him, against him, soft, quick; the same. Her lips found him, kept him. He was stunned. Now that the baby was gone, upstairs, out of the room, she began to breathe again, live again. She was free. She was whispering, rapidly, endlessly.

'Thank you, thank you, darling. For being yourself, always. Dependable, so very dependable!'

He had to laugh. 'My father told me, "Son, provide for your family!"'

Wearily, she rested her dark, shining hair against his neck. 'You've overdone it. Sometimes I wish we were just the way we were when we were first married. No responsibilities, nothing but ourselves. No – no babies.'

She crushed his hand in hers, a supernatural whiteness in her face.

'Oh, Dave, once it was just you and me. We protected each other, and now we protect the baby, but get no protection from it. Do you understand? Lying in the hospital I had time to think a lot of things. The world is evil –'

'Is it?'

'Yes. It is. But laws protect us from it. And when there aren't laws, then love does the protecting. You're protected from my hurting you, by my love. You're

266

vulnerable to me, of all people, but love shields you. I feel no fear of you because love cushions all your irritations, unnatural instincts, hatreds and immaturities. But – what about the baby? It's too young to know love, or a law of love, or anything, until we teach it. And in the meantime be vulnerable to it.'

'Vulnerable to a baby?' He held her away and laughed gently.

'Does a baby know the difference between right and wrong?' she asked.

'No. But it'll learn.'

'But a baby is so new, so amoral, so conscience-free.' She stopped. Her arms dropped from him and she turned swiftly. 'That noise? What was it?'

Leiber looked around the room. 'I didn't hear –'

She stared at the library door. 'In there,' she said, slowly.

Leiber crossed the room, opened the door and switched the library lights on and off. 'Not a thing.' He came back to her. 'You're worn out. To bed with you – right now.'

Turning out the lights together, they walked slowly up the soundless hall stairs, not speaking. At the top she apologized. 'My wild talk, darling. Forgive me, I'm exhausted.'

He understood, and said so.

She paused, undecided, by the nursery door. Then she fingered the brass knob sharply, walked in. He watched her approach the crib much too carefully, look down, and stiffen as if she'd been struck in the face. 'David!'

Leiber stepped forward, reached the crib.

The baby's face was bright red and very moist; his small pink mouth opened and shut, opened and shut;

267

his eyes were a fiery blue. His hands leapt about on the air.

'Oh,' said Dave, 'he's just been crying.'

'Has he?' Alice Leiber seized the crib-railing to balance herself. 'I didn't hear him.'

'The door was closed.'

'Is that why he breathes so hard, why his face is red?'

'Sure. Poor little guy. Crying all alone in the dark. He can sleep in our room tonight, just in case he cries.'

'You'll spoil him,' his wife said.

Leiber felt her eyes follow as he rolled the crib into their bedroom. He undressed silently, sat on the edge of the bed. Suddenly he lifted his head, swore under his breath, snapped his fingers. 'Damn it! Forgot to tell you. I must fly to Chicago Friday.'

'Oh, David.' Her voice was lost in the room.

'I've put this trip off for two months, and now it's so critical I just *have* to go.'

'I'm afraid to be alone.'

'We'll have the new cook by Friday. She'll be here all the time. I'll only be gone a few days.'

'I'm afraid. I don't know of what. You wouldn't believe me if I told you. I guess I'm crazy.'

He was in bed now. She darkened the room; he heard her walk around the bed, throw back the cover, slide in. He smelled the warm woman-smell of her next to him. He said 'If you want me to wait a few days, perhaps I could –'

'No,' she said, unconvinced. 'You go. I know it's important. It's just that I keep thinking about what I told you. Laws and love and protection. Love protects you from me. But, the baby –' She took a breath. 'What protects you from him, David?'

Before he could answer, before he could tell her how

silly it was, speaking of infants, she switched on the bed light, abruptly.

'Look,' she said, pointing.

The baby lay wide-awake in its crib, staring straight at him, with deep, sharp blue eyes.

The lights went out again. She trembled against him.

'It's not nice being afraid of the thing you birthed.' Her whisper lowered, became harsh, fierce, swift. 'He tried to kill me! He lies there, listens to us talking, waiting for you to go away so he can try to kill me again! I swear it!' Sobs broke from her.

'Please,' he kept saying, soothing her. 'Stop it, stop it. Please.'

She cried in the dark for a long time. Very late she relaxed, shakingly, against him. Her breathing came soft, warm, regular, her body twitched its worn reflexes and she slept.

He drowsed.

And just before his eyes lidded wearily down, sinking him into deeper and yet deeper tides, he heard a strange little sound of awareness and awakeness in the room.

The sound of small, moist, pinkly elastic lips.

The baby.

And then – sleep.

In the morning, the sun blazed. Alice smiled.

David Leiber dangled his watch over the crib. 'See, baby? Something bright. Something pretty. Sure. Sure. Something bright. Something pretty.'

Alice smiled. She told him to go ahead, fly to Chicago, she'd be very brave, no need to worry. She'd take care of baby. Oh, yes, she'd take care of him, all right.

The aeroplane went east. There was a lot of sky, a lot of sun and clouds and Chicago running over the horizon. Dave was dropped into the rush of ordering, planning, banqueting, telephoning, arguing in conference. But he wrote letters each day and sent telegrams to Alice and the baby.

On the evening of his sixth day away from home he received the long-distance phone call. Los Angeles.

'Alice?'

'No, Dave. This is Jeffers speaking.'

'Doctor!'

'Hold onto yourself, son. Alice is sick. You'd better get the next plane home. It's pneumonia. I'll do everything I can, boy. If only it wasn't so soon after the baby. She needs strength.'

Leiber dropped the phone into its cradle. He got up, with no feet under him, and no hands and no body. The hotel room blurred and fell apart.

'Alice,' he said, blindly, starting for the door.

The propellers spun about, whirled, fluttered, stopped; time and space were put behind. Under his hand, David felt the doorknob turn; under his feet the floor assumed reality, around him flowed the walls of a bedroom, and in the late afternoon sunlight Dr Jeffers stood, turning from a window, as Alice lay waiting in her bed, something carved from a fall of winter snow. Then Dr Jeffers was talking, talking continuously, gently, the sound rising and falling through the lamplight, a soft flutter, a white murmur of voice.

'Your wife's too good a mother, Dave. She worried more about the baby than herself...'

Somewhere in the paleness of Alice's face, there was a sudden constriction which smoothed itself out before it was realized. Then, slowly, half-smiling, she began to talk and she talked as a mother should about this, that and the other thing, the telling detail, the minute-by-minute and hour-by-hour report of a mother concerned with a dollhouse world and the miniature life of that world. But she could not stop; the spring was wound tight, and her voice rushed on to anger, fear and the faintest touch of revulsion, which did not change Dr Jeffers' expression, but caused Dave's heart to match the rhythm of this talk that quickened and could not stop:

'The baby wouldn't sleep. I thought he was sick. He just lay, staring, in his crib, and late at night he'd cry. So loud, he'd cry, and he'd cry all night and all night. I couldn't quiet him, and I couldn't rest.'

Dr Jeffers' head nodded slowly, slowly. 'Tired herself right into pneumonia. But she's full of sulphur now and on the safe side of the whole damn thing.'

David felt ill. 'The baby, what about the baby?'

'Fit as a fiddle; cock of the walk!'

'Thanks, Doctor.'

The doctor walked off away and down the stairs, opened the front door faintly, and was gone.

'David!'

He turned to her frightened whisper.

'It was the baby again.' She clutched his hand. 'I try to lie to myself and say that I'm a fool, but the baby knew I was weak from the hospital, so he cried all night every night, and when he wasn't crying he'd be much too quiet. I knew if I switched on the light he'd be there, staring up at me.'

David felt his body close in on itself like a fist. He remembered seeing the baby, feeling the baby, awake in the dark, awake very late at night when babies should be asleep. Awake and lying there, silent as thought, not crying, but watching from its crib. He thrust the thought aside. It was insane.

Alice went on. 'I was going to kill the baby. Yes, I was. When you'd been gone only a day on your trip I went to his room and put my hands about his neck; and I stood there, for a long time, thinking, afraid. Then I put the covers up over his face and turned him over on his face and pressed him down and left him that way and ran out of the room.'

He tried to stop her.

'No, let me finish,' she said, hoarsely, looking at the wall. 'When I left his room I thought. It's simple. Babies smother every day. No one'll ever know. But when I came back to see him dead, David, he was alive! Yes, alive, turned over on his back, alive and smiling and breathing. And I couldn't touch him again after that. I left him there and I didn't come back, not to feed him or look at him or do anything. Perhaps the cook tended to him. I don't know. All I know is that his crying kept me awake, and I thought all through the night, and walked around the rooms and now I'm sick.' She was almost finished now. 'The baby lies there and thinks of ways to kill me. Simple ways. Because he knows I know so much about him. I have no love for him; there is no protection between us; there never will be.'

She was through. She collapsed inward on herself and finally slept. David Leiber stood for a long time over her, not able to move. His blood was frozen in his body, not a cell stirred anywhere, anywhere at all.

The next morning there was only one thing to do. He did it. He walked into Dr Jeffers' office and told him the whole thing, and listened to Jeffers' tolerant replies:

'Let's take this thing slowly, son. It's quite natural for mothers to hate their children, sometimes. We have a label for it – ambivalence. The ability to hate, while loving. Lovers hate each other, frequently. Children detest their mothers –'

Leiber interrupted. 'I never hated my mother.'

'You won't admit it, naturally. People don't enjoy admitting hatred for their loved ones.'

'So Alice hates her baby.'

'Better say she has an obsession. She's gone a step further than plain, ordinary ambivalence. A Caesarian operation brought the child into the world and almost took Alice out of it. She blames the child for her near-death and her pneumonia. She's projecting her troubles, blaming them on the handiest object she can use as a source of blame. We *all* do it. We stumble into a chair and curse the furniture, not our own clumsiness. We miss a golf stroke and damn the turf or our club, or the make of ball. If our business fails we blame the gods, the weather, our luck. All I can tell you is what I told you before. Love her. Finest medicine in the world. Find little ways of showing your affection, give her security. Find ways of showing her how harmless and innocent the child is. Make her feel that the baby was worth the risk. After a while, she'll settle down, forget about death, and begin to love the child. If she doesn't come around in the next month or so, ask me. I'll recommend a good psychiatrist. Go on along now, and take that look off your face.'

When summer came, things seemed to settle, become easier. Dave worked, immersed himself in office detail, but found much time for his wife. She, in turn, took long walks, gained strength, played an occasional light game of badminton. She rarely burst out any more. She seemed to have rid herself of her fears.

Except on one certain midnight when a sudden summer wind swept around the house, warm and swift, shaking the trees like so many shining tambourines. Alice wakened, trembling, and slid over into her husband's arms, and let him console her, and ask her what was wrong.

She said, 'Something's here in the room, watching us.'

He switched on the light. 'Dreaming again,' he said. 'You're better, though. Haven't been troubled for a long time.'

She sighed as he clicked off the light again, and suddenly she slept. He held her, considering what a sweet, weird creature she was, for about half an hour.

He heard the bedroom door sway open a few inches.

There was nobody at the door. No reason for it to come open. The wind had died.

He waited. It seemed like an hour he lay silently, in the dark.

Then, far away, wailing like some small meteor dying in the vast inky gulf of space, the baby began to cry in his nursery.

It was a small, lonely sound in the middle of the stars and the dark and the breathing of this woman in his arms and the wind beginning to sweep through the trees again.

Leiber counted to one hundred, slowly. The crying continued.

Carefully disengaging Alice's arm he slipped from

bed, put on his slippers, robe, and moved quietly from the room.

He'd go downstairs, he thought, fix some warm milk, bring it up, and –

The blackness dropped out from under him. His foot slipped and plunged. Slipped on something soft. Plunged into nothingness.

He thrust his hands out, caught frantically at the railing. His body stopped falling. He held. He cursed.

The 'something soft' that had caused his feet to slip, rustled and thumped down a few steps. His head rang. His heart hammered at the base of his throat, thick and shot with pain.

Why do careless people leave things strewn about a house? He groped carefully with his fingers for the object that had almost spilled him headlong down the stairs.

His hand froze, startled. His breath went in. His heart held one or two beats.

The thing he held in his hand was a toy. A large cumbersome patchwork doll he had bought as a joke, for –

For the baby.

Alice drove him to work the next day.

She slowed the car halfway downtown; pulled to the kerb and stopped it. Then she turned on the seat and looked at her husband.

'I want to go away on a holiday. I don't know if you can make it now, darling, but if not, please let me go alone. We can get someone to take care of the baby, I'm sure. But I just have to get away. I thought I was growing out of this – this *feeling*. But I haven't. I can't stand being in the room with him. He looks up at me as if he hates me, too. I can't put my finger on it; all I know is I want to get away before something happens.'

He got out on his side of the car, came around, motioned to her to move over, got in. 'The only thing you're going to do is see a good psychiatrist. And if he suggests a holiday, well, okay. But this can't go on; my stomach's in knots all the time.' He started the car. 'I'll drive the rest of the way.'

Her head was down; she was trying to keep back tears. She looked up when they reached his office building. 'All right. Make the appointment. I'll go talk to anyone you want, David.'

He kissed her. 'Now, you're talking sense, lady. Think you can drive home okay?'

'Of course, silly.'

'See you at supper, then. Drive carefully.'

'Don't I always? 'Bye.'

He stood on the kerb, watching her drive off, the wind taking hold of her long, dark, shining hair. Upstairs a minute later, he phoned Jeffers and arranged an appointment with a reliable neuropsychiatrist.

The day's work went uneasily. Things fogged over; and in the fog he kept seeing Alice lost and calling his name. So much of her fear had come over to him. She actually had him convinced that the child was in some ways not quite natural.

He dictated long, uninspired letters. He checked some shipments downstairs. Assistants had to be questioned, and kept going. At the end of the day he was exhausted, his head throbbed, and he was very glad to go home.

On the way down in the lift he wondered, What if I told Alice about the toy – that patchwork doll – I slipped on the stairs last night? Lord, wouldn't *that* back her off? No, I won't ever tell her. Accidents are, after all, accidents.

Daylight lingered in the sky as he drove home in a taxi. In front of the house he paid the driver and walked slowly up the cement walk, enjoying the light that was still in the sky and the trees. The white colonial front of the house looked unnaturally silent and uninhabited, and then, quietly, he remembered this was Thursday, and the hired help they were able to obtain from time to time were all gone for the day.

He took a deep breath of air. A bird sang behind the house. Traffic moved on the boulevard a block away. He twisted the key in the door. The knob turned under his fingers, oiled, silent.

The door opened. He stepped in, put his hat on the chair with his briefcase, started to shrug out of his coat, when he looked up.

Late sunlight streamed down the stairwell from the window near the top of the hall. Where the sunlight touched it took on the bright colour of the patchwork doll sprawled at the bottom of the stairs.

But he paid no attention to the toy.

He could only look, and not move, and look again at Alice.

Alice lay in a broken, grotesque, pallid gesturing and angling of her thin body, at the bottom of the stairs, like a crumpled doll that doesn't want to play any more, ever.

Alice was dead.

The house remained quiet, except for the sound of his heart.

She was dead.

He held her hands in his hands, he felt her fingers.

He held her body. But she wouldn't live. She wouldn't even try to live. He said her name, out loud, many times, and he tried, once again, by holding her to him, to give her back some of the warmth she had lost, but that didn't help.

He stood up. He must have made a phone call. He didn't remember. He found himself, suddenly, upstairs. He opened the nursery door and walked inside and stared blankly at the crib. His stomach was sick. He couldn't see very well.

The baby's eyes were closed, but his face wax red, moist with perspiration, as if he'd been crying long and hard.

'She's dead,' said Leiber to the baby. 'She's dead.'

Then he started laughing low and soft and continuously for a long time until Dr Jeffers walked in and out of the night and slapped him again and again across his face.

'Snap out of it! Pull yourself together!'

'She fell down the stairs, doctor. She tripped on a patchwork doll and fell. I almost slipped on it the other night, myself. And now –'

The doctor shook him.

'Doc, Doc, Doc,' said Dave, hazily. 'Funny thing. Funny. I – I finally thought of a name for the baby.'

The doctor said nothing.

Leiber put his head back in his trembling hands and spoke the words. 'I'm going to have him christened next Sunday. Know what name I'm giving him? I'm going to call him Lucifer.'

It was eleven at night. A lot of strange people had come and gone through the house, taking the essential flame with them – Alice.

David Leiber sat across from the doctor in the library.

'Alice wasn't crazy,' he said slowly. 'She had good reason to fear the baby.'

Jeffers exhaled. 'Don't follow after her! She blamed the child for her sickness, now you blame it for her death. She stumbled on a toy, remember that. You can't blame the child.'

'You mean Lucifer?'

'Stop calling him that!'

Leiber shook his head. 'Alice heard things at night, moving in the hall. You want to know what made those noises, Doctor? They were made by the baby. Four months old, moving in the dark, listening to us talk. Listening to every word!' He held to the sides of the chair. 'And if I turned the lights on, a baby is so small. It can hide behind furniture, a door, against a wall – below eye-level.'

'I want you to stop this!' said Jeffers.

'Let me say what I think or I'll go crazy. When I went to Chicago, who was it kept Alice awake, tiring her into pneumonia? The baby! And when Alice didn't die, then he tried killing me. It was simple; leave a toy on the stairs, cry in the night until your father goes downstairs to fetch your milk, and stumbles. A crude trick, but effective. It didn't get me. But it killed Alice dead.'

David Leiber stopped long enough to light a cigarette. 'I should have caught on. I'd turn on the lights in the middle of the night, many nights, and the baby'd be lying there, eyes wide. Most babies sleep all the time. Not this one. He stayed awake, thinking.'

'Babies don't think.'

'He stayed awake doing whatever he *could* do with

his brain, then. What in hell do we know about a baby's mind? He had every reason to hate Alice; she suspected him for what he was – certainly not a normal child. Something – different. What do you know of babies, doctor? The general run, yes. You know, of course, how babies kill their mothers at birth. Why? Could it be resentment at being forced into a lousy world like this one?'

Leiber leaned towards the doctor, tiredly. 'It all ties up. Suppose that a few babies out of all the millions born are instantaneously able to move, see, hear, think, like many animals and insects can. Insects are born self-sufficient. In a few weeks most mammals and birds adjust. But children take years to speak and learn to stumble around on their weak legs.

'But suppose one child in a billion is – strange? Born perfectly aware, able to think, instinctively. Wouldn't it be a perfect setup, a perfect blind for anything that baby might want to do? He could pretend to be ordinary weak, crying, ignorant. With just a *little* expenditure of energy he could crawl about a darkened house, listening. And how easy to place obstacles at the top of stairs. How easy to cry all night and tire a mother into pneumonia. How easy, right at birth, to be so close to the mother that *a few deft manoeuvres might cause peritonitis!*'

'For God's sake!' Jeffers was on his feet. 'That's a repulsive thing to say!'

'It's a repulsive thing I'm speaking of. How many mothers have died at the birth of their children? How many have suckled strange little improbabilities who cause death one way or another? Strange, red little creatures with brains that work in a bloody darkness we can't even guess at. Elemental little brains, aswarm with racial memory, hatred, and raw cruelty, with no more thought than self-preservation. And self-preservation in this case consisted of eliminating a mother who realized what a horror she had birthed. I ask you, doctor, what is there in the world more selfish than a baby? Nothing!'

Jeffers scowled and shook his head helplessly.

Leiber dropped his cigarette down. 'I'm not claiming any great strength for the child. Just enough to crawl around a little, a few months ahead of schedule. Just enough to listen all the time. Just enough to cry late at night. That's enough, more than enough.'

Jeffers tried ridicule. 'Call it murder, then. But murder must be motivated. What motive had the child?'

Leiber was ready with the answer. 'What is more at peace, more dreamfully content, at ease, at rest, fed, comforted, unbothered, than an unborn child? Nothing. It floats in a sleepy, timeless wonder of nourishment and silence. Then, suddenly, it is asked to give up its berth, is forced to vacate, rushed out into a noisy, uncaring, selfish world where it is asked to shift for itself, to hunt, to feed from the hunting, to seek after a vanishing love that once was its unquestionable right, to meet confusion instead of inner silence and conservative slumber! And the child *resents* it! Resents the cold air, the huge spaces, the sudden departure from familiar things. And in the tiny filament of brain the only thing the child knows is selfishness and hatred because the spell has been rudely shattered. Who is responsible for this disenchantment, this rude breaking of the spell? The mother. So here the new child has someone to hate with all its unreasoning mind. The mother has cast it out, rejected it. And the father is no better, kill him, too! He's responsible in *his* way!'

Jeffers interrupted. 'If what you say is true, then every woman in the world would have to look on her baby as something to dread, something to wonder about.'

'And why not? Hasn't the child a perfect alibi? A thousand years of accepted medical belief protects him. By all natural accounts he is helpless, not responsible. The child is born hating. And things grow worse, instead of better. At first the baby gets a certain amount of attention and mothering. But then as time passes, things change. When very new, a baby has the power to make parents do silly things when it cries or sneezes, jump when it makes a noise. As the years pass, the baby feels even that small power slip rapidly, forever away, never to return. Why shouldn't it grasp all the power it can have? Why shouldn't it jockey for position while it has all the advantages? In later years it would be too late to express its hatred. *Now* would be the time to strike.'

Leiber's voice was very soft, very low.

'My little boy baby, lying in his crib at night, his face moist and red and out of breath. From crying? No. From climbing slowly out of his crib, from crawling long distances through darkened hallways. My little boy baby. I want to kill him.'

The doctor handed him a water glass and some pills. 'You're not killing anyone. You're going to sleep for twenty-four hours. Sleep'll change your mind. Take this.'

Leiber drank down the pills and let himself be led upstairs to his bedroom, crying, and felt himself being put to bed. The doctor waited until he was moving deep into sleep, then left the house.

Leiber, alone, drifted down, down.

He heard a noise. 'What's – what's *that?*' he demanded, feebly.

Something moved in the hall.

David Leiber slept.

Very early the next morning, Dr Jeffers drove up to the house. It was a good morning, and he was here to drive Leiber to the country for a rest. Leiber would still be asleep upstairs. Jeffers had given him enough sedative to knock him out for at least fifteen hours.

He rang the doorbell. No answer. The servants were probably not up. Jeffers tried the front door, found it open, stepped in. He put his medical kit on the nearest chair.

Something white moved out of sight at the top of the stairs. Just a suggestion of a movement. Jeffers hardly noticed it.

The smell of gas was in the house.

Jeffers ran upstairs, crashed into Leiber's bedroom.

Leiber lay motionless on the bed, and the room billowed with gas, which hissed from a released jet at the base of the wall near the door. Jeffers twisted it off, then forced up all the windows and ran back to Leiber's body.

The body was cold. It had been dead quite a few hours.

Coughing violently, the doctor hurried from the room, eyes watering. Leiber hadn't turned on the gas himself. He *couldn't* have. Those sedatives had knocked him out, he wouldn't have wakened until noon. It wasn't suicide. Or was there the faintest possibility?

Jeffers stood in the hall for five minutes. Then he

walked to the door of the nursery. It was shut. He opened it. He walked inside and to the crib.

The crib was empty.

He stood swaying by the crib for half a minute, then he said something to nobody in particular.

'The nursery door blew shut. You couldn't get back into your crib where it was safe. You didn't plan on the door blowing shut. A little thing like a slammed door can ruin the best of plans. I'll find you somewhere in the house, hiding, pretending to be something you are not.' The doctor looked dazed. He put his hand to his head and smiled palely. 'Now I'm talking like Alice and David talked. But, I can't take any chances. I'm not sure of anything, but I can't take any chances.'

He walked downstairs, opened his medical bag on the chair, took something out of it and held it in his hands.

Something rustled down the hall. Something very small and very quiet. Jeffers turned rapidly.

I had to operate to bring you into this world, he thought. Now I guess I can operate to take you out of it. . .

He took half a dozen slow, sure steps forward into the hall. He raised his hand into the sunlight.

'See, baby! Something bright – something pretty!'

A scalpel.

Joan Aiken (1924–   )

Furry Night

*So, finally, and a little reluctantly on my part because I
have had a tremendous amount of pleasure reading and
re-reading a whole host of chilling ghost and horror stories,
to the last item in the book. In the genre of the modern
macabre tale I, along with a great many others, hold Joan
Aiken to be the most accomplished and imaginative fe-
male writer at work – indeed there are very few men who
can match her ability, either! Her writing is a marvellous
mixture of the everyday and the extraordinary, an inter-
mingling of the people and places we all know, with the
most remarkable fantasies. In this final tale she brings us
face to face with the last major figure of horror literature
we have yet to encounter, the werewolf, but in a shape and
form you've never dreamt of before – not even in your
strangest nightmares.*

THE deserted aisles of the National Museum of
Dramatic Art lay very, very still in the blue autumn
twilight. Not a whisper of wind stirred the folds of
Irving's purple cloak; Ellen Terry's ostrich fan was
smooth and unruffled; the blue-black gleaming breast-
plate that Sir Murdoch Meredith, founder of the
Museum, had worn as Macbeth, held its reflections as
quietly as a cottage kettle.

And yet, despite this hush, there was an air of strain,
of expectancy, along the narrow coconut-matted gal-

leries between the glass cases; a tension suggesting that some crisis had taken or was about to take place.

In the total stillness a listener might have imagined that he heard, ever so faintly, the patter of stealthy feet far away among the exhibits.

Two men, standing in the shadow of the Garrick showcase, were talking in low voices.

'This is where it happened,' said the elder, white-haired man.

He picked up a splinter of broken glass, frowned at it, and dropped it into a litter-bin. The glass had been removed from the front of the case, and some black tights and gilt medals hung exposed to the evening air.

'We managed to hush it up. The hospital and ambulance men will be discreet, of course. Nobody else was there, luckily. Only the Bishop was worried.'

'I should think so,' the younger man said. 'It's enough to make anybody anxious.'

'No, I mean he was *worried*. Hush,' the white-haired man whispered. 'Here comes Sir Murdoch.'

The distant susurration had intensified into soft, pacing footsteps. The two men, without a word, stepped farther back in the shadow until they were out of sight. A figure appeared at the end of the aisle and moved forward until it stood beneath the portrait of Edmund Kean as Shylock. The picture, in its deep frame, was nothing but a square of dark against the wall.

Although they were expecting it, both men jumped when the haunted voice began to speak.

> *You may as well use question with the wolf*
> *Why he hath made the ewe bleat for the lamb —*

A sleeve of one of the watchers brushed against the

wall, the lightest possible touch, but Sir Murdoch swung round sharply, his head out-thrust, teeth bared. They held their breath, and after a moment he turned back to the picture.

> *The currish spirit*
> *Governed a wolf, who, hang'd for human slaughter*
> *Even from his gallows did his fell soul fleet. . .*

He paused, with a hand pressed to his forehead, and then leaned forward and hissed,

> *Thy desires*
> *Are wolvish, bloody, starv'd, and ravenous!*

His head sank on his chest. His voice ceased. He brooded for a moment, and then resumed his pacing and soon passed out of sight. They heard the steps go lightly down the stairs, and presently the whine of the revolving door.

After a prudent interval the two others emerged from their hiding-place, left the gallery, and went out to a car which was waiting for them in Great Smith Street.

'I wanted you to see that, Peachtree,' said the elder man, 'to give you some idea of what you are taking on. Candidly, as far as experience goes, I hardly feel you are qualified for the job, but you are young and tough, and have presence of mind; most important of all, Sir Murdoch seems to have taken a fancy to you. You will have to keep an unobtrusive eye on him every minute of the day; your job is a combination of secretary, companion, and resident psychiatrist. I have written to Dr Defoe, the local G.P. at Polgrue. He is old, but you will find him full of practical sense. Take his advice . . . I think you said you were brought up in Australia?'

'Yes,' Ian Peachtree said. 'I only came to this country six months ago.'

'Ah, so you missed seeing Sir Murdoch act.'

'Was he so very wonderful?'

'He made the comedies too macabre,' said Lord Hawick, considering, 'but in the tragedies there was no one to touch him. His Macbeth was something to make you shudder. When he said,

Alarum'd by his sentinel, the wolf,
Whose howl's his watch, thus with his stealthy pace
With Tarquin's ravishing strides, towards his design
Moves like a ghost —

he used to take two or three stealthy steps across the stage, and you could literally see the grey fur rise on his hackles, the lips draw back from the fangs, the yellow eyes begin to gleam. It made a cold chill run down your spine. As Shylock and Caesar and Timon he was unrivalled. Othello and Antony he never touched, but his Iago was a masterpiece of villainy.'

'Why did he give it up? He can't be much over fifty.'

'As with other sufferers from lycanthropy,' said Lord Hawick, 'Sir Murdoch has an ungovernable temper. Whenever he flew into a rage it brought on an attack. They grew more and more frequent. A clumsy stage-hand, a missed cue, might set him off; he'd begin to shake with rage and the terrifying change would take place.

'On stage it wasn't so bad; he had his audiences completely hypnotized and they easily accepted a grey-furred Iago padding across the stage with the handkerchief in his mouth. But off stage it was less easy; the claims for mauling and worrying were beginning to mount up; Equity objected. So he retired and, for some time, founding the Museum absorbed him. But now it's finished, his temper is becoming uncertain again. This afternoon, as you know, he pounced on the Bishop for innocently remarking that Garrick's Hamlet was the world's greatest piece of acting.'

'How do you deal with the attacks? What's the treatment?'

'Wolf's-bane. Two or three drops given in a powerful sedative will restore him for the time. Of course, administering it is the problem, as you can imagine. I only hope the surroundings in Cornwall will be sufficiently peaceful so that he is not provoked. It's a pity he never married; a woman's influence would be beneficial.'

'Why didn't he?'

'Jilted when he was thirty. Never looked at another woman. Some girl down at Polgrue, near his home. It was a real slap in the face; she wrote two days before the wedding saying she couldn't stand his temper. That began it all. This will be the first time he's been back there. Well, here we are,' said Lord Hawick, glancing out of his Harley Street doorstep. 'Come in and I'll give you the wolf's-bane prescription.'

The eminent consultant courteously held the door for his young colleague.

The journey to Cornwall was uneventful. Dr Peachtree drove his distinguished patient, glancing at him from time to time with mingled awe and affection. Would the harassing crawl down the A.30, the jam in Exeter, the flat tyre on Dartmoor, bring on an attack? Would he be able to cope if they did? But the handsome profile remained unchanged, the golden eyes in their deep sockets stayed the eyes of a man, not those of a wolf, and Sir Murdoch talked entertainingly, not at all discomposed by the delays. Ian was fascinated by his tales of the theatre.

There was only one anxious moment, when they reached the borders of Polgrue Chase. Sir Murdoch glanced angrily at his neglected coverts, where the brambles grew long and wild.

'Wait till I see that agent,' he muttered, and then, half to himself, 'O, thou wilt be a wilderness again, peopled with wolves.'

Ian devoutly hoped that the agent would have a good excuse.

But the Hall, hideous Victorian-Gothic barrack though it was, they found gay with lights and warm with welcome. The old housekeeper wept over Sir Murdoch, bottles were uncorked, the table shone with ancestral silver. Ian began to feel less apprehensive.

After dinner they moved outside with their nuts and wine to sit in the light that streamed over the terrace from the dining-room french windows. A great walnut tree hung shadowy above them; its golden, aromatic leaves littered the flagstones at their feet.

'This place has a healing air,' Sir Murdoch said. 'I should have come here sooner.' Suddenly he stiffened. 'Hudson! Who are those?'

Far across the park, almost out of sight in the dusk, figures were flitting among the trees.

'Eh,' said the housekeeper comfortably, 'they're none but the lads, Sir Murdoch, practising for the Furry Race. Don't you worrit about them. They won't do no harm.'

'On my land?' Sir Murdoch said. 'Running across my land?'

Ian saw with a sinking heart that his eyes were turning to gleaming yellow slits, his hands were stiffening and curling. Would the housekeeper mind? Did she know her master was subject to these attacks? He felt in his pocket for the little ampoules of wolf's-bane, the hypodermic syringe.

There came an interruption. A girl's clear voice was heard singing:

> *Now the hungry lion roars,*
> *And the wolf behowls the moon –*

'It's Miss Clarissa,' said the housekeeper with relief.

A slender figure swung round the corner of the terrace and came towards them.

'Sir Murdoch? How do you do? I'm Clarissa Defoe. My father sent me up to pay his respects. He would have come himself, but he was called out on a case. Isn't it a gorgeous night?'

Sitting down beside them she chatted amusingly and easily, while Ian observed with astonished delight that his employer's hands were unclenching and his eyes were becoming their normal shape again. If this girl was able to soothe Sir Murdoch without recourse to wolf's-bane they must see a lot of her.

But when Sir Murdoch remarked that the evening was becoming chilly and proposed that they go indoors, Ian's embryonic plan received a jolt. He was a tough and friendly young man who had never taken a great deal of interest in girls; the first sight, in lamplight, of Clarissa Defoe's wild beauty came on him with a shattering impact. Could he expose her to danger without warning her?

More and more enslaved he sat gazing as Clarissa played and sang Ariel's songs. Sir Murdoch seemed completely charmed and relaxed. When Clarissa left, he let Ian persuade him up to bed without the topic of the Furry Race coming up again.

Next morning, however, when Ian went down to the village for a consultation with cheerful, shrewd-eyed old Dr Defoe, he asked about it.

'Heh,' said the Doctor. 'The Furry Race? My daughter revived it five years ago. There's two villages, ye see, Polgrue, and Lostmid, and there's this ball, what they call the Furry Ball. It's not furry; it's made of applewood with a silver band round the middle, and on the band is written,

> Fro Lostmid Parish iffe I goe
> Heddes will be broke and bloode will flowe.

'The ball is kept in Lostmid and on the day of the race one of the Polgrue lads has to sneak in and take it and get it over the parish boundary before anybody stops him. Nobody's succeeded in doing it yet. But why do you ask?'

Ian explained about the scene the night before.

'Eh, I see; that's awkward. You're afraid it may bring on an attack if he sees them crossing his land? Trouble is, that's the quickest short cut over the parish boundary.'

'If your daughter withdrew her support, would the race be abandoned?'

'My dear feller, she'd never do that. She's mad about it. She's a bit of a tomboy, Clarissa, and the rough-housing amuses her – always is plenty of horseplay, even though they don't get the ball over the boundary. If her mother were still alive now . . . Bless my soul!' the old doctor burst out, looking troubled, 'I wish Meredith had never come back to these parts, that I do. You can speak with Clarissa about it, but I doubt you'll not persuade her. She's out looking over the course now.'

The two villages of Lostmid and Polgrue lay in deep adjacent glens, and Polgrue Chase ended on the stretch of high moorland that ran between them. There was a crossroads and a telephone box, used by both villages. A spinney of wind-bitten beeches stood in one angle of the cross, and Clarissa was thoughtfully surveying this terrain. Ian joined her, turning to look back towards the Hall, and noticing with relief that Sir Murdoch was still, as he had been left, placidly knocking a ball round his private golf-course.

It was a stormy, shining day. Ian saw that Clarissa's hair was exactly the colour of the sea-browned beech leaves and that the strange angles of her face were emphasized by the wild shafts of sunlight glancing through the trees.

He put his difficulties to her.

'Oh, dear,' she said, wrinkling her brow. 'How unfortunate. The boys are so keen on the race. I don't think they'd ever give it up.'

'Couldn't they go some other way?'

'But this is the only possible way, don't you see? In the old days, of course, all this used to be common land.'

'Do you know who the runner is going to be – the boy with the ball?' Ian asked, wondering if a sufficiently heavy bribe would persuade him to take a longer way round.

But Clarissa smiled with innocent topaz eyes. 'My dear, that's never decided until the very *last* minute. So that the Lostmidians don't know who's going to dash in and snatch the ball. But I'll tell you what we *can* do – we can arrange for the race to take place at night, so that Sir Murdoch won't be worried by the spectacle. Yes, that's an excellent idea; in fact it will make it far more exciting. It's next Thursday, you know.'

Ian was not at all sure that he approved of this idea, but just then he noticed Sir Murdoch having difficulties in a bunker. A good deal of sand was flying about, and his employer's face was becoming a dangerous dusky red. 'Here, in the sands, Thee I'll rake up,' he was muttering angrily, and something about murderous lechers.

Ian ran down to him and suggested that it was time for a glass of beer, waving to Clarissa as he did so. Sir Murdoch noticed her and was instantly mollified. He invited her to join them.

Ian, by now head over heels in love, was torn between his professional duty, which could not help pointing out to him how beneficial Clarissa's company was for his patient, and a strong personal feeling that the elderly wolfish baronet was not at all suitable company for Clarissa. Worse, he suspected that she guessed his anxiety and was laughing at it.

The week passed peacefully enough. Sir Murdoch summoned the chairmen of the two parish councils and told them that any trespass over his land on the day of the Furry Race would be punished with the utmost rigour. They listened with blank faces. He also ordered mantraps and spring-guns from the Dominion and Colonial Stores, but to Ian's relief it seemed highly unlikely that these would arrive in time.

Clarissa dropped in frequently. Her playing and singing seemed to have as soothing an effect on Sir Murdoch as the songs of the harpist David on touchy old Saul, but Ian had the persistent feeling that some peril threatened from her presence.

On Furry Day she did not appear. Sir Murdoch spent most of the day pacing – loping was really the word for it, Ian thought – distrustfully among his far spinneys, but no trespasser moved in the bracken and dying leaves. Towards evening a fidgety scuffling wind sprang up, and Ian persuaded his employer indoors.

'No one will come, Sir Murdoch, I'm sure. Your notices have scared them off. They'll have gone another way.' He wished he really did feel sure of it. He found a performance of *Caesar and Cleopatra* on TV and switched it on, but Shaw seemed to make Sir Murdoch impatient. Presently he got up, began to pace about, and turned it off, muttering:

> *And why should Caesar be a tyrant, then?*
> *Poor man! I know he would not be a wolf!*

He swung round on Ian. 'Did I do wrong to shut them off my land?'

'Well,' Ian was temporizing, when there came an outburst of explosions from Lostmid, hidden in the valley, and a dozen rockets soared into the sky beyond the windows.

'That means someone's taken the Furry Ball,' said Hudson, coming in with the decanter of sherry. 'Been long enough about it, seemingly.'

Sir Murdoch's expression changed completely. One stride took him to the french window. He opened it, and went streaking across the park. Ian bolted after him.

'Stop! Sir Murdoch, stop!'

Sir Murdoch turned an almost unrecognizable face

and hissed, 'Wake not a sleeping wolf!' He kept on his way, with Ian stubbornly in pursuit. They came out by the crossroads and, looking down to Lostmid, saw that it was a circus of wandering lights, clustering, darting this way and that.

'They've lost him,' Ian muttered. 'No, there he goes!'

One of the lights broke off at a tangent and moved away down the valley, then turned and came straight for them diagonally across the hillside.

'I'll have to go and warn him off,' Ian thought. 'Can't let him run straight into trouble.' He ran down-hill towards the approaching light. Sir Murdoch stole back into the shade of the spinney. Nothing of him was visible but two golden, glowing eyepoints.

It was at this moment that Clarissa, having established her red-herring diversion by sending a boy with a torch across the hillside, ran swiftly and silently up the steep road towards the signpost. She wore trousers and a dark sweater, and was clutching the Furry Ball in her hand.

Sir Murdoch heard the pit-pat of approaching foot-steps, waited for his moment, and sprang.

It was the thick fisherman's-knit jersey with its roll collar that saved her. They rolled over and over, girl and wolf entangled, and then she caught him a blow on the jaw with the heavy applewood ball, dropped it, scrambled free, and was away. She did not dare look back. She had a remarkable turn of speed, but the wolf was overtaking her. She hurled herself into the telephone box and let the door clang to behind her.

The wolf arrived a second later; she heard the impact as the grey, sinewy body struck the door, saw the gleam of teeth through the glass. Methodically, though with shaking hands, she turned to dial.

Meanwhile Ian had met the red-herring boy just as his triumphant pursuers caught up with him.

'You mustn't go that way!' Ian gasped. 'Sir Murdoch's waiting up there and he's out for blood.'

'Give over that thurr ball,' yelled the Lostmidians.

''Tisn't on me,' the boy yelled back, regardless of the fact that he was being pulled limb from limb. 'Caught ye properly, me fine fules. 'Tis Miss Clarissa's got it, and she'm gone backaway.'

'*What?*'

Ian waited for no more. He left them to their battle, in which some Polgrue reinforcements were now joining, and bounded back up the murderous ascent to where he had left Sir Murdoch.

The scene at the telephone box was brilliantly lit by the overhead light. Clarissa had finished her call, and was watching with detached interest as the infuriated wolf threw himself repeatedly against the door.

It is not easy to address your employer in such circumstances.

Ian chose a low, controlled, but vibrant tone.

'Down, Sir Murdoch,' he said. 'Down, sir! Heel!'

Sir Murdoch turned on him a look of golden, thunderous wrath. He was really a fine spectacle, with his eyes flashing, and great ruff raised in rage. He must have weighed all of a hundred and thirty pounds. Ian thought he might be a timber-wolf, but was not certain. He pulled the ampoule from his pocket, charged the syringe, and made a cautious approach. Instantly Sir Murdoch flew at him. With a feint like a bullfighter's, Ian dodged round the callbox.

'Olé,' Clarissa shouted approvingly, opening the door a crack. Sir Murdoch instantly turned and battered it again.

'Avaunt, thou damned doorkeeper!' shouted Ian. The result was electrifying. The wolf dropped to the ground as if stunned. Ian seized advantage of the moment to give him his injection, and immediately the wolf-shape vanished, dropping off Sir Murdoch like a label off a wet bottle. He gasped, shivered, and shut his eyes.

'Where am I?' he said presently, opening them again. Ian took his arm, gently led him away from the door, and made him sit on a grassy bank.

'You'll feel better in a minute or two, sir,' he said, and, since Shakespeare seemed so efficacious, added, 'The cure whereof, my lord, 'Tis time must do.' Sir Murdoch weakly nodded.

Clarissa came out of her refuge. 'Are you all right now, Sir Murdoch?' she asked kindly. 'Shall I sing you a song?'

'All right, thank you, my dear,' he murmured. 'What are you doing here?' and he added to himself, 'I really must not fly into these rages. I feel quite dizzy.'

Ian stepped aside and picked up something that glinted on the ground.

'What's that?' asked Sir Murdoch with awakening interest. 'It reminds me – May I see it?'

'Oh, it's my medallion,' said Clarissa at the same moment. 'It must have come off. . .' Her voice trailed away. They both watched Sir Murdoch. Deep, fearful shudders were running through him.

'Where did you get this?' he demanded, turning his cavernous eyes on Clarissa. His fingers were rigid, clenched on the tiny silver St Francis.

'It was my mother's,' she said faintly. For the first time she seemed frightened.

'Was her name Louisa?' She nodded. 'Then your father –?'

'Here comes my father now,' said Clarissa with relief. The gnarled figure of the doctor was approaching them through the spinney. Sir Murdoch turned on him like a javelin.

'O thou foul thief!' he hissed. 'My lost Louisa! Stol'n from me and corrupted by spells and medicines.'

'Oh, come, come, come,' said the doctor equably, never slowing his approach, though he kept a wary eye on Sir Murdoch. 'I wouldn't put it quite like that. She came to me. *I* was looking forward to bachelorhood.'

'For the which I may go the finer, I will live a bachelor,' murmured Ian calmingly.

'And I'll tell ye this, Sir Murdoch,' Dr Defoe went on, tucking his arm through that of Sir Murdoch like an old friend, 'You were well rid of her.' He started strolling at a gentle but purposeful pace back towards the Hall, and the baronet went with him doubtfully.

'Why is that?' Already Sir Murdoch sounded half convinced, quiescent.

'Firstly, my dear sir, Temper. Out of this world! Secondly, Macaroni Cheese. Every night till one begged for mercy. Thirdly, Unpunctuality. Fourthly, long, horrifying Dreams, which she insisted on telling at breakfast. . .'

Pursuing this soothing, therapeutic vein, the doctor's voice moved farther away, and the two men were lost in the shadows.

'So that's all right,' said Clarissa on a deep breath of relief. 'Why, Ian!'

Pent-up agitation was too much for him. He had

grabbed her in his arms like a drowning man. 'I was sick with fright for you,' he muttered, into her hair, her ear, the back of her neck. 'I was afraid – oh well, never mind.'

'Never mind,' she agreed. 'Are we going to get married?'

'Of course.'

'I ought to find my Furry Ball,' she said presently. 'They seem to be having a pitched battle down below; there's a good chance of getting it over the boundary while everyone's busy.'

'But Sir Murdoch –'

'Father will look after him.'

She moved a few steps away and soon found the ball. 'Come on; through the wood is quickest. We have to put it on the Polgrue churchyard wall.'

No one accosted them as they ran through the wood. Fireworks and shouting in the valley suggested that Lostmid and Polgrue had sunk their differences in happy saturnalia.

'Full surgery tomorrow,' remarked Clarissa, tucking the Furry Ball into its niche. 'Won't someone be surprised to see this.'

When Ian and Clarissa strolled up to the terrace, they found Sir Murdoch and the doctor amiably drinking port. Sir Murdoch looked like a man who had had a festering grief removed from his mind.

'Well,' the doctor said cheerfully, 'we've cleared up some misunderstandings.'

But Sir Murdoch had stood up and gone to meet Clarissa.

'As I am a man,' he said gravely, 'I do think this lady to be my child.'

The two pairs of golden eyes met and acknowledged each other.

'That'll be the end of his little trouble, I shouldn't wonder,' murmured the doctor. 'Specially if she'll live at the Hall and keep an eye on him.'

'But she's going to marry me.'

'All the better, my dear boy. All the better. And glad I shall be to get rid of her, bless her heart.'

Ian looked doubtfully across the terrace at his future father-in-law, but he recalled that wolves are among the most devoted fathers of the animal kingdom. Sir Murdoch was stroking Clarissa's hair with an expression of complete peace and happiness.

Then a thought struck Ian. 'If *he's* her father –'

But Dr Defoe was yawning. 'I'm off to bed. Busy day tomorrow.' He vanished among the dark trees.

So they were married, and lived happily at the Hall. Clarissa's slightest wish was law. She was cherished equally by both father and husband, and if they went out of their way not to cross her in any particular, this was due quite as much to the love they bore her as to their knowledge that they had dangerous material on their hands.

Some Other Peacocks

Enid Bagnold   National Velvet
Hal Borland   When The Legends Die
D. K. Broster   The Flight Of The Heron
D. K. Broster   The Gleam In The North
D. K. Broster   The Dark Mile
Beverly Cleary   Fifteen
Jim Corbett   Man-eaters Of Kumaon
Monica Dickens   Cobbler's Dream
Geza Gardonyi   Slave Of The Huns
Leon Garfield   Drummer Boy
John Gordon   The House On The Brink
Helen Griffiths   The Wild Heart
Esther Hautzig   The Endless Steppe
A. P. Herbert   The Water Gipsies
Janet Hitchman   The King Of The Barbareens
James Vance Marshall   Walkabout
L. M. Montgomery   Anne Of Green Gables
Andre Norton   The Beast Master
Andre Norton   Lord Of Thunder
Patrick O'Brian   The Golden Ocean
Stephanie Plowman   To Spare The Conquered
Marjorie Kinnan Rawlings   The Yearling
Jack Schaefer   Shane And Other Stories
Polly Toynbee   A Working Life
Stanley J. Weyman   The House Of The Wolf
Stanley J. Weyman   Under The Red Robe
Eric Williams   Great Escape Stories